A Concrete Case of Murder

Also by Patrick C. Walsh

The Mac Maguire detective mysteries

The Body in the Boot

The Dead Squirrel

The Weeping Women

The Blackness

23 Cold Cases

Two Dogs

The Match of the Day Murders

The Chancer

The Tiger's Back

The Eight Bench Walk

Stories of the supernatural

13 Ghosts of Winter

The Black Vaults Experiment

All available in Amazon Books

Patrick C. Walsh

A Concrete Case of Murder

The eleventh 'Mac' Maguire mystery

Garden City Ink

A Garden City Ink book
www.gardencityink.com

First published in Great Britain in 2021
All rights reserved
Copyright © 2021 Patrick C. Walsh

ISBN: 9798733701585

A CIP record for this title is available from the Library

Cover art © Patrick C Walsh 2021

Garden City Ink Design

"Love is like a brick. You can build a house, or you can sink a dead body."
  — **Lady Gaga**

For my consultant, Mr. Vasdev, who is a dab hand at Robotic-assisted Laparoscopic Prostatectomies for which I'm grateful. Also, for Jim who gave me the idea in the first place.

A Murder

He lay back feeling totally happy. He knew that he had just made her happy too. She was good in bed but then again so was he. He was now certain that she was totally in love with him and that was exactly what he wanted. It's what he had been working towards for the last few months.

He didn't love her but then he had never loved anyone. He thought love was a weakness to be avoided at all costs. He had married for money, not love, and now he was going to leave his wife for even more money. A lot more money.

He pictured himself as the boss of one of the biggest construction companies in the world. He had thought that politics might be the way to money and power but this way was better. Who knows, perhaps with her money, he could do both? He happily pictured himself opening massive new buildings all over the world and then walking out of the door of Number Ten as the country's most beloved Prime Minister to give a press conference to his adoring public.

She looked over at his contented face and then lay back in the bed letting the lovely warm glow spread through her body. She had just had the best sex ever with the man she loved. As she lay there, she knew that she loved him deeply and with all her heart. In fact, she loved him more than she'd loved any man in her life. Except for daddy, of course.

Yes, she loved him and that was why she was going to kill him. Her love for him made her feel vulnerable and it was a feeling that she detested. Then there was the other thing, seeing him and the slut together. Even thinking about it made her feel sick. If she had any doubts then all she had to do was to remember seeing the two of them at it together.

She hugged him and told him how much she loved him. He told her that he loved her too and that she was the only woman in the world that he cared about.

'Am I really the only one?' she asked as her hand went underneath the pillow.

'Yes, of course,' he said with a false smile. 'Cross my heart and hope to die.'

He did indeed cross his heart and that's where she plunged the knife. She stabbed him again. And again. She kept stabbing.

He somehow managed to get up and push her away. She fell to the floor on the other side of the bed. She picked herself up and followed him down the stairs. She found him in the kitchen near the back door. He was lying on the floor and the life blood was seeping out of him. She knelt down, held his hand and cried. Then he stopped breathing.

Even in her grief a part of her was bitterly exultant. He had lied and cheated and humiliated her and this was the inevitable result. He deserved this.

The tears eventually stopped and she stood up and looked around her. There was blood everywhere. What was she going to do? She had planned the murder meticulously and had even figured out the perfect place to get rid of the body but, for some reason, she hadn't thought about all the other evidence. With a shiver she realised that, besides all the blood, there must be traces of her all over the house.

It was as though she'd been gripped by some sort of madness and she was only waking from it now. She cried again but, this time, it was for herself. She was in deep trouble and she knew it. She panicked for a moment as she imagined the trial and the endless years in prison. She decided that she'd sooner die. There was only one thing to do.

She sighed, sat down and composed herself. She then did what she always did when she was in trouble.

She called daddy.

Chapter One

That Monday morning Mac awoke with a start. The church bells were ringing and they were echoing around his head. He turned over and wrapped the pillow around his ears. It took him a few seconds to realise that it wasn't the bells after all, it was his phone. He'd not long returned from his holiday in Cyprus and, after three weeks of living next door to a church that had an exceptionally enthusiastic and early rising bell ringer, he was expecting every sound to be that of a bell.

He wearily sat up and looked over at the clock as he reached for his phone. It had just gone ten o'clock. He didn't normally sleep in this late but he'd had a bad night and sleep had proved elusive. As Tim had been away for the weekend on a buying trip, he hadn't gone to the pub on Sunday evening as usual. Instead, he'd gone to bed early and that had probably been a mistake.

He had given up on sleep around three o'clock and had gone into the living room to drink hot chocolate and watch TV for a while. He must have gotten some sleep after that but, right now, he felt as if he hadn't slept at all. He was still groggy and, once he'd spoken to whoever it was, he was going to go straight back to bed.

He was surprised when he saw that the call was from Detective Inspector Toni Woodgate.

'Mac, I need you to do me favour. There's a case that I could do with you taking on for me. I hope that you've got nothing on right now?' Toni asked.

Mac was now fully awake and assured her that he hadn't.

'That's great! Dan Carter said that you'd be up for it,' Toni said. 'There'll be two people waiting for you in the Major Crime Unit's team room. I'll tell them that you're on

3

your way. I promise you that this will be the strangest story about a theft that you'll have ever heard.'

Mac immediately wondered why the Major Crime Unit or the local detective team weren't dealing with the case.

'I take it that something's happened?' he asked.

'Unfortunately, it has,' Toni replied. 'We're dealing with a multiple murder not far from Cromer. A mother, son, two daughters and the family dog were killed with a shotgun sometime last night. We're looking for the father now. Although it's Dan Carter's case, he's asked for the whole of the local detective team to assist in the search. I was just on my way out of the door when these two walked in. His name is Peter Stirling and her name is Mrs. Ellen Mowbray. Best of luck.'

'You too,' Mac replied.

He stood up and checked the pain level in his back, just as he did every morning. It wasn't too bad so he got himself shaved and dressed in double quick time. While he did this, he thought about the multiple murder enquiry. Thankfully, familicides were not all that common in the UK although, having said that, he counted them up and realised that he'd investigated five cases in his time. He knew the exact number as they were all cases that he would never forget.

It's also called 'family annihilation' which Mac always thought was a much better name for it. In all the cases, except one, a controlling and often violent father had killed his entire family as punishment for his wife wanting to leave him. In the other case a mild-mannered family man had lost his job and decided that death was the best out-come for him. He had also decided that it would be unkind to leave anyone behind and so he'd poisoned his wife and their four children before cutting his own throat.

Mac had seen a lot of bad things in his career as a police-man but these crimes were always the worst. He pushed the dark memories out of his head. They would be of no help to him today. He had a theft of some sort to deal with and, from what Toni had intimated, it would be an unusual one.

He took his dog Terry for a very short walk and promised him an longer walk that evening. However, from his dog's pitiful whines when he closed the door, he wasn't sure that he was believed. He felt better when he remembered that his neighbour Amanda would be along to take Terry for his daily walk in the country in a couple of hours anyway.

Ten minutes later he walked into the Major Crime Unit's team room at Letchworth police station. Martin Selby, the team's computer specialist, was crouched over his laptop. He gave Mac a little wave and then returned to his laptop screen.

Toni had put the couple in Dan Carter's office with a uniformed officer to keep them company. The woman was in her forties but she dressed older. She had short brown hair and she wore glasses and a disapproving expression. He could see her sitting patiently, lips pursed and both hands tightly clutching her handbag, through the glass office windows. He also noticed that she was sitting as far away from the man as possible. He was in his thirties and had slicked back hair and a fake tan. He was sharply dressed in a blue suit, white shirt and pink tie. He had a puzzled look on his face and he couldn't seem to keep still.

Mac opened the door, sat down and introduced himself.

'Have you had an accident or something?' the woman asked on seeing Mac's crutch.

Mac decided to ignore her question. He didn't want to go through the long explanation regarding the damage to his lower spine and how this had led to his long-term pain. No-one ever understood it anyway.

'Something like that. Do you mind telling me exactly what's happened?' he asked. 'Mrs. Mowbray first, if you don't mind.'

'No, I don't mind at all,' she replied. 'I accompanied this man here in good faith to view a house that I was interested in buying. He's supposed to be an estate agent.'

She paused, pursed her lips again and glared at the man before continuing.

'He drove me to where he said the house would be but there was nothing there, nothing at all. He stopped the car in a cul-de-sac in the middle of nowhere and so I knew that he was up to no good. I called the police immediately.'

'Did he actually do anything?' Mac asked.

'Well, no,' she replied with a shake of her head, 'but that was only because I had my pepper spray out. I knew that he was up to something underhand. He looks the type, doesn't he?'

Mac turned to look at Mr. Stirling. His eyes were raised to the ceiling and he was muttering to himself.

'I wasn't trying anything on!' he said in exasperation. 'I was just trying to sell a house. Anyway, you're not my type.'

She gave him a scathing look.

'What do you mean, I'm not your type?'

'You're a woman,' he replied.

'Oh,' was all she could think to say by way of reply.

Mac turned to Mr. Stirling.

'I take it that you're an estate agent?'

'Yes, I was just taking this lady here to view a house and…God, this sounds so silly…it wasn't there.'

It was Mac's turn to look puzzled.

'What had happened to the house?'

'That's what I'd like to know!' he said too loudly. 'It's disappeared, disappeared without a bloody trace. It was only a three-bedroomed country cottage with a nice conservatory on the side but how can a whole house disappear just like that?'

Mac was really confused now.

'What exactly do you mean by 'disappeared'?' he asked.

'I mean it's gone!' Mr. Stirling replied. 'Every single roof tile, brick, window, door and whatever else have all gone. All that's there now is a green field. It's as though the house had never existed.'

It was now Mac's turn to give a look of disbelief. Martin opened the door and walked inside with his open laptop.

'Toni asked me to take a quick look,' Martin explained.

'And did you find anything?' Mac asked.

'Well, there definitely used to be a house just where Mr. Stirling said it was. You can see it here on Google Earth.'

He turned the laptop around and showed them an aerial view of a narrow country lane. He expanded the view and they could all see a dark-blue slated roof at the end of a little driveway.

'How long ago was this photo taken?' Mac asked.

'Just over seven months ago,' Martin replied. 'I've also found a record of the property on the Land Registry.'

'So, it definitely existed then,' Mac said turning to Mr. Stirling. 'Where exactly is, or was, the house?'

'It's called Hoar's Cottage and it's on a little lane called Down's Bottom which is just off the King's Walden Road,' he replied. 'It's not far from Great Offley.'

Mac had seen signs for Great Offley on the main Hitchin to Luton road when he was on his way to the airport but that was as close as he'd ever come to it.

'Mrs. Mowbray, I want to assure you that we'll be giving this our most serious attention. However, you can go for now, if you like,' Mac said in as soothing a tone as he could muster. 'We've got your details and we'll be in touch if we need to speak to you. Do you need a lift anywhere?'

'No, that's alright. I'm parked just down the road. Thank you so much, Mr. Maguire.'

She gave the estate agent another scalding look as she left.

Mac looked at Mr. Stirling for a moment. He decided to trust him.

'I'd like you to take me and show me where the house was. Is that okay?'

'Well, yes I suppose so. Knowing my bloody luck, the damn thing will be standing there in all its glory,' he said as he shook his head. 'I'm sorry but it's been a strange sort of day.'

Mac could only agree with him. Before setting off, he got the exact co-ordinates from Martin and loaded them onto his phone. As they drove, he wondered what he'd find when he reached Down's Bottom.

After a few minutes of silence Mr. Stirling said, 'You think I'm mad, don't you?'

'No, but...' Mac paused. 'Well, you have to admit that it's a very strange story.'

'Oh, I'm not blaming you for thinking that,' he replied. 'The thought that I might be mad has occurred to me too. I was the one who did the initial evaluation and took all the photos when it was first put on the market.'

'How long ago was that?' Mac asked.

'About six weeks ago, I'd guess. Mrs. Mowbray was the first bite that we'd had since then.'

'Why was that?'

'Well, it's a bit of a hard sell even though it's going at a good price. Although it's only fifteen minutes from a main road, it's feels as if it's quite isolated. There are no other houses nearby and the nearest shop is a couple of miles away and that seems to be putting people off. To be honest, the market's a bit slow anyway at the moment. So, when I heard that someone was interested in Hoar's Cottage, I got her out there straight away.'

'Who owns the house?' Mac asked.

'I've no idea,' the estate agent said with a shrug. 'It's been put on the market by a company called Ricard and Montefiore Property Agents. They act as middle-men for people who want to sell their houses discreetly. I did ask if they could divulge the owner but they said that they couldn't.'

If the house really had gone then Mac knew who he'd be calling on next.

They turned left off the main road towards Great Offley. The village at this point was old and interesting. Then they passed by a really picturesque pub that was dripping with hanging flower baskets. Mac looked at this with even more interest. However, they soon found themselves passing by lots of newer, and far less picturesque, houses. Mac guessed that they would still cost an arm and a leg though.

A few minutes later they had left the houses behind and were driving down a narrow country lane. It was only wide enough for one car but it had passing places every few hundred yards. Luckily, traffic was light and they only had to stop once to let a car go by. They drove past green fields for a few miles before the satnav pointed them towards an even narrower lane that was partly hidden behind a hedge. Mac looked at the map on his phone. It looked as if they were in the right place.

The little lane was full of potholes so they had to drive quite slowly. They pulled up about two hundred and fifty yards down the lane and came to a stop. Mac couldn't see anything but hedges and green fields. He and Mr. Stirling got out.

'It used to be right there,' Mr. Stirling said pointing to a hedge. 'There used to be a little picket fence and a gate and behind that there was the house. Here, I'll show you.'

He pulled out a large tablet and searched for a photo. He then handed the tablet to Mac. He could see a pretty white-painted cottage sitting behind a low wooden white picket fence. It had ornamental shrubs in the front garden. Mac looked about and could still only see hedges and green fields.

'You're absolutely sure that this is the right spot?' Mac asked with some disbelief.

'Yes, I've checked and re-checked the co-ordinates. Anyway, if you look here,' he said scrolling to a particular photo. It was a shot of the house from the lane. 'There on the right,' Mr. Stirling said as he pointed to a tree.

On the right of the photo there was a tree. It was old and gnarled and looked as if it was splitting in two. Mac looked up and there was the tree. There could be no doubt about it. Only the house was missing from the photo. He pulled out his own phone and got up the estate agency's website. He searched for Hoar's Cottage and clicked on the results. He easily found the photo he was looking for. He hadn't really doubted Mr. Stirling but he thought that it would be wise to check anyway.

'I didn't see any 'For Sale' signs in these photos,' Mac said.

'Well, I couldn't see the point of putting one up,' the estate agent replied. 'After all, it's in the middle of nowhere and this road's a dead end. So, who would see it?'

Mac could see his point.

'Did you ask the property agents if they knew anything?' he asked.

'They were the first people I rang,' Mr. Stirling replied. 'They thought I'd gone mad. As far as they were concerned, the house should still be here. I asked if the owner might have been responsible for its disappearance but they checked and assured me that they weren't.'

Mac looked around and could see nothing out of the ordinary, except for one thing that is. There was a rectangular patch in the road surface that looked quite new. He had no idea what this might mean so he took a photo and made a mental note of it.

Mac walked over and had a look at the hedge. It looked old and as if it belonged there. From what he'd seen so far, he was having great difficulty believing that a house ever stood on that spot. He walked up the road to where there was a gap in the hedge. He then went into the field and very carefully walked back to the spot where the house had been before stopping to look down at the grass. If the ground had been undisturbed then he was definitely going to consider taking the estate agent to the nearest doctor.

However, it wasn't. New turf had obviously been laid as the joins between the strips were just about visible. There was an awful lot of it too and Mac thought that it could easily cover the footprint of a house. He walked around the field for some minutes but that was the only evidence he found. He stood there motionless thinking. He hadn't noticed that Mr. Stirling had followed him.

'Mr. Maguire, are you alright?' he eventually asked.

'Oh, I'm sorry. I was just thinking,' Mac replied waking from his trance.

'It doesn't seem possible that there was once a house here, does it?' the estate agent said in something like wonder.

'At first sight you might be right but it looks as if there's quite a lot of new grass here. You can just about see the joins between the strips of turf.'

The estate agent looked down.

'Oh yes, I must admit that I hadn't noticed that,' he said looking somewhat relieved. 'So, what happens now?'

'Well, I'm not altogether certain that a crime has been committed as yet but I'll follow up on it anyway.'

He was almost certain that there must have been some sort of mix-up somewhere but he found that he was getting quite intrigued by the case. After all, it's not every day that someone steals a whole house.

'So, what are you going to do? There doesn't seem to be much to go on,' the estate agent said looking around him.

'Well, I'm going to take some photos and call someone I know who might be able to tell me roughly how long ago the turf was laid down,' Mac said. 'Then I'm then going to contact someone in the Archaeological Department at the local university. They helped us out a while back when we were looking for a grave. They should be able to confirm if the soil in this area has been disturbed and whether or not some, or all of your house, might be right underneath where we're standing.'

'So, you're taking it seriously then?' he asked with some surprise.

'I am,' Mac assured him.

'Thank you, Mr. Maguire,' Mr. Stirling said, looking somewhat relieved. 'I think that I'm going to go home and lie down, if that's alright. I suddenly feel very tired.'

Mac took his photos and then Mr. Stirling dropped him back at the station. The Major Crime Unit's room was now totally empty. He sat down at an empty desk, pulled his phone out and selected a number.

'Hello, Mac,' a man's voice said.

'Hello, Jimmy. How's the gardening going?'

'Great. How can I help you?'

Jimmy Stourton was nothing if not to the point. He had been a safebreaker when Mac had first met him but now, after learning his skills in an open prison, he was a gardener. Not just any gardener though, he now owned a small company that catered to the highest end of the landscaping market.

'I'm sending you a photo now of some turf that looks as if it was laid down fairly recently. I was wondering if you could tell me how long it's been down for?' Mac asked.

'Has it been regularly watered since it was laid?' Jimmy asked.

'Possibly not.'

Mac was guessing that whoever had made the house disappear wouldn't be hanging around to water the grass.

'Well, we've had a lot of rain over the last couple of months anyway. I'm looking at the photo now and my best guess would be five to six weeks perhaps,' Jimmy replied.

Mac said his thanks and rang off. Jimmy had never been one for small talk. At least this gave him a time frame. He remembered that the estate agent had said that he'd done the initial evaluation some six weeks ago. So, the house must have disappeared shortly after that.

He next called the Archaeology Department at the local university. It took him a while before he was finally put through to a Professor Sid Cowans. Mac had to tell him the story several times before the Professor understood exactly what Mac wanted from him. He finally agreed to send a research student who would meet him on site at ten o'clock the next morning. He told Mac that the research student was the best surveyor that they had.

Mac sat back and thought.

He knew that a house had once existed and now it didn't. He needed to find out exactly what it might take to make a whole house totally disappear

.

Since he'd called her, he'd been in a sort of demented fever. He still couldn't believe it. He loved her and he thought that she'd really cared for him. He would have done anything for her, anything, but now all he wanted to do was kill her.

A few nights ago, after they had made love, he had signed the land over to her company. She had promised him a slice of the action, a slice that would make him richer than he had ever imagined. She had told him that, once they'd signed the contract, they would both have enough money to disappear abroad and live a life of luxury together.

He had been played though.

He had given her the land and then, nothing. The one and only time that he'd managed to get through to her by phone, she had made it plain that the land was the only thing that she'd ever wanted. She told him not to bother calling her again as she was blocking his number. He'd then gone to her company's offices in London. He'd been forcibly escorted off the premises and thrown into the street.

He still couldn't believe it. He'd given away his main asset for nothing. How could he have been so stupid?

Without that land his asset sheet would have a big black hole in it and his company would go bust. Everything he'd worked so long and hard for would be gone overnight. He realised that he had been a fool and that was the bitterest thing of all. He couldn't stand the thought of people looking at him, pointing at him and saying how stupid he had been. His own family most of all.

They would all be better off dead, he told himself.

This idea took root and, after thinking about it for a while, he reached the conclusion that it was indeed the only thing to do. A bottle of vodka eventually helped him to work up the courage up to do it. He cried as he killed his children but he felt little or nothing when he shot his wife. Shooting the poor dog was the hardest part though. He loved that dog and killing him broke his heart but he told himself that it had to be done.

Afterwards, he drove around in a delirium for some hours. There was one more killing that he had to carry out but he found that this one was the hardest of all. He drank more vodka and then parked up and fell asleep. He woke up and found himself staring at a tree in a field. He had no idea where he was except that this was the place where he was going to die.

He wearily climbed over a gate and stumbled across the field, hypnotised by the tree ahead. It was an oak and the sun was rising behind it. It had a broad symmetrical canopy covered with lush green leaves and it was beautiful. A good place to end it all then.

He sat down with his back against the trunk of the tree and looked up at the greenery above. The sunlight flashing through the waving leaves almost hypnotised him.

Now, that is really something, he thought. Why hadn't he ever looked at a tree like this before?

He sat and drank until the bottle was empty. Then he thought of her again. His anger and foolishness felt like an acid bile in his stomach as he manoeuvred the shotgun into position just underneath his chin.

'See you in hell, Nessa,' he said.

Then he pulled the trigger.

The sound caused a flock of startled birds to rise into the sky. They circled for a few moments before settling back down again. The birds' complaints quickly died down and everything was once again quiet.

Chapter Two

Mac had consulted his friend Tim about two matters. The first, and most important, was arranging the time that they were going to meet in the Magnets for their evening refreshment. The second was a request for information. Luckily for Mac, Tim knew a lot of the local building firms and he suggested that Mac should talk to someone called Jez Manning who owned a company in Stevenage. He called and arranged to meet him at his office. He left a note for Dan Carter telling him where he was going.

As Mac drove down the motorway towards Stevenage, he thought about his conversation with Tim. It was a little on the strange side and, strangest of all, Tim said that he'd call at Mac's house first before they went to the pub.

There was something strange in Tim's voice. Mac was sure that something was wrong but what?

They'd only been back from Cyprus for just over a week and, on holiday, Tim had been his usual self if not more so. They had both had a great time but then Mac suddenly remembered that Tim hadn't been drinking quite as much as he normally would have.

He'd explained it away as gas in his stomach making him feel a little bloated. Mac had been having such a good time that he hadn't paid it that much attention.

Was Tim ill? he thought. Is that why he wants to see me at home and not the pub?

He quickly pushed that thought away. He reassured himself by thinking that, even if Tim was ill, it couldn't be anything that serious. After all, he looked so well.

A little voice reminded him that so did his own wife just months before she died.

He firmly banged down the lid on that train of thought and started thinking about what questions he was going to ask Mr. Manning. He decided that he was most interested in exactly what would be required to demolish a whole house without leaving a trace. He had no idea of how big a job that might be and what would it might take to make it happen.

The firm of 'J. Manning and Sons - Master Builders' was situated just off the motorway in an industrial area of the town not far from the football ground. It was hidden away between a car wash and a large do-it-yourself store. The office was a portacabin in the corner of a busy site.

Two over-sized forklift trucks were buzzing around an articulated lorry carefully manipulating what looked like six wooden roof supports onto a low-loader. They were massive and he wondered what type of house they might be going into.

Mac opened the door of the portacabin and a young woman glanced up at him and smiled. She was in her mid-twenties and she looked as if she was happy in her work.

'Mr. Maguire?' she asked. 'My dad will speak to you once he's finished with his call.'

She nodded towards a grizzled grey-haired man in his fifties who was sitting on a desk behind her. He was dressed in a pair of old blue overalls, a checked shirt and high-laced boots that were caked in mud.

'I take it that you're Miss Manning then?' Mac asked as he took a seat.

'Well, I was until six months ago. I'm Mrs. Dawkins now,' she said with a smile.

'It looks as if married life is suiting you.'

'It is that,' she replied her smile getting even wider.

'Mr. Maguire?' a gruff voice said.

It was almost a shout. The man came towards him and held out a huge calloused hand. He was only about Mac's height but he was much stockier.

'How can I help the police?' Jez Manning said as he gestured towards a chair.

Mac sat down but Jez perched himself on the corner of his desk. He obviously wasn't one for sitting down much.

Mac explained the case as it stood and awaited Jez's reaction.

'Well, I must admit that I've never heard of that before,' Jez said as he scratched his head.

'What a house being demolished and leaving virtually no trace?' Mac asked.

'No not that, I mean the fact that it was done without the owner or the property agents knowing,' Jez replied. 'I've done some reinstatement work over the years. It usually happens when some bright spark buys a bit of farm land cheap and then they think that they can build a house on it without getting caught. Land with planning permission to build on is really expensive, especially around here, so they reckon that they're getting a bargain. However, they never seem to understand that it's actually quite hard to hide a house.'

'What do you mean by reinstatement work?' Mac asked.

'Well, if someone builds a house where they shouldn't have, and the local council planning people find out, then they can issue an Enforcement Order,' Jez replied. 'If the order calls for complete reinstatement then the land has to be returned to the state it was in before the house was built or as near to it as possible. So, the house has to be demolished and everything taken away. That includes driveways, patios and fences too. Then the site might have to be re-covered in grass and any hedges or trees would have to be reinstated too.'

'That sounds like quite a job,' Mac said.

'It certainly can be and it's usually a very expensive one too,' Jez replied. 'So, after trying to pull a fast one, all they usually end up with is an empty bank account and a bit of farming land that they can't do anything with.'

'What would it take to demolish a house like that?' Mac asked. 'I mean in terms of men and equipment.'

Jez gave this some thought.

'I can do you a proper calculation if you like but, off the top of my head, you'd need at least a couple of excavators and five or six tipper lorries for a house like the one you described. With that and a small team, I'd guess that you could do it in two to three days.'

That was a lot quicker than Mac would have thought. He remembered something.

'I saw a patch on the road near where the house used to be. It looked new.'

Mac took out his phone and showed Jez the photo he'd taken.

'That was probably where they disconnected the property from the mains,' Jez replied. 'For a reinstatement they'd have to dig all the cables up too.'

It looks as if they did a thorough job then, Mac thought.

'If you had to make a house disappear without the owner knowing, how would you go about it?'

Jez gave this some thought.

'Well, from what you've told me there were no neighbours to witness the demolition or get annoyed about it, so that's a great help. I suppose the two main things I'd be worried about would be the men who carried out the demolition and where the house might eventually end up.'

'So, how would you deal with that?' Mac asked.

The builder scratched his head again.

'Well, if it was being done illegally, you wouldn't want any record to exist linking the waste to where it actually came from. Now, we're not a massive operation here but, if we were already legally demolishing something a bit larger, then you could lose a house worth of waste materials fairly easily. You have to raise a Waste Transfer Note for every load that goes to landfill saying what it is and where the waste has come from. I've never done it myself but I've known some companies who haven't always been truthful when it comes to their waste documentation.'

'So, you're saying that, if someone already had a big demolition project underway, then they could simply slip the waste from the house into landfill and claim that it came from that project?' Mac asked.

'Yes, that's about it,' Jez replied. 'If you were knocking down a tower block say, then trucks would be moving waste day and night. A few more truckloads wouldn't be noticed.'

'What about the men? What if you were asking them to do something that wasn't quite legal?'

'Well, it's not something I'd ever do personally but I'd guess that you could spin them a line. You could tell them that a friend had been served with an Enforcement Order and that he was a bit embarrassed about it. I'd say that he wanted the house removed with as little fuss as possible. I'd pay them double time and in cash.'

'Would that be enough to keep them from telling anyone else?' Mac asked.

'I suppose that would depend on the type of men you used for the job. However, if I wanted to be extra careful, I'd use men who were going home.'

'Going home?'

'Unfortunately for us builders, a lot of experienced men are going back home now that Brexit is here,' Jez replied. 'They're mostly from Eastern Europe; Poland, Bulgaria, Romania and the like. They reckon that it will be a lot easier working in the EU than trying to work here so most of them will soon be looking for work in Germany and Holland. We'll be losing a lot of good men.'

Mac gave this some thought.

'Who might be capable of arranging all that? If the demolition was done illegally, I mean.'

'My guess is that it could be someone with their own building business and probably a fairly big business at that,' Jez replied. 'In that instance, all they'd need to do to make it happen is to make a few phone calls.'

As luck would have it, Mac's phone rang at that precise moment. It was Dan Carter.

'Mac, how's the case of the disappearing house going? Toni told me that she'd passed the case over to you.'

'Nothing much to report on as yet. I take it that you've found the father then,' Mac said.

He knew that Dan wouldn't have been giving his case a second thought unless the hunt was already over.

'Yes, we found what was left of him lying at the foot of an oak tree in a field near Babb's Green,' Dan replied.

'That's not far from Ware, isn't it?' Mac asked.

'That's right. We've no idea why he picked that particular spot. Perhaps he just drove around until he'd worked his courage up. Anyway, the forensics people reckon that he'd used both barrels just under his chin. He practically blew his head off.'

'How did you find him?'

'He'd left his car on the side of the road. A farmer called it in as it was blocking access to one of his fields. So, there's just the paperwork left to do really.'

'Have you any idea yet as to why he did it?' Mac asked.

'It looks as if was all about money,' Dan replied. 'He ran a fairly big building business and, apparently, it was going bust although no-one seems to know why.'

'I'm with a builder now. Do you want me to ask him if he knows anything?' Mac suggested.

'Yes, please. Every bit of information will help. Oh, talking of help, Leigh's more or less free now that the panic's over if you want some help. I'd feel better if you had someone with you.'

'Thanks, having Leigh on board would be great,' Mac said.

'Good, she's on her way as we speak.'

Dan gave him the details of the builder who had killed himself before he ended the call. Mac looked up. Jez was still sitting on the desk.

'I'm sorry about that,' Mac said as he put his phone away. 'Tell me, have you heard about Josh Wolfe yet?'

Jez slowly nodded his head.

'One of my sons told me that he'd killed his wife and kids. I still can't believe it. Have you found him yet?'

'Yes, we have. Unfortunately, he's dead too.'

'Why on earth would a man do something like that?'

'We think that it was about money,' Mac replied, 'and being seen as a failure too, I'd guess. For some people they identify themselves so closely with their job or company and they can't envisage living without it. If they lose that then they feel that life's not worth living.'

'But why kill the whole family?' Jez asked giving Mac a sad look.

'For the controlling types, they honestly believe that their family are their property to do with as they like. For some, the pain of failing is so devastating that they think that they're actually doing their family a favour. Saving them from a fate worse than death, I suppose.'

'It doesn't make any sense to me,' Jez said as he shook his head again.

'No, me neither if I'm being honest. Did you know Josh Wolfe personally?' Mac asked.

'We've had some dealings over the years. I learned to keep my distance from him in the end.'

Mac was interested.

'Why was that?'

Jez paused and scratched his head again.

'See us here, we're a niche business. We specialise in projects that most other builders wouldn't touch with a bargepole. They're usually one-offs and that requires real skill. We'll never get any bigger than we are and we're happy with that. We actually enjoy what we do, especially the really hard challenges. We're building three eco-houses at the moment, all different and all brand-new designs. We're really enjoying it but builders like Josh would run a mile from work like that. They're only in it for the money. We worked together on a project some years ago and let's just say that he cut a few too many corners for my liking.'

'What do you mean by 'too many corners'?' Mac asked.

'He always had his eye on the bottom line, did Josh. He'd use cheaper materials when he could get away with it and he was always late paying his suppliers even when he had the money. But, when he started mucking about with site Health and Safety, that's where I drew the line. I pulled my men off the job and paid up the contract. We survive as a business because of the skills of our men and I wasn't about to leave their welfare in the hands of the like of Josh Wolfe,' Jez said indignantly.

They were interrupted by the door opening. A slim young woman with shoulder-length blonde hair walked in. She was wearing a black tailored trouser suit and a white blouse. She smiled on seeing Mac.

'So, this is the right place then,' she said. 'I was having some doubts.'

'This is my partner, Leigh Marston,' Mac said.

Seeing Jez's puzzled look, Mac rephrased his introduction.

'I should have said that this is my police colleague, Detective Constable Leigh Marston.'

Jez smiled at his mistake and shook his head. He then shook Leigh's hand.

'We were just talking about Josh Wolfe,' Mac said.

'Well, thankfully, I missed meeting him in person. I was still interviewing some of his neighbours in Cromer when they found his body,' Leigh said with a frown.

Mac thought that she'd been lucky. Shotgun suicides are never a nice sight.

'Dan said that he thought that it was all about money. Is that right?'

'We need to do a bit more digging but it seems that his business was on its last legs for some reason. He was doing okay just a few months ago so something dramatic must have happened.'

Mac turned to Jez, 'Have you heard anything recently about Josh Wolfe's business dealings?'

'Not really,' Jez replied. 'But, as I said, I've been keeping him at arm's length for quite a while.'

'I heard that he's been bragging about how he was going to become a multi-millionaire soon.'

They all turned around and looked at Jez's daughter.

'I know someone who does his office admin and she said that he'd been walking on air recently. Then, last Thursday, he left the office with a face like thunder and no-one's seen him since.'

'Did she say anything else?' Mac asked.

'Not really,' she replied, 'only that, just before he disappeared, he went into his office as happy as you like and then, just a half an hour later, he came out looking like death. She's still got no idea why.'

Mac made sure that he got the name of the admin assistant. He then said his goodbyes and left Jez a card in case he, or his daughter, thought of anything else.

As they walked to the car Leigh asked, 'Did you find out much?'

'Yes, I did. Mr. Manning was quite helpful although he wasn't all that complimentary about Mr. Wolfe. Does that match with what you've learned about him so far?' Mac asked.

'Well, to be honest, not many people have had a good word to say about him,' Leigh replied. 'It looks like he was the controlling type and violent with it at times. His poor wife was often seen with black eyes and bruises. Killing his own kids is something that I'll never understand though. I've seen the family photos and they all looked so sweet.'

'No, that's something that I've never been able to understand myself.'

'Have you had any leads about the disappearing house yet?' Leigh said wanting to change the subject.

'Not really but Mr. Manning has given me some ideas,' Mac replied. 'He thinks that it was probably another builder who did it and, in all likelihood, one with a much bigger business than his.'

Mac looked at his watch. It had gone two o'clock.

'Anyway, let's go back to the station. We can park up there and pop around to the Magnets for a bite to eat. After that we'll need to get our thinking caps on.'

Chapter Three

Mac felt better with some food inside him. He sat in the Major Crime Unit's room gazing up at a blank whiteboard. For the moment they had the room to themselves.

'Where do we start then?' Leigh asked.

'I was just wondering why someone might want to make a whole house disappear,' Mac said. 'Why do you think they did it?'

Leigh looked up at the ceiling as she thought.

'Well, it could be revenge, I suppose.'

'Revenge against who though?' Mac asked as he stood up and wrote it down on the whiteboard.

'Well, the owner, I'd guess. Who else might it be revenge against?' Leigh reasonably asked.

'Against someone who had once lived there, perhaps, or even against the house itself. It might have been a constant reminder of some terrible trauma for instance,' Mac said not terribly convinced by his own argument.

He shrugged and wrote that down too anyway.

'What about a mistake?' Leigh suggested. 'Perhaps they demolished the wrong house and whoever did it just doesn't want to admit it.'

Mac wrote that down too.

'That's certainly a possibility. What else?' he asked.

Leigh screwed her face up as she thought. It made Mac smile.

'To cover something up,' she said eventually. 'It would be a bit extreme but, if the house was a crime scene, then a good way of getting rid of the evidence might be to get rid of the entire house.'

Mac wrote this down on the board too and underlined it.

'That's what I think might be going on here,' Mac said. 'However, we can't ignore it being revenge or a mistake either, just in case.'

He then wrote Josh Wolfe's name down.

'Is it just a co-incidence that a man who owns a fairly big building company kills himself just weeks after the house disappeared?' Mac said as he turned to Leigh. 'I don't always like coincidences. We'll need to check with Dan once he's had a chance to interview Mr. Wolfe's staff and see if his company are currently involved in any big demolition projects.'

'So, what do we do now?' she asked.

Mac stood and stared at the board. Right now, they had absolutely nothing to go on. He took out his phone and made the only call he could. Leigh gathered that he was talking to the property agents.

'That was Ricard and Montefiore,' Mac said. 'They said that they'll see us now. It sounds as if they're wondering where Hoar's Cottage has gone too.'

'Where are they?' Leigh asked as they walked towards the car park.

'They're in Hitchin, in the old part of town just past the Priory,' Mac replied.

Mac climbed in the passenger seat. He was happy to let Leigh drive while he had a think.

It didn't take them long before they were in Hitchin and driving past the Priory. They then drove down a street that looked as if it were the backdrop for a period costume drama. A hundred yards or so further on a very discreet green and gold sign told them that they had arrived at their destination. The offices of Ricard and Montefiore was comprised of a large and quite beautiful Georgian town house. The wide front door was surrounded by ornately carved white stone with a triangular pediment on the top.

Leigh followed a sign and drove through an archway and into a car park at the rear of the building. A sign sternly warned that the car park was solely for its customers' use and that any car parked there illegally would be towed away. It still didn't say what they did which Mac found puzzling.

They pulled up in a vacant space and a man immediately came out of the building and approached them.

'I'm sorry but you can't park there,' he said in a loud voice. 'Please move your car immediately.'

Mac looked him over. He was well over six feet tall with short-cropped hair and lots of muscles under an expensive suit.

Mac didn't bother answering. He took his warrant card out and showed it to the man.

'Do you have a search warrant?' the man asked.

'A search warrant?' Mac asked giving the man a puzzled look. 'Why would we need a search warrant? We just want to talk to someone about a disappearing house.'

The man gave them a sceptical look before going back inside. He came out a few minutes later. He attempted a smile but didn't quite succeed.

'My apologies,' he said. 'I thought that you were someone else. Mr. Smyth will see you now.'

They followed him inside. The interior mirrored the Georgian exterior with its antique patterned wallpapers, ornate mirrors and portraits of long dead aristocrats. They were shown into a room that contained a gleaming dark wooden oval-shaped table and six mahogany chairs with carved backs. The walls were painted heritage green and cream and at the far end of the room there was a painting of a starched woman in her forties who was dressed like something out of Jane Austen. She seemed to be looking down her nose at them.

Mac wondered what his friend Tim would make of it. Was it all for real or just a stage set?

This reminded him of his friend and his worry moment-arily returned. He had to stop and push all thoughts of Tim from his mind. He had work to do.

Mac and Leigh sat down and waited. They didn't have to wait long. A tall rangy man in his forties entered the room. He sat down and gave Mac and Leigh a long look. Mac looked back. The man was very elegantly dressed in a formal grey three-piece suit topped off with lavender-blue shirt and what looked like an old school tie. He had a long face and fashionably floppy black hair that was turning grey.

'Is it true that Hoar's Cottage has disappeared?' he asked with some disbelief in a cut-glass upper-class accent.

He took a card from an ornate silver card case and passed it to Mac.

Before answering Mac read the card. It said, 'Jon Adams-Smyth, Partner - Ricard and Montefiore - Property Gurus.' Mac introduced himself and Leigh and took out his warrant card. He slipped the card he'd been given to Leigh who looked at it with interest.

'On the card it says that you're a partner,' Mac said. 'What does that mean?'

'Well, the company was started by just the two of us and, before you ask, neither of us are called Ricard or Monte-fiore. We just thought that it sounded better than Smyth and Jenkins. So, what's happened to Hoar's Cottage then?'

'That's what we'd like to know,' Mac replied. 'It looks as if someone's demolished it and then took everything away. Have you informed your client yet?'

'We've contacted the client's representatives and they were as surprised about it as we were. They've assured us that it's not their client's doing.'

'Your operation here seems quite up-market. Is Hoar's Cottage typical of the type of properties that you manage?'

'No, not really. The cottage came as part of a package that the owner wanted to divest themself of as quickly as possible. We personally managed the sale of the other, more desirable properties, but we felt that the smaller components might be better dealt with by a local estate agency. Our clientele wouldn't be interested in a remote cottage.'

'And exactly who are your clientele?' Mac asked.

'People with large properties to sell and people with money, lots of money,' Mr. Smyth said with a little smile. 'We act as a sort of very discreet property broker. People approach us when they want to sell and we put them in contact with people who might want to buy. We basically guide our clients on both sides through the whole process.'

Mac gave Mr. Smyth a long look. He was getting an inkling of what his business was really about.

'When you say discreet, what does that mean exactly?'

'It means that everything is done very confidentially, usually via our clients' representatives. We rarely get to meet our clients in the flesh or even know who they actually are most of the time.'

'You don't know who they are?' Mac asked looking puzzled.

'Well, most often, the entities involved in a transaction are not people per se but their companies,' Mr. Smyth explained. 'Very often these companies are set up solely to facilitate the sale of a property.'

Again, that small smile. What he'd said confirmed what Mac had been thinking.

'Shell companies, I take it?' Mac asked.

Mr. Smyth shrugged.

'So, I take it that all this discretion and confidentiality is really aimed at keeping any of the money changing hands from going to the tax man?' Mac asked.

Another shrug and a deprecating smile.

'Nothing we do here is illegal. We merely follow our clients' wishes.'

'Who owns Hoar's Cottage?' Mac asked.

'I couldn't say,' Mr. Smyth replied with an excellent poker face.

'I could get a court order…'

Mr. Smyth interrupted, 'When I said that I couldn't say what I meant was that I don't know. In this case they haven't even furnished me with the name of a company as such. I get my instructions and keep in touch via an encrypted app. We've sold two large properties already and the funds were sent to several accounts all in different locations.'

'What were the locations?' Mac asked. 'Were they tax havens?'

Mr. Smyth thought for a while and then said, 'Well, let me just say that you're not too far off the mark there.'

'I'd like you to produce all the records you have with regards to the package of the properties that included Hoar's Cottage,' Mac asked.

He wasn't all that hopeful that it would help but he had to ask anyway.

'Well, you will need a court order for that but, if I were you, I wouldn't waste my time,' Mr. Smyth replied with a sympathetic smile. 'As I said everything was done via an encrypted app. All we could do was respond to messages with a one-time code. I dare say that everything on the app was automatically deleted as we went along.'

'But you must have had some records?' Mac asked.

'Yes but, on our client's instructions, they were all forwarded electronically as each sale was completed. We kept nothing otherwise.'

'Is that usual?' Mac asked.

'It's not unusual shall I say,' Mr. Smyth replied. 'Many of our clients value the discreet way we operate.'

Mac would bet that they did.

As they walked back to the car Leigh asked, 'So, are we going to ask for a court order then?'

'There's no point really, is there? Property gurus indeed! Tax avoidance gurus more like it.' As he said this Mac had a thought. 'I think that I'll give Colin Furness a call when I get a minute.'

'Colin Furness? Wasn't he the financial wizard from the Fraud Squad who helped you with the Cyprus case?' Leigh asked.

'Yes, that's him. If anyone can help then it will be him.'

Mac looked at his watch. It was nearly four thirty.

'We might as well call it a day,' Mac said. 'I'm meeting with Tim at six.'

'You're not meeting Tim at the pub by any chance?' Leigh asked hopefully.

'Sorry, no. We're meeting up at my house.'

Leigh looked a little disappointed.

'Oh well, Netflix it is then.'

Once again, dark thoughts insinuated themselves into Mac's head as he made his way home. For some reason he wasn't looking forward to seeing his friend.

He stood in the centre of the room and looked around him. He could remember exactly what it had looked like before it had been so desecrated. He'd used the cottage several times for an affair that he'd been having with a married woman. It had suited him then. While being within a reasonable driving distance from London, it was still quite remote. As the woman involved was the wife of a business friend of his, being remote was good. They both wanted to keep it all as secret as possible.

He sighed. He hadn't thought about her for a while now. He hadn't wanted it to end, that was all her idea. He'd asked her to leave her husband and damn the consequences but she said that she couldn't. She had children, two of which were still at home. She'd told him that she and her husband's family were also very close and, if she left her husband, then she'd be leaving them too.

And so, the affair had ended and it had really hurt. Besides his mother and his daughter, she'd only been the third woman in his life that he'd truly loved. They had visited the little cottage every second Thursday during their affair and it had always been pristine. It was far from pristine now.

There were three bloodied hand-prints on one wall of the living room and the white-painted walls by the stairs looked as if they had been sprayed with red wine. A trail of blood ran across the white carpet in front of him. He stared down at the dark red blotches. He could see it in his mind's eye. The man running down the stairs in a panic, trying to get away. Yet, there was nowhere to run to. He was already dead.

He followed the blood trail into the kitchen. Here it was even worse. He'd made it all the way to the back door before collapsing. A red pool had formed in a slight hollow in the tiled floor and there, in the middle of it, lay a body. He was naked. There were cuts all over the upper part of his body and he could count at least five stab wounds. The expression on the dead man's face was one more of surprise than horror.

He sat down heavily on a chair and shook his head. He had seen dead bodies before, after all construction can be a risky business, but never one like this.

He had brought something to wrap the body in and, on his way here, he had figured out a way of disposing of the evidence. At least he thought he had. The amount of blood around the house meant that he would have to think again. He thought of what he should do.

He knew that he had a decision to make but he'd been putting it off until the last moment. This was unlike him but his daughter's life was at stake here.

She'd told him that the man, whose body was now lying lifeless on the floor, had been violent with her and that she'd been afraid and had no choice but to kill him. However, he'd now seen the damage that she'd inflicted on him. It had been a frenzied attack and yet there hadn't been a single scratch on her.

He thought about calling the police and washing his hands of the whole thing. That would be the right thing to do, and the easiest. He'd get her a good barrister, the best that money could buy, and perhaps she'd get off lightly. However, looking around him, he didn't see how that would be possible. It would be a massive gamble and, if he lost, his daughter would hate him forever. Picturing his daughter, who he fiercely loved, wasting away in jail for a lifetime made him think again.

He knew that he only had two choices; give her up to the police or believe what she'd said to him and cover up her part in a killing.

He knew in his heart that he would never be able to give her up and so he prayed to God for forgiveness. He then tried to think of what he should do next.

It didn't take him long. He had a reputation for thinking clearly in even the most pressurised situations and that reputation was well-earned. His idea was simple enough.

34

He'd done it once before and that had worked out well enough. He made a single phone call. That was all that was needed. He then put it out of his mind. He had total trust that everything would be done exactly as he'd asked.

He wrapped the body in plastic sheeting and carried it out to the van where he placed it on another plastic sheet. It was a dead weight but he was strong and it was no problem for him. He had no fear of anyone seeing him as the road was a dead end and there wasn't another house for miles.

He then locked the door of the house behind him and took off his bloodied clothes and shoes. He carefully wiped his hands and arms with several wet wipes. He placed the clothes, shoes and wipes on top of the body and then wrapped it all up in the plastic sheet. He securely taped it all up and then shut and locked the van's back door. He took a bag from the front passenger seat and changed into some new jogging bottoms, a T shirt and some trainers. Now, he was ready to go.

He stood and looked back at the house before he left. He had some good memories of the place and his many visits there and he felt sad. He knew that this would be the last time that he'd ever see it.

Chapter Four

Mac picked up his car at the police station and drove home. It was still only five-twenty so he had some time before his meeting with Tim. He felt butterflies as big as bats flapping around in his stomach as he went to make a pot of coffee. He stood and looked at the birds squabbling over the bird feeder. The sight of their antics usually cheered him up but today Mac paid them little attention.

Had Tim lost some weight recently? He remembered jokingly saying how fetching he'd looked in his swimming trunks. Now he wondered. Looking back, he also wondered if Tim had been enjoying himself as much as he'd thought when they were in Cyprus. He'd caught him being a bit thoughtful a few times. Not that Tim couldn't be thoughtful now and again but, generally, it was unlike him.

A word kept popping into his head. Mac thought it the most horrible word in the English language. He quickly pushed it away.

He was helped in this by Terry. On hearing a little whine, he looked down to see his dog looking up at him with the most soulful eyes. Had he sensed Mac's dark mood somehow?

He looked at the clock. It was only five thirty. He decided that he needed some air.

All Mac had to do was walk towards the front door to see the energy levels in Terry build up. By the time his hand was on the dog lead Terry was bouncing up and down as though on springs. Once outside, Mac breathed in deeply.

I'm just making mountains out of molehills, he told himself.

He walked past the graveyard but, this time, he didn't go in. Seeing all those lines of headstones set his teeth on edge. He'd talk to Nora tomorrow. He wondered what he'd have to tell her. Mac ended up walking further than he'd planned and he hoped that his back wouldn't object to it later. He looked at his watch. It was time to go home.

Tim was a little early. Mac gave him a wave as they converged on his house from opposite directions. Terry was happy to see Tim too and bounced up and down, only staying still long enough to allow himself to be patted.

'Beer?' Mac asked once they'd gotten themselves inside.

'Err...no. You're alright there, Mac,' Tim replied.

Now Mac was really worried. He sat down and looked at his friend.

'What is it, Tim?'

Tim gave him a look that turned his stomach to ice.

'It's, well...it's...'

Mac waited patiently while Tim searched for the words. His heart had speeded up and he could hear it in his ears. Thump, thump, thump.

'I'm afraid that I lied to you,' Tim said avoiding looking at Mac directly. 'I didn't miss the first week of our holiday because I'd mixed up Hertfordshire and Herefordshire. I...I had to be somewhere.'

'Where?' Mac asked as the thumping got louder.

'The hospital,' Tim replied. 'They needed me in for the pre-op.'

'Pre-op?'

'It's a pre-operative assessment,' Tim explained. 'It's to check that you're okay to be operated on.'

'I know that but why would you need an operation? Christ, Tim what haven't you been telling me?'

'You were so happy to be going on holiday and I didn't want to spoil your mood. Then you solved the Harold Jones case[1] and you were so made up over that too. I just didn't want to ruin our holiday. So, I lied a little.' Tim shrugged and looked at Mac with eyes every bit as soulful as Terry's had been.

Thump, thump, thump.

---

[1] The Eight Bench Walk – the tenth Mac Maguire mystery

'It's cancer, Mac.'

There was a pause in the thumping in his ears and then it raced off again.

That word. That horrible, filthy word. It had taken his wife, the only woman he'd ever loved and now. And now.

Please God, not again, he said to himself.

He felt the blackness that had enveloped him for many months after his wife's death hovering somewhere nearby.

'It's not quite as bad as you might think,' Tim said quickly. 'It's prostate cancer and it hasn't spread. My consultant thinks that the operation should do the trick. If it works out then I should be cancer free in three days from now.'

'The operation is in three days?' Mac asked. 'Why didn't you tell me all this earlier? We've been back from our holiday for a while now. Why?'

Mac felt as though he had some sort of motion sickness. He could feel the world spinning violently through space.

Tim looked back at him with a shame-faced look.

'I'm sorry. You're right, I should have told you but I just couldn't. I knew how you'd feel and I just couldn't see the point of putting you through the wringer for any longer than was necessary.'

'I could have helped,' Mac said.

'I'm hoping that you still can,' Tim said. 'As it's a fairly major operation, I'll need to recuperate for a while and I'll need to have someone around during the day too.'

'You can stay here,' Mac quickly said. 'I'll look after you.'

'Thanks, Mac,' a slightly tearful Tim said. 'I'll be more than happy to take you up on your offer.'

'I'll get Amrit to help too...'

The look on Tim's face made Mac stop mid-sentence.

'You've already told Bridget, haven't you?'

Another shame-faced look from Tim.

'Well, I needed someone to talk to and she is a doctor. I could have gone for radiotherapy or hormone treatment but, after talking it through with Bridget, I chose the operation. She told me that the consultant who'll be doing the surgery is very highly thought of. Anyway, she's already talked to Amrit and she'll be coming in every day to help out until I have the catheter removed.'

'You'll have a catheter in?' Mac said with a concerned expression.

'Yes, but it's just for two weeks or so until it all heals up. Bridget said that I might feel a bit banged up for a while afterwards.'

'What's the operation?' Mac asked. 'I mean what do they do?'

As soon as he'd asked the question, he wasn't sure that he wanted to hear the answer.

'It's called a...' Tim screwed up his face in concentration. He then said very slowly, 'It's called a Robotic-assisted Laparoscopic Prostatectomy.'

Mac could see why Tim had needed to think for a while. Seeing his friend's blank look, Tim carried on.

'It's keyhole surgery of a sort but they have to make six incisions to be able to get all of the prostate out.'

Six! Tim hadn't been lying when he said it was major surgery.

'Christ!' Mac said softly.

The world spun even faster as the reality of the situation started to sink in. Tim put a reassuring hand on Mac's knee.

'It will be okay, Mac. It will be okay.'

Mac looked up at his friend and he could see the worry in his face. His reaction was only making things worse.

Pull yourself together, he said to himself.

'Of course, it will,' Mac said trying to smile. 'They can do absolute wonders these days, can't they? What's the plan of action then?'

'I'd be grateful if you could drive me to the hospital,' Tim said. 'I'll be bringing a bag with everything I'll need while I'm there and a suitcase that you can take back with you for when I come out. I'll be on a special diet from tomorrow until I go in. No food, just water and these special little drinks they've given me.'

'Of course, I'll drive you. How long will you be in for?'

'If it all goes well then I should be out on Saturday,' Tim replied.

'That soon?' Mac asked with some surprise.

'Bridget said that they don't keep you hanging about in hospital these days. They'll have me sitting up in a chair and walking a bit the day after the operation.'

That seemed a bit too soon to Mac but he guessed that the doctors knew what they were doing.

'I'll leave you now, Mac,' Tim said holding his hand out. 'I've got quite a bit of work to square away before the operation.'

Mac shook his friend's hand. Tim must have seen the fear he felt.

'It will be okay, Mac,' Tim said. 'It will.'

Mac sat there for quite a while after Tim had gone. He knew that he'd have to do better. It had ended up with Tim consoling him which was definitely the wrong way around.

He told himself that lots of people survive cancer, lots. For Tim's sake, he needed to stay strong. Yes, Tim would make it and, before he knew it, they would be back down the pub discussing their favourite football team's latest failures.

He didn't notice until sometime afterwards that his face was wet with tears.

Chapter Five

The next morning Mac found himself sitting in the Major Crime Unit's room staring at the blank whiteboard. It was blank because he had no idea of where the investigation might go next.

Members of the team came and went but those who knew him best left him to his thoughts. The Josh Wolfe case was over, bar the paperwork, but a recent pub brawl in Dunstable, which had left one man in hospital with serious injuries, and an aggravated burglary in Huntingdon were keeping the team more than busy.

Mac had asked Dan if Josh Wolfe had been involved in any major demolition works recently but it didn't seem that he had. Perhaps Josh Wolfe and Hoar's Cottage weren't connected after all, Mac thought.

Despite Tim's news, Mac had slept well but he'd found himself wide awake just after six o'clock. Even after taking Terry for a walk and having a leisurely breakfast he still found himself driving towards the station just after seven o'clock. He needed to be doing something and he hoped that he'd be able to use the time to come up with some ideas. He did have one idea though but he was unsure how practical it might be. He looked up some information on the internet anyway.

Leigh was a little late that morning.

'I haven't slept that well for ages,' Leigh said with a smile as she walked in. 'I went to bed early too so I must have been tired.'

'I've been in for a while,' Mac said turning to look again at the blank whiteboard. 'I was hoping to have a few ideas up on the board for what we might do next but, as you can see, I'm struggling.'

In truth he'd spent more time thinking about Tim than the case. Bridget had come around to see him not long after

Tim had left and they'd had a very long chat. Mac had felt a little better after that. His daughter had persuaded him to accept the fact that Tim was unlikely to die any time soon. She said that if the operation worked then it will have been as if the cancer had never been there. If not, then there were other treatments.

Mac had believed her. Almost.

'Yes, we've not got much to go on, have we?' Leigh said bringing Mac back to the present.

'You can say that again but something will turn up. I've asked Martin if he could find out who the previous owners of Hoar's Cottage were. You never know but they might be able to tell us something,' Mac said with a shrug. 'Coffee?'

Martin had the answer before they had finished their drinks.

'Apparently, the cottage was sold five years ago by a Mrs. Petra Furlong,' Mac said reading from the print-out. 'She sold it to a company called Syncote Holdings which ceased to exist shortly afterwards. The only name associated with the company is that of Ferrer and Garnet Solicitors. I'll ring Colin Furness now and see if he knows anything about them.'

Leigh tried to make out what was being said but, as Mac was mostly listening to what Colin was saying, she had to wait until he'd finished. His glum expression as he put his phone away told her most of what she needed to know.

'Colin says that Ferrer and Garnet are basically in the same business as Ricard and Montefiore. He doesn't think that we'll learn anything from them either,' Mac said. 'He says that they've got the use of shell companies down to a fine art these days when it comes to property sales. With all the loopholes in the law, it appears that most of what they do is legal anyway.'

'Why don't the government close the loopholes then?' Leigh asked. 'I don't get any choice about whether I pay tax or not, they take it straight out of my salary.'

'Colin mentioned that too. He said that they could close the loopholes overnight but, unfortunately, a lot of people in the government like using shell companies too.'

'Somehow, I'm not all that surprised,' Leigh said with a scowl. 'So, what's next then?'

'Well, I've arranged for someone from the university to survey the site this morning,' Mac replied. 'We can go there first, if that's alright?'

'Yes, sure. What is it they'll be looking for exactly?'

'Well, some confirmation that a house did actually exist there once, I suppose,' Mac replied. 'They should also be able to tell us if there's anything buried where the house used to sit. I'm not sure if it will be any help even if they do find something but we'll see.'

'What do you think will be buried there?' Leigh asked.

'Nothing really, if I'm being honest. Unless all the men who took part in the demolition were in on it, which I doubt, then I guess that they would have treated it the same as any other reinstatement. Jez Manning told me that, if that was the case, then everything would have to be taken away.'

Mac called Mrs. Furlong, who said that she'd be happy to see them. He arranged to meet her in an hour and a half. First, they had to meet the archaeological student who was going to survey the site of the missing house for them.

'Where does Mrs. Furlong live?' Leigh asked as they walked towards the car park.

'Furlong Farm. It's near Offley Hoo, just down the road from the cottage. You'll see the sign as we pass by.'

Mac remembered Furlong Farm from his previous visit to the missing cottage. The entrance to the farm was on a tight bend so you had to slow down. That, plus the fact that there was a large sign, meant that you really couldn't miss it.

'Anyway, I'm glad that Mrs. Furlong could see us today,' Mac said. 'Other than meeting with the surveyor, I've no idea what we'd be doing otherwise.'

A small white van was parked in the lane near where the cottage had stood. A young woman got out. She was very practically dressed in a waterproof jacket, jeans and green wellingtons. Her fair complexion and her long blonde hair, that was braided into an intricate plait that lay over one shoulder, gave her a very Scandinavian look.

'Hi, I'm Jenny Lindstrom,' she said with a cheery smile.

Mac introduced Leigh and himself.

'So, what are you going to use for the survey?' Mac asked.

Jenny opened the back of the van.

'I'll be using this,' she said pointing inside the van.

Mac saw something that looked like two short scaffolding tubes connected by another in the form of a 'H'. In the centre of the connecting pole there was a box of electronic equipment. He'd seen something like it before.

'How does it work then?' Leigh asked.

'I'll be doing a GPR survey and that stands for Ground Penetrating Radar. It's a bit like the radar that aircraft use but we point it down into the ground instead. If there's anything down there then this will pick it up. It's really simple to use. I just turn it on and then walk up and down making sure that I cover the whole area that you want surveyed,' Jenny replied.

Mac took her through the gap in the hedge and showed her where he wanted her to survey.

'So, basically it's all of the area that's been newly grassed over then?' she asked.

'That's right. How long do you think it will take?' Mac asked.

'I'll have to go out a bit beyond this area to make sure that I don't miss anything. Two to three hours I should think, no more,' Jenny replied.

'And how long before we get the results?'

'I can do you a proper report, if you want, but I can tell you if there's anything down there more or less straight after I've finished the survey.'

This was exactly what Mac had wanted to hear.

'Call me as soon as you've got some results,' Mac said as he gave her a card.

They left Jenny to her work and drove back towards the farm. Mac was quiet and Leigh left him to his thoughts.

They turned off the narrow road at the sign for Furlong Farm and drove down a lane that was somewhat wider than the road for around a quarter of a mile. The farmhouse was large and, judging from the different building styles, had obviously been added to over the years. Behind the house there were four massive barns and some smaller out-houses. The farm looked solid and prosperous and as if it had been around for some time.

The front door of the house opened as they pulled up and a middle-aged woman wearing a dark-green pullover, jeans and wellingtons waved at them. She was sturdily-built and looked every inch the farmer's wife.

'Mrs. Furlong, no doubt,' Mac said.

In that he was right. Tea and biscuits were ready for them as they walked in. The kitchen was in one of the oldest parts of the house and he had to be careful as he had to take a step down as he went in. The floor was covered with large flagstones that had been worn right down in places. That, plus the large black timber roof beams, whitewashed walls and ancient fireplace, gave Mac the idea that the farmhouse went back a lot further than he had first thought.

They sat down at a long and very robust looking kitchen table that also had the patina of great age. On it stood a teapot, that had a knitted woollen cosy on it, cups and saucers and a large plate of chocolate biscuits. Tea was poured before any questions were asked. It was Mrs. Furlong who asked the first one.

'I've heard all about Hoar's Cottage from the postie,' she said. 'I take it that's why you're here?'

'That's right,' Mac replied. 'We've been asked to look into its disappearance by the estate agency that was trying to sell it. Is there anything that you can tell us about it?'

'About it disappearing, no,' she replied with a shake of her head. 'That's just about the strangest thing that's ever happened around here, I can tell you. I popped down there this morning and had a look for myself. You'd never have guessed that a house had ever been there at all.'

'We think that the cottage was demolished around five to six weeks ago. You didn't see or hear anything different around that time?'

'I've been thinking about that ever since the postie told me about it but no. We're a good bit away but, even so, you'd think that we would have heard something if lots of heavy lorries had been going up and down the road there.'

Mac gave this some thought.

'Who else lives here with you?'

'Just my son, his wife and their two children but they were away on holiday around that time,' she said. 'I remember because it felt so strange being by myself in the house at night and I didn't sleep all that well. I used to go out and check on the cows and pigs for something to do. As I said, we're a good bit away from the road but you can still hear a car go by at night as it's so quiet.'

'So, you'd have definitely heard a lorry going by?' Mac asked.

'Yes, if I'd have been awake that is,' she replied.

Mac thought that the idea he'd had earlier might have some mileage in it after all.

'Do you mind me asking where Mr. Furlong is?'

Mac knew the answer from her expression before she even said a word.

'He died. Just over five years ago now.'

'I'm sorry to hear that,' Mac said. 'The cottage was sold five years ago too. Did that have something to do with your husband's death?'

'Yes, in a way,' she replied. 'We bought the house from a farm down the road about twenty-five years ago as soon as it came on the market. We rented it to one of our employees, Bob Hartley. He'd worked with us for years and he was getting fed up of driving in every day from Hexton where he lived. So, he and his wife moved in and lived quite happily there until my husband died. He loved my husband and I think that his heart went out of the job after that. He was well above retirement age anyway and so he and his wife bought a caravan by the sea and they decided to retire there. None of our other employees wanted the cottage and so I sold it.'

'Did you ever have any contact with the people who bought the cottage?'

Mrs. Furlong shook her head.

'No, the estate agency dealt with everything.'

'Do you still have any of the paperwork related to the sale?' Mac asked.

'Yes, of course. Do you want me to copy it for you?'

Mac did. While she was away Mac tucked into the chocolate biscuits. A couple of minutes later she handed Mac several sheets of paper.

'Why is it called Hoar's Cottage, do you know?' Mac asked seeing the name prominently on the first page.

It was something that had been niggling him ever since he'd heard the name.

Mrs. Furlong smiled widely.

'Well, as I said we bought it from a farm just down the road some time ago. Her husband had died too but she got a bit of a shock when the will was read. She hadn't even known that her husband owned the cottage until then and for a very good reason. He'd bought the house some twenty years before and he'd very quietly installed his mistress in it. His wife only discovered after he died that all those overnight fishing trips with friends were just an excuse for him to pop down the road and get cosy with another woman. To rub it in, the will stated that the cottage had to be sold and all the money given to his mistress. It was a cruel thing to do to anyone. The poor woman had to organise selling the house knowing that the proceeds would all be going to her

47

husband's floozy. That why she called it Hoar's Cottage. I'm afraid that her spelling skills weren't all that good.'

Mac had to think for a while before he smiled too.

'Well, she got it phonetically right anyway.'

After leaving Mrs. Furlong they sat in the car in silence for a while. Leigh didn't attempt to start up the engine, she knew that Mac was thinking. He pulled out his tablet and looked at it for a while.

'I think we should go that way,' Mac eventually said pointing towards the road.

'What? Back towards the cottage?' Leigh asked.

'Yes, but don't turn off the road. Keep going until we get to the next house or farm. According to the figures that Jez Manning sent me, they would have had to make at least fifty trips to a tip to get rid of all the demolition waste. As Mrs. Furlong didn't hear anything at all then it's probably a safe assumption that they didn't come this way.'

Leigh gave this a little thought before smiling.

'So, you're trying to trace the direction that the trucks went in. Will that help?'

'It might,' Mac replied. 'With such narrow roads, I'd guess that they'd only move the waste at night. With any luck, someone will have heard them. While I was waiting for you, I discovered that the nearest sites that would take demolition waste are Luton, not far from the airport, and Stevenage. If they took the waste anywhere further away than that then we're probably sunk.'

They drove past Down's Bottom and went on for over half a mile before they came to a small house that stood just a few yards back from the road. Mac was hopeful.

He rang the bell. Nothing. He then rang it again. After a third time he could see a figure through the frosted glass in the door slowly approaching them. An old man opened the door and seemed surprised to see them.

'We're from the police and I was wondering...'

Mac stopped at seeing the man's puzzled expression.

'I'm deaf,' he said too loudly while pointing at one of his ears. 'I'll go and get my hearing aid.'

Mac signed for him not to bother and gave him a thumbs-up as thanks.

'People don't wear hearing aids in bed,' Mac said to himself as they walked away.

They did better at the next house. Although it was at least a hundred yards away from the road the old woman who lived there remembered the trucks going by.

'They woke me up,' she said. 'I thought that it was thunder at first. Fairly made my windows rattle so they did. I never heard anything like it before or since.'

Mac knew that they were on the right track.

They drove on and came to a fork in the road.

'Which way?' Leigh asked.

Mac looked at a map on his phone.

'Let's go right,' he suggested. 'If we draw a blank then we can always come back and try the other way.'

They didn't need to. They found two more houses where the occupants said that the sound of lorries had kept them awake at night.

'They were going to Luton then,' Mac said. 'Here's the address of the waste site.'

Leigh fed it into the satnav and they were off. Mac called the site while they were on the road and got his instructions. Around ten minutes later they were driving past a long queue of tipper trucks all of which had full loads. They drove through the gates and pulled up outside a large portacabin.

They could hear that some sort of argument was going on well before they stepped inside. Once they did, they saw two red-faced men in dusty overalls shouting at each other and waving around pieces of paper. Behind them a bald-headed man with a long-suffering expression on his face sat behind a desk. He forlornly shook his head as he looked over at the two men. He then noticed Mac and came over.

'Mr. Tapper?' Mac asked as he showed him his warrant card.

The man nodded.

'Come on, let's find somewhere a bit quieter, shall we?'

He led them outside to where a picnic bench had been set up on a patch of grass. The sun had come out and it was now pleasantly warm.

'That's better,' Mr. Tapper said with a smile as he sat down.

'What was all that about?' Mac asked as he and Leigh joined him.

'Wrong paperwork. We keep telling them but they keep doing it anyway. If they don't bring along the correct documentation then they have to take their load back and get it. As they get paid by the load, they can get a bit upset about it. Anyway, I checked for any waste documentation around the dates you that gave me but there was nothing on the system that would match your house. We don't get many visits from the police. Do you mind me asking what this is all about?'

Mac told him all about the house that wasn't there.

He rubbed the top of his bald dome as he thought.

'And you're sure that the trucks must have come here?' he asked.

'We're fairly sure,' Mac replied.

The man shrugged.

'You've seen the queues of trucks as you came in, well, it's been like that for the last couple of months or so. They come in twenty-four hours a day, seven days a week, so fifty or so loads could easily get slipped in, if that's what someone wanted to do.'

'So, there's no way that you might be able to track the waste that came from the house?' Mac asked with more hope than anything else.

'Are you okay to walk a hundred yards or so?' Mr. Tapper asked looking at Mac's crutch. When Mac nodded, he continued, 'Follow me.'

Mac and Leigh followed Mr. Tapper over a grassy field until they came to a high metal fence.

'That's where it all goes,' he said.

Mac looked down into a vast hole in the ground. It must have been a good half a mile across and nearly that deep.

Mac frowned as he looked at it. It was obviously an old worked-out quarry.

'Even if we knew roughly where it was, which we don't,' Mr. Tapper said, 'it would now be covered in thousands of tons of demolition waste.'

'Is the site always this busy?' Leigh asked.

'No, not usually but we have three major building projects on the go not far from here and that's where most of the waste is coming from.'

Mac was interested in this.

'Where are these projects?' he asked.

'Well, the biggest one's probably over at Dunstable where they're redeveloping most of the old hospital site. Then there's the new retail centre at Bury Park and the other one's at the University campus in Luton where they're demolishing the old student housing blocks and lecture halls.'

Mac took his phone out and looked at the map of the area. He smiled.

'Thank you, Mr. Tapper. You've been most helpful.'

'Have I?' he replied looking mystified.

As they walked back to the car Mac said, 'That was a very good question you asked back there.'

'What, about the site being busy?' Leigh replied.

'That's right. Drive slowly as we go back. I want...'

Leigh had to wait to hear what Mac wanted as his phone went off. It was Jenny Lindstrom. She had finished the survey.

Leigh glanced over at Mac as they drove out of Luton. He was peering out of the windscreen at the side of the road. Leigh guessed what he was looking for and she pulled to a halt without being asked. Mac smiled at her as she turned the car's hazard lights on.

Mac quickly got out and noted down a number that had been painted onto the lamppost.

'Do you really think there's a chance that the traffic camera might have caught our trucks?' Leigh asked as she drove on.

'I'm hoping that's the case. I'm also hoping that the camera might have caught their number plates too,' Mac replied as he pulled out his phone.

Mac was on his phone most of the way back to where Hoar's Cottage used to stand. From what Leigh could make out, the police unit responsible for the speed cameras were going to check and see if they had anything around the time that the cottage was demolished. Mac confirmed this after he'd finished talking.

'I checked where the other three building projects are on the map,' Mac explained. 'They're all to the west of the waste site...'

'So, any trucks coming from the east of Luton are likely to be ours.'

'That's it,' Mac said with a smile.

A possible lead at last, Leigh thought, unconsciously smiling too.

They could see Jenny as they turned into Down's Bottom. The back doors of her van were open and she was sitting on the tailgate as she keyed into a laptop.

She smiled brightly when she saw them coming.

'Have you found anything?' Mac asked without saying 'hello' first.

'No,' Jenny replied. 'There's absolutely nothing down there except earth.' Seeing Mac's and Leigh's disappointed expressions she carried on. 'However, I can confirm that the earth has been disturbed over the entire area that has been grassed over and to a depth of around two to three metres in places.'

'So, there was definitely something there once?' Mac asked.

Jenny nodded.

'Whoever demolished your house did a good job though. There were some bits of what might be rubble deep down but nothing much bigger than a brick, I'd say.'

Mac thanked her and asked her to send all the data to Martin Selby for the case file. He then said goodbye.

'Where to now?' Leigh asked.

'Back to the station,' Mac said as he looked at his watch. 'But first, let's go to the Magnets and get something to eat. I'm starving.'

Leigh felt a little hungry too. She looked at the clock when she got back into the car and was surprised to find that it was now after three o'clock.

She felt a little frisson of excitement as she drove back. It was definitely the most puzzling case that she'd ever been involved with but now they had a lead.

She smiled as she glanced over at her passenger.

She also had Mac and that was even better.

Chapter Six

They ate their sandwiches in silence. Mac stared out of the pub window at the people passing by outside but his thoughts were elsewhere.

'What is it, Mac?' Leigh eventually asked.

Mac turned to look at her.

'Is it that obvious?' he asked.

She nodded.

'I'm just a bit worried about something,' he continued. 'Tim's going in for an operation on Thursday and...'

With some prompting Leigh got the whole story out of him.

'Well, it could be worse,' she said with a shrug of her shoulders.

Mac gave her a puzzled look.

'My uncle went in for that same operation about two years ago,' Leigh explained. 'He's my favourite relative so I helped him out as much as I could. As he's a widower, I went to some of his medical appointments with him to keep him company. I learned a fair bit about prostate cancer through that. Basically, so long as the cancer hasn't spread anywhere else then Tim will probably be okay.'

'How is your uncle these days?' Mac asked with great interest.

'He's great. He still has the occasional blood test and they keep checking his PSA levels but, thankfully, they've been next to nothing ever since the operation.'

'PSA levels?' Mac asked.

Leigh's forehead crinkled up as she thought.

'Sorry, I've forgotten what it stands for but it's a sort of marker in the blood that's specific to the prostate. Anyway, what I'm saying is that prostate cancer's really easy to test for.'

'I must admit that, when Tim told me that it was cancer, I could only think the worst. However, I spoke to my daughter last night and she explained that not all cancers are the same. The one that killed my wife was very aggressive and they caught it too late but Bridget said that prostate cancers can be quite slow growing and some hardly grow at all.'

'That's right,' Leigh said. 'My uncle was told by his consultant that he might have lived for four or five years without any intervention but, now that he's had the operation, I'm hoping that he'll be around for quite a lot longer than that.'

Mac sat back and thought about this. He decided that he was being an idiot about the whole thing. Tim needed his support now and not his self-pity.

'Has that helped a bit?' Leigh asked.

Mac nodded. It had.

'I'll be seeing Tim here a bit later on. Want to join us?'

'Sure, I've got nothing else on.'

Mac was curious so, as they walked back to the station, he asked her a question.

'I thought that you were going out with someone. What was his name?'

'Jerome,' Leigh replied as she pulled a pretend sad face. 'No, we split up a couple of weeks ago.'

'Oh, I'm sorry...'

'Don't be,' Leigh said quickly. 'No-one got dumped, it just sort of fizzled out.'

'So, you don't mind being single again?'

'Not at all. In fact, I'm really looking forward to having some time to myself again,' she said with a smile. 'I've got some friends here now that I go out with every week so I'm not totally by myself.'

'You've been in Letchworth what, just over a year or so now?' Mac said.

'Yes, I arrived just in time for the Case of the Letchworth Poisoner[2],' she said with a laugh. 'God, I was so nervous back then; about the move, about working with you, about everything really. I wasn't even sure that I wanted to stay in the police, if I'm being honest.'

'And now?'

She gave this a little thought.

'I love my little flat and I love Letchworth. It's such an unusual place and it still surprises me at times. I also love working with Dan and the team. At the last place I worked the team was, well, toxic is the word I'd use. Everyone seemed to be playing mind games with everyone else.'

'Well, you were lucky there,' Mac said, 'and luckily for us all, Dan Carter had total control over who he recruited to join the Major Crime Unit. We're also lucky that he's not the type who would tolerate a bad apple in the team for more than five minutes anyway.'

'Don't get me wrong, I'd gladly give up my single life if the right man came along. I look at couples like Jo and Gerry and Kate and Toni and I do feel a little envious at times but not enough to make me jump into a relationship just for the sake of it.'

'You're being very wise,' Mac said.

'Anyway, I've already got a double date lined up. Tonight, with you and Tim,' she said with a smile.

This made Mac laugh out loud.

Back at the empty Major Crime Unit's team room they wrestled with the blank whiteboard. After half an hour or so it became obvious that the whiteboard was well ahead on points.

'I really hope that we get something from the traffic cameras,' Mac said with some exasperation. 'Anyway, let's have a look at the three companies who are carrying out the demolition work around Luton.'

---

[2] The Dead Squirrel – The second Mac Maguire mystery

He pulled out his notebook. He'd gotten the names of the companies from Mr. Tapper before they left the waste site.

'So, first up is the company who are redeveloping the university site,' Mac said. 'They're called Aldereds.'

They found that Aldereds was a new company that had been put together just for the university project. It was a consortium of four other companies; two were British, one was German and the last was Japanese.

'God, I hope it's not them!' Leigh exclaimed. 'There'd be far too many suspects by half.'

Mac could only agree. They tried T.B. Power next.

'They must be quite a big company,' Leigh said. 'I've seen loads of their lorries around.'

'I guess that they must be. From what Mr. Tapper told us, redeveloping the old hospital site is a very big project. Let's see what we can find out about them.'

T.B. Power was the opposite to Aldereds. The company was over twenty-five years old and was more or less wholly owned by one man. Mr. Power didn't seem to be into self-publicity much as they found very little on the man himself. There was plenty about his company though. It turned out that the redevelopment of the hospital site, big as it was, was dwarfed by comparison to some of the company's other projects. One of the biggest was the building of a hundred and twenty floor skyscraper on the South Bank. It was going to be the highest building in London by far.

'It says here that they completed the biggest concrete pour in Europe not long ago,' Leigh said. 'It took them four days to pour fourteen thousand cubic metres of concrete for the skyscraper's foundation.'

'That's a lot of concrete alright,' Mac said trying to picture what fourteen thousand cubic metres might look like and failing.

The last company was called 'Florenz Construction'. It was building the new retail park at Bury Park. It turned out to be a German-Italian company based in Strasbourg. Even after half an hour on Google that still remained the sum of their knowledge.

Mac sat back and shook his head.

'We'll get nowhere by ourselves,' Mac said. 'We need some help.'

He called Jez Manning who was thankfully able to suggest someone. Jez had been interviewed a year or so before by a journalist who worked for a specialist construction magazine. The journalist was called Sam Ellis and Jez thought that she really knew her stuff. Mac called her and she agreed to take a video call just after six o'clock.

'So, we've got an hour or so to play with,' Mac said. 'Any ideas?'

'If you have any, could you give us some?' a grumpy looking Dan Carter said as he entered the room.

He was followed in by DS Adil Thakkar, DI Jo Dugdale and DI Andy Reid. They all looked tired and mildly exasperated.

'I take it that your cases aren't going all that well?' Mac observed.

Dan sat on the corner of a desk.

'Well, the man who was injured in the pub brawl died three hours ago, so it's now a murder case. The problem is that we've got too many suspects as there were at least twenty men involved in the fracas and it looks as if all of them are lying to us. As for the burglary, we've got next to nothing as yet. A woman in a wheelchair was quite badly injured during the robbery so, as you can guess, it's all over the newspapers. I thought that we'd take some time out, get our heads together and see if we could come up with something new. How's your case going?'

'Not much better, if I'm being honest,' Mac replied. 'We're guessing that the house ended up in a great big hole just outside of Luton but, unfortunately for us, it now has a few thousand tons of building waste sitting on top of it.'

'So, no leads at all?' Dan asked.

'Just the one. We're waiting to hear back from the traffic camera people in Luton. We're hoping that they might have caught some of the trucks carrying the rubble from the house demolition on camera as they came towards the waste site but other than that...'

Mac shrugged.

'Well, the best of luck to all of us then,' Dan said as he stood up. 'It looks as if we'll need it.'

Mac watched as they all filed into Dan's office.

'I think Dan might well be right there,' Leigh said.

Mac turned to see her looking glumly at the blank whiteboard. Martin came in and gave them both a little wave as he walked to his desk. They watched as he set up his laptop before inserting a memory stick. Mac was surprised when, a few minutes later, he placed the stick in front of Mac.

'I had some free time on the train just now so I thought that I'd try my luck,' Martin said pointing at the memory stick. 'I'm not sure how useful it will be but it's got a case file on there.'

Mac immediately plugged the stick in and they both started reading.

The case file started off with a statement given by an eighteen-year-old man called Edward Haskell some ten months earlier. He stated that, at the age of twelve, he had been lured away from a children's home in Luton with the promise of a 'party' and some easy money to be made. He said that he hated the home and he was just glad to get away for a while. Along with three other young boys, he was driven in a big black car to a cottage with a big glass conservatory. In this cottage a number of men were waiting for them. All four boys were stripped and tied up and then repeatedly raped by the men and made to do some truly disgusting things. All the men were naked and all wore masks on their faces.

Edward was driven back to the children's home early the next morning and he was told that he would be killed if he told anyone about what had happened that night.

A month or so after this the big black car pulled up alongside him as he was on his way back from school and rough hands dragged him inside. He was taken to yet another 'party' at the house with two boys he'd never seen before. Again, they were all raped and forced to do whatever disgusting acts turned the men on. He said that one boy refused and had a knife held to his throat.

Edward did as he was told and just hoped that it would soon end. He said that he saw the black car once or twice again but he somehow managed to keep away from it.

Edward had kept it all to himself for nearly six years but something had finally made him tell the police. It wasn't clear what had triggered this but the police started an investigation anyway. As he couldn't identify any of the men who attacked him then that just left the man who drove him and the house itself.

They had no luck with the driver. His description didn't match anyone on the criminal database so they had Edward look at hundreds of photos of men who had been involved in paedophile activity just in case. They drew a blank. They next tried to find the house.

Edward said that the windows on the car had been blacked out but, as they drove, he remembered hearing the sounds of aircraft taking off nearby. They carried on for about half an hour after that. The car stopped and started three or four times just before they arrived at their destination. He said that the house itself was quite small but it had a large conservatory on the side and this is where the 'parties' took place.

The investigators had made the assumption that the boys had been driven past the airport and then, at some point, had gone down a road with passing places. They had taken photos of around forty houses in the area that had conservatories. One of them was of Hoar's Cottage and it exactly fitted Edward's description of the house. However, when they went to show Edward Haskell the photographs, they discovered that a neighbour had found him dead that very morning. His body had been found surrounded by empty pill packets and there was an empty bottle of vodka. The coroner had ruled it as suicide and no foul play was suspected.

With their only source of information gone, the investigation ground to a halt but they decided not to close the case. This made Mac wonder.

'There's something missing from the file, isn't there?' he said.

'What?' Leigh asked.

'Why didn't they interview the other young men who'd been at the children's home at around the same time as Edward Haskell? It seems like an obvious step to me and that way they might have gotten someone to back up Edward's story.'

It was clear from Mac's reaction that this had seriously annoyed him.

'That poor lad!' Leigh said giving Mac a sad look. 'He didn't have much of a chance in life, did he?'

'No, he didn't. However, it looks as if our investigation might have gotten a little more serious,' Mac said as he got his phone out.

Annoying as it was, reading the case file had given him an idea. He called Mrs. Furlong and asked her a single question.

'So, the conservatory wasn't there when she sold the house. That means that someone put it there around five years ago,' Mac said giving Leigh a knowing look.

'And, if we can find out who, then we might have a real lead,' she said with a smile.

'The only problem is that there must be hundreds of firms within fifty miles or so of the cottage who do double glazing and conservatories,' Mac said. 'Not only that but, considering what it was going to be used for, I'd doubt that they'd use anyone local anyway. So, we might be looking at thousands.'

Mac looked again at the photo. The conservatory wasn't like any that he'd seen before. It was old-fashioned, perhaps Edwardian in design, octagonal in shape and far too big for such a small house. He looked over at Martin.

'I know that you have an app that can identify people's faces,' Mac said. 'Do you think it would be any good for conservatories?'

Martin gave this some thought.

'It wouldn't be the same software but I could give it a go. I take it that you want me to use the photo of Hoar's Cottage that's in the case file?'

'If you could,' Mac replied. 'It looks a quite a bit more expensive than the average conservatory so I'm hoping that might reduce the number of firms we might have to contact.'

Martin said that he would do his best and that was more than good enough for Mac.

Chapter Seven

They just had time for a coffee before the video meeting started. Sam Ellis proved to be an attractive woman in her late thirties. Her hair had been stylishly cut and she was freshly made up. She was also wearing a shimmering turquoise evening dress so Mac guessed that she was going out somewhere after the call.

Mac introduced himself and Leigh and gave Sam a brief outline of the case.

'So, you're interested in finding out if Aldereds, T.B. Power or Florenz might have been involved in helping your house to disappear?' she asked with a bemused expression.

'That's right,' Mac replied. 'The demolition waste had to go somewhere so we're guessing that it went to a waste site with documentation from one of those construction companies.'

Sam gave this some thought.

'I'd forget Florenz. As far as I know they've got no local connections plus they do a lot of work for the European Union so they like to keep things squeaky clean when it comes to abiding by the rules. Aldereds are new and I'm not sure I can really tell you anything at all about them. If I had to bet though, I'd put my money on T.B. Power.'

'Why is that?'

'Well, they've got a reputation for sailing close to the wind at times plus they might have some previous,' Sam said.

'Previous?' Mac asked looking puzzled.

'Stories abound about T.B. and his associates and a lot of them are actually true,' Sam replied. 'I heard this one from one of T.B.'s lieutenants a couple of years ago. It appears that, when T.B. was first starting up, he took over a construction contract for just one pound. It was so cheap because the companies who had originally signed it had made a right mess of it and there were some quite severe penalty clauses if the contract wasn't completed on time. Somehow T.B. managed it though. T.B.'s company made their name doing just that, buying up failing building contracts on the cheap and then, against all the odds, making them work. However, there was a major stumbling block to this particular contract. A court injunction had been taken out by one of the partners of the company who had previously tried to make the project work. Let's call him Mr. Smith. Although T.B. was sure that they would win the case in court, the injunction would inevitably delay the project. Mr. Smith was hoping that a legal battle would indeed delay the work long enough so that the contract would fail completely. A bit of schadenfreude on his part, I'd guess.'

She stopped and took a sip of white wine from an outsize glass.

'I'm going to a party given by the publishers of the magazine,' Sam explained, 'and, as it's usually as boring as hell, I find that a little pre-drinking helps enormously. Now, where was I?'

'T.B. Power and previous,' Mac replied.

'Oh, yes. So, T.B. had a problem and, being T.B., he quickly came up with a solution. He found a way to get Mr. Smith to drop the injunction. T.B. discovered that Mr. Smith had just built himself a brand-new house, one that he was very proud of. So, while he and his family were in Spain on holiday, T.B. got a few of the boys to demolish Mr. Smith's house and then take everything away. It was all done as quietly and discreetly as possible and, while nothing ever led directly to T.B., when Mr. Smith returned to find a green field where his house used to be, he got the message. The injunction was dropped the very next day.'

Mac perked up on hearing this.

'Who runs the hospital site? I take it that it's not T.B. himself?' Mac asked.

'No, T.B. has several massive projects on the go at the moment so one of his most trusted lieutenants is running the project. His name is Liam Flahavan and he's worked for TB for nearly thirty years now.'

'You've used that word 'lieutenant' a couple of times now. It makes it sound as though T.B.'s organisation is based along military lines or something.'

Sam gave this some thought.

'Probably more along Mafia lines, I'd guess. Not that I think that T.B. is often on the wrong side of the law but, if circumstances warranted it, I don't think he'd hesitate. At the highest level, all of his employees are hand-picked and they're all intensely loyal too. If they had to kill someone to protect him, I honestly don't think they'd hesitate either.'

'Tell me about T.B.,' Mac said getting interested.

Sam looked at her watch before taking another sip from her glass.

'As I said, stories about T.B. abound but this is what I think might be true about him. A boy named Christy Power came over to England from Dublin when he was just fourteen. His mother had just died and, even when she was alive, his life was tough as his father was a drunk who used to beat him up regularly. So, the night after his mother died, he emptied the contents of his father's wallet, left home and headed for the night boat to Holyhead. He then caught the train to London. Once there, he lied about his age and tried to get a job on the buildings.

He didn't have much luck until someone offered him a job carrying bricks. They said that if he could match their champion hod carrier then they'd give him some work. Now, this hod carrier was a giant of a man, and his hod was outsize too, so it was clear that they were just having a laugh. The laugh was on them though. The story goes that Christy watched this giant load up his hod with bricks and then carry it on his shoulder up several ladders to where the bricklayers were working. He'd then dump the bricks in a huge pile. Now, even at that age, Christy was clever. In fact, I think that he's probably the cleverest man that I've ever met. Anyway, he worked it out that, in the time that the giant filled his hod, he could half fill a much smaller hod and make enough trips to come somewhere close to equalling the amount that the giant had carried.'

Another sip of wine.

'The bricklayers loved him. He brought just enough bricks for each course and he stacked them right where the brickies could easily get at them. Even though he might have been slower than the giant, the contractor soon realised that the brickies were laying far more brick and so Christy Power got the job. He and the giant, Tony O'Halloran, became good friends. So much so that he later employed Tony as his assistant and bodyguard. A year or so later young Christy became a bricklayer himself and he became the fastest and the best that there was. That's how he got his nickname. They called Christy 'The Brick' which was shortened to T.B. and that's what he's been called ever since. He liked going to the pub as much as anyone else, I'd guess, but he also made sure that he educated himself. He invested in a Quantity Surveying university course and ended up with a first. Not long after that he started his own business.'

'How did he get to be so successful?' Mac asked.

'As I said, he's the cleverest man I've ever met but at least part of it is down to how he recruits his top-level staff,' Sam replied.

'His lieutenants?'

'That's right. Like many other industries in this country, construction's quite class-ridden. If you start at the bottom then there's usually a massive glass ceiling that stops you getting anywhere near to the top, unless you're T.B., of course. However, he didn't recruit the usual chinless wonders fresh out of university. His lieutenants are almost always Irish or of Irish descent and they've all started at the bottom. I'd say that he's a genius at finding talent and then fitting that talent into his organisation. They all know that, if it wasn't for T.B., they'd still be brickies or labourers or whatever, so the loyalty they show him is immense. They would do anything for him and that's very rare in the construction business.'

'Has he any family?' Mac asked.

'Yes, he married twice but both wives died on him. He has two children, Nessa from his first wife, and Eoin from the second. I've only met Nessa once, she's a director of the company and a right bitch by all accounts. Eoin, on the other hand, is really nice. I did an article on him for the magazine not too long ago and I really liked him. Unlike Nessa, he doesn't work for his dad. He left home when he went to university and he hasn't been back since.'

She looked at her watch and then took a gulp of wine.

'I'm sorry but I've got to go. I can send you some articles I've written about T.B., if you think that might help?'

Mac said that it would. He looked at his watch too. It was time for the pub. He texted Tim and told him that he'd be there in ten minutes. He then glanced over at Martin who was still hard at work.

'Any luck?' he asked.

'No, not yet but it's an interesting challenge,' Martin replied without looking up. 'I've just tweaked the parameters a bit so I'm hoping to get something soon.'

'Don't work too late,' Mac said. 'If you fancy a pint we'll be at the Magnets for a while.'

Martin stopped working and thought for a moment.

'I might just take you up on that.'

Tim had already occupied table thirteen and Mac could see that a pint of lager and a large glass of wine were waiting for them. Tim took a sip from his glass of water.

'Are you on water now until your operation?' Mac asked as he took his seat.

'Nice to see you too, Mac,' Tim said a little sarcastically. 'Anyway, I like to think of it as 'Adam's Ale' if you don't mind.' He then turned to Leigh, gave her a smile and said, 'However, it's always wonderful to see you.'

'I think that you might be interested in what she's got to tell you,' Mac said. 'A couple of years ago her uncle went through the same operation that you're due to have on Thursday.'

Tim looked up and said with real interest, 'And how is your uncle?'

Leigh told him all about the operation and how it had affected him.

'You're saying that he felt as though he'd been beaten up after the operation?' Tim asked.

'Yes, but that was only for a few days,' Leigh replied. 'After all, they will put six holes in you so it's not exactly a minor operation, but my uncle recovered fairly quickly.'

'And he's okay now?' Tim asked looking at Leigh keenly.

'Yes, he's better than okay. He has to have a blood test every six months but that's it really. He's really happy as the operation worked and that means that he doesn't need to be on any long-term medication.'

Mac and Leigh kept their silence while Tim processed what Leigh had told him.

Mac thought that some of what she'd said, about how he'd feel after the operation and having to use a catheter for a while, didn't sound all that great. But, overall, it had been a positive message.

He knew that Tim thought so too when he could see his shoulders relax and a real smile return to his face.

'Thanks Leigh,' Tim said. 'That's really helped. Another drink?'

He drove the van straight into the heart of London and across the river to the South Bank. As he crossed over the bridge, he could see his destination on the other side. The huge open expanse of the building site was floodlit and it was surrounded by lines of cement trucks that, from a distance, looked like bees buzzing around a hive.

To the right of the site there were patches of darkness. He was heading for one of these.

The biggest concrete pour in Europe was happening right in front of his eyes and he should have been excited about it but he wasn't. There was going to be a small addition to the concrete base of the skyscraper and he'd only feel better once it was finally off his hands.

He wondered for a moment about the timing of it all. Was it just a coincidence that he had a dead body to dispose of just at the very time that he had the perfect place to put it? Knowing his daughter, he doubted it.

He drove past the bulky concrete trucks, their huge churns rotating, keeping the concrete inside mixed and stable. No-one paid him any attention. He was in a works van, one of a hundred or more that serviced the site. They were pouring on the opposite side of the site and he knew that he had some time before the concrete trucks would once again converge on this side.

Concrete blocks and rusty steel tie-rods formed a sort of fence around the concrete pool below. However, there were a few gaps and he pulled up as close to one of them as he could. It was dark and he was grateful for that. He got out and looked around. There was no-one about. He went and looked down at the concrete pool some fifteen feet below him. He knew that it should still be liquid enough for his purposes.

He looked around again. Still no-one.

He opened the back doors of the van and pulled out the body. He manoeuvred it so that he could give it a fireman's *lift and then he made his way to the edge. He then let the body slip and fall into the concrete below. The body didn't sink though. Instead, it half-floated on the surface of the concrete pool.*

He cursed himself for being a fool and looked around. He found what he needed almost immediately. He took the twenty-foot length of scaffolding tube and used it to push the body under the surface. Air trapped inside the plastic sheets made it a harder job than he'd have thought.

The feet were still just above the surface when he heard somebody coming!

He pushed down hard on the tube and, as the footsteps got closer, he saw the last inch of the body disappear under the cement pool's surface.

'Couldn't keep away now, could you?' a deep voice said.

He knew who it was. It was Paddy Sullivan, the man who he'd put in control of the concrete pour. He had to think quickly. Why exactly was he standing there with a long piece of scaffolding tube in his hand? He instantly knew what to do. He pulled the tube up and then slathered his left hand with concrete. He threw the tube away and then squeezed the viscous concrete between the palms of his hand and rubbed then together.

'Is it okay?' Paddy asked looking a little concerned.

What he'd just done had been the old way of testing the quality of concrete. One that he'd used for years.

'Yes, it feels fine,' he replied. 'Sorry, I shouldn't be butting in but I just couldn't sleep tonight.'

They both leaned on one of the concrete blocks and looked over the vast flat pool of concrete.

'You know, it feels good to get my hands dirty with a bit of concrete again.'

'Years ago, when we were shifting bricks and digging trenches, who'd have thought that we'd end up here, running the whole show?' Paddy said with a smile.

'Yes, we've come a long way together, haven't we?' he said as he picked up a rag from the floor and started wiping his hands. 'Is it all going to schedule still?'

'Yes, we're bang on to finish later today around five,' Paddy replied. 'You know, when we started, I envisaged all sorts of problems but it's all gone to plan so far.'

He looked at Paddy keenly.

'That's because you envisaged all those problems, Paddy. You were put in charge of all this because I knew you would make it happen. I know how hard you and your men have worked. Tell them that there'll be a nice bonus for all of them when they're finished.'

'I'll do that. Will I see you down the pub later?'

'Now that I wouldn't miss for any money and all the drinks will be on me.'

Paddy watched as his friend got into the van. He shook his head and smiled. He could drive any fancy car he liked but, instead, he chose an old Transit van that had seen better days. He waved at his friend as he drove off.

Paddy turned and looked down at the concrete pool below. He wondered who it was that was now lying under the concrete's surface. He didn't wonder for too long. He decided that, whoever it was, they probably had it coming to them. If he'd have been asked, he'd have gladly lent the boss a hand. One thing was for certain, they would have a lovely gravestone. All one hundred and twenty floors of it.

Oh well. He thought of the end of the pour and of the relief he'd feel and of the celebrations that would ensue.

As he walked away, he'd already forgotten about the body in the concrete. It would stay forgotten.

Chapter Eight

Mac had been dreaming about bells again but it was the beep-beep-beep of his alarm clock that woke him up. Before he opened his eyes, he tried to capture his dream.

Tim had been in it and, together, they were trying to pull on a bell-rope but it wouldn't budge an inch. Around them other people were easily pulling down their ropes and the air was filled with the sound of bells large and small. Mac pulled harder on the rope but it still wouldn't move and he was now starting to feel a bit silly. That's when he woke up.

Mac opened his eyes and wondered if there was any truth in dreams. Some people thought that they could reveal the future or, at least, your true inner self. Whatever that was. He decided that there was no answer to this question and so he sat up. He then stood up and said his daily silent prayer that his back pain wouldn't be too bad. Thankfully, it wasn't.

He smiled when he remembered that they finally had a lead. Martin had joined them for the last drink and he'd brought along some print-outs. Luckily for them, the style was unusual, and so Martin had only found seven companies that produced conservatories of the type that had been erected at Hoar's Cottage. This had cheered Mac up as seven was a lot better than the hundreds, or even thousands, of companies they might have had to contact.

He thought about this as he had a shower. Two of the companies were in Scotland and one was in Durham. These were probably a bit too far away to be likely candidates so they'd contact the other four first. He mentally crossed his fingers. This was proving to be one of his more difficult cases as they had so little hard evidence to go on but he still desperately wanted to crack it.

He then thought about Tim. Even though he'd been on water all night, he'd still been good company. A little worm of dark worry burrowed into his mind. He stamped on it immediately.

Tim will be alright, he told himself. He'll be alright.

He watched the birds fluttering around the feeders as he drank his first cup of coffee. Their shenanigans made him smile. He then heard the front door opening. He hadn't been expecting anyone this early so he went to investigate. Amrit was standing in the hallway, resplendent in a purple and gold sari and sparkling jewelled sandals.

'You're a bit early today,' Mac said.

Amrit was a retired nurse who had agreed to look after Mac long term. She came in two days a week, monitored his pain, cleaned his house and made sure that he didn't poison himself by eating out of date food. To Mac, she was completely indispensable.

'Well, I am a lady who lunches today,' Amrit replied. 'I'm meeting some old friends who I haven't seen for quite a while. We'll be having lunch and, hopefully, a few drinks too.'

'If you don't mind me saying, you look a bit overdressed for cleaning,' Mac said.

'Don't worry, I have my apron with me. I'll be fine.'

'While you're here, there was something I wanted to talk to you about...'

'I take it that it's about Tim,' she said.

Mac wasn't surprised that Amrit knew about Tim. Tim had told Bridget and Amrit and Bridget were friends.

'It seems that everyone knew except me,' Mac said with a touch of self-pity.

'Well, I did work on a urology ward for a while so Bridget wanted to pick my brains. Anyway, just listen to yourself,' Amrit admonished. 'I can understand why Tim didn't tell you until he had to. He was trying to be kind to you, Mac. He didn't want you worrying about him.'

'I'm afraid that I can't help but worry.'

'I know,' Amrit said, her expression softening. 'It would help Tim if you didn't show it though. He'll have a lot to cope with after the operation and worrying about you won't help his recovery.'

Amrit was, of course, right. She usually was. Whatever he was feeling didn't really matter. Getting his friend well again was all that was really important.

He sat in the car thinking about his conversation with Amrit for a while before he started the car. He then remembered that they had a lead and he thought about whether they might be able to track down the company who had installed the conservatory.

He thought of Amrit again and then of the conservatory. It was like two live wires touching and producing sparks. He'd had another idea. He drove the short distance to the police station with a smile on his face.

Leigh had beaten him to it this morning. When he walked into the Major Crime Unit's room, she was already hard at work on her computer, a half-empty cup of coffee beside her. Dan, Andy, Jo and Adil were in Dan's office in some sort of high-level huddle. Mac gave them a wave.

'Want another one?' Mac asked gesturing towards the cup.

'Yes, please,' she replied. 'This one's gone cold.'

She noticed Mac looking at Dan's now empty office when he returned.

'They left in a bit of a rush,' she explained. 'I think that they've got a new lead in the pub stabbing case.'

'Let's hope that they're not the only ones,' Mac said. 'What have you found so far?'

'I've been looking at the four companies we decided on last night. I've got the contact details for three of them but, unfortunately, the last one's gone out of business.'

Mac frowned. He hoped that it wasn't the company who had gone bust who had erected the conservatory. That might complicate things.

'Let's hope it's one of the other ones then,' Mac said.

Leigh put the phone on speaker and called the first company. They immediately struck out as the company had only been in existence for three years. They had no better luck with their next call. This company, which was situated in the town of Dedham, near Colchester, insisted that they were a small family firm and they only ever worked in the Essex and Suffolk areas. They had never done any work in Hertfordshire and they had no plans to start anytime soon.

'Well, that doesn't bode well for the last one, does it?' Mac said. 'It's even further away.'

Leigh frowned as she entered the last company's number. The phone was answered by a young man who had a soft Norfolk burr.

'Hindsome's Windows,' he said. 'Gary speaking.'

Leigh explained who she was and why she was calling.

'Five years ago, you say?' the young man said. 'I've only been working here for four years so I'm afraid that I wouldn't know.'

'Who would?' Leigh asked.

'Oh, my dad will know. I'll go and get him.'

They heard some indistinct rustlings and thumps and then two distant voices. It sounded as if the son was trying to explain to his father who was calling. They heard steps and then someone picked up the phone.

'Hello, Barry Hindsome here,' a man's voice said too loudly. 'My son said that you're the police. Is that right?'

Leigh explained again who she was and why she was calling.

'A conservatory job in Hertfordshire? That's a bit too far for us, love,' he said. 'We normally only work in the Norfolk area. When was it again?'

'Five years ago,' Leigh replied.

'Five years?'

There was a long pause. This at first gave Mac some hope but then it got even longer. They'd probably just lost him.

'Mr. Hindsome, are you still there?' Leigh eventually asked.

'Oh yes, I'm still here. I'm just trying to remember something.' They then heard him say to his son, 'Go and get your uncle.'

'Sorry but the old brainbox isn't quite as good as it used to be but my brother Harry will know.'

Another muted discussion, this time with someone new.

'Hello, Harry Hindsome here.'

Leigh explained who she was and why she was calling for the third time. She pulled an exasperated face at Mac when she'd finished.

'Oh yes, that sounds like one of ours alright,' Harry said.

Another pause.

'Well, what can you tell us about it?' Leigh said her voice rising a notch or two.

'It was a strange one that. We were rung up by this chap who said that we had come highly recommended by a friend of his. I told him that the job was a bit too far away for us but he said that he'd pay fifty percent on top to cover our travelling costs.'

'What was his name?' Leigh asked.

There was a lengthy silence followed by Harry asking Barry if he'd ever gave them a name.

'Sorry love, but he never gave us a name,' Harry eventually said.

'What about his friend, the one who he said had recommended you?' Leigh asked hopefully.

'He never said who he was either,' Harry replied.

'Isn't that unusual? I mean taking on a job without knowing who's paying you?'

'Oh, we knew who was paying us. The day after we spoke, we received a money transfer from some company in the Bahamas for half of the sum agreed. I remember it was the Bahamas because I always said that I'd love to take the wife there one day on a cruise.'

Another shell company, Mac guessed.

'What did he sound like, the man who called you?' Mac asked.

'He wasn't young, forty or fifty I'd guess,' Harry replied. 'He had quite a posh accent too.'

It wasn't much but it was something, Mac thought.

'So how did it work?' Mac asked.

'Well, we received a key in the post and me and Barry went down there first to have a look. We found the house, a bit small for such a big conservatory I thought, but that's what they wanted and there weren't any problems as far as we could see. The next day we got a team down to start on the groundwork, laying the floor and the brickwork and so on. By the end of the week, it was finished. We popped the key in the letter box and left. Three days later the rest of the money arrived and that was that.'

'Were any special requests made?'

There was another pause and another discussion between Harry and Barry.

'Yes, Barry here remembered something. They asked for special glass to be fitted throughout. With this glass you can see outside but no-one can see inside. People only usually order it for privacy if they're overlooked by another property. We were surprised when we got there as there didn't seem to be another property within a mile of that house.'

Mac asked if they could send him copies of all the paperwork they had and then thanked Harry, Barry and Gary for their help.

'Harry, Barry and Gary!' Leigh said with a wide smile. 'A rhyming family.'

Mac smiled too but it didn't last long.

'Frustrating, isn't it? We finally find the company but all we learn is that the man who called them was middle-aged and posh sounding. It's not a lot to go on, is it? Anyway, as I was driving in, I had an idea.'

Leigh perked up on hearing this.

'How did they keep the house clean?' Mac said. 'Did they do all the cleaning themselves? If the man was as posh as Harry said then I'd rather doubt it.'

'You think that they might have employed a cleaner?' Leigh asked.

'It's possible and, if they did, they'd have to be fairly local, wouldn't they? I'd guess that they'd employ a contract cleaning service rather than having the same person coming time after time. It would be more impersonal that way.'

Leigh frowned as she said, 'But doesn't that leave us in the same position we were in with the window companies? I mean there must be hundreds of cleaning companies within twenty or thirty miles of the cottage.'

'Yes, I thought about that too,' Mac replied. 'However, we do have a contact in the area so, you never know, we might get lucky.'

Mac called Mrs. Furlong again and asked her if she'd ever seen any vehicles belonging to cleaning companies in the vicinity of Hoar's Cottage. She hadn't but she agreed to call all her friends in the neighbourhood and ask them the same question.

'So, what now?' Leigh asked.

'We wait,' Mac replied. 'While we're waiting let's have a look at what we know so far.'

When he'd finished, they sat down and gazed at the whiteboard. It was full but it didn't really amount to much.

'This all has to have something to do with the paedophile ring,' Leigh said with some certainty.

'You might well be right,' Mac replied. 'However, if they wanted to get rid of the evidence, whoever owned it could have simply had the cottage demolished months ago and no-one would been any the wiser. Instead of that, they put it on the market. There's got to be something more to this...'

Mac was interrupted by his phone ringing. He looked at the number. It was Mrs. Furlong.

'Mr. Maguire, I might just have something for you,' she said.

Mac listened avidly to what she had to say. Leigh knew that he'd learned something by the little smile on his face.

'One of Mrs. Furlong's friends, who lives in Great Offley, said that she saw a small van drive into Down's Bottom more than once,' Mac said as he put his phone away. 'It had the firm's name on the side, Little Miss Mop-up Cleaners.'

'Thank God for nosy neighbours,' Leigh said as her fingers flew over the keyboard. 'They've got an office in Luton.'

A few seconds later and they were both listening to the phone ringing at the other end.

A man's deep and gravelly voice said, 'Little Miss Mop-up Cleaners, Mark speaking. How can I help?'

They both looked at each other in surprise before Leigh introduced herself.

'We believe that your company had a contract to clean a house called Hoar's Cottage near Great Offley. Is that right?'

They both waited for the response with bated breath.

'Is that the house with the big conservatory in the middle of nowhere?' he asked.

'Yes, that's it,' Leigh replied. 'We need to speak to you about it. Can we come now?'

'Well, my wife Amy will be back in a couple of hours. It's really her business so it might be better if you talk to her about it.'

Leigh got the address and then put the phone down.

'Yes!' she said raising her right fist in celebration.

Mac thought that she was right to celebrate. He wondered if this finally might be the tipping point for the case. He could only hope.

Chapter Nine

As they drove towards Luton, Mac scratched an itch. He rang the lead investigator in the Edward Haskell case and had a chat with him. He wanted to know why no further interviews had been carried out.

'What did he say?' Leigh asked when Mac had finished the call.

'Nothing really,' Mac replied. 'He was quite evasive and then ended the call saying that he had an urgent meeting he had to attend.'

Leigh looked over and could see that Mac was quite puzzled by the call.

When they finally found it, it proved to be not so much an office as a semi-detached house in the Round Green area of Luton. A small van with a bright pink sign on the side that said 'Little Miss Mop-up Cleaners' was parked outside.

Mac guessed that the wife was home.

The front door of the house opened as they got out of the car and a tall bearded man in his thirties wearing light blue and pink striped overalls appeared.

He looked at Mac and Leigh looking back at him and shrugged. 'It's a living. I take it that you're the police?'

Mac showed him his warrant card.

'I'm the change of shift. Go straight in. You'll find Amy inside,' he said as he made his way towards the van.

They let themselves in and found Amy stretched out flat on the settee. She sat up and looked surprised for a moment.

'Oh, I'm sorry. Mark did say that the police were coming but I forgot. I've had a hard day. One of my staff is ill and the other left giving no notice. I'm meeting myself coming back at the moment.'

Mac could well believe it. She looked exhausted and she still had her work clothes on, a stained version of the same overalls that her husband had on.

'We won't keep you long,' Mac said as he sat down. 'We believe that you used to clean at a place called Hoar's Cottage. It's on a lane called Down's Bottom not far from Great Offley.'

She had to think and it looked painful.

'Are you on about that little house in the middle of nowhere just off the main road to Hitchin?'

'Yes, that's the one,' Mac replied.

'I didn't know that it had a name,' she said. 'Yes, that was a strange one.'

'In what way?'

'Lots of ways, I suppose. For instance, we ran that contract for just over four years and yet I never met the man I worked for. I usually get to meet my customers but all I got for that one was a phone call.'

'Did he give you a name?' Mac asked.

'No, he never did which was another strange thing. He said something about the house being owned by a company.'

'Do you know the company's name?'

'Yes, I've got it in my records somewhere,' she replied. 'It's in the Bahamas believe it or not, at least that's where we got our payments from.'

Mac frowned. It was probably the same shell company that had paid the Hindsomes for the conservatory.

'How did the contract end?' Mac asked.

'It didn't end officially, we just stopped getting paid. We carried on for a month or so and then gave up. We never heard from them again.'

'While you were cleaning the cottage did you ever come across anything unusual or anything that might help us identify who owned it?' Mac asked.

Amy looked at him with some puzzlement.

'Why do you need to know?'

Mac told her about the house being demolished.

'Really? So, someone just came along, knocked the whole house down and took everything away?' she said with some surprise. 'I'd have thought that the owner should be the one contacting you in that case.'

'Yes, you'd have thought that, wouldn't you? However, it seems that the owner of Hoar's Cottage wants to keep everything secret and they've gone to great lengths to ensure that no-one knows about them. We have information that some very serious crimes may have occurred in that house but, so far, we've encountered nothing but secrecy and obstruction. We need something, a clue that might lead us in the right direction,' Mac said hoping that he wasn't sounding too desperate.

Amy thought about this for a while.

'I never really found anything out of the ordinary but I often had the feeling that parts of the house had been tidied up before I got there.'

'Which parts?'

'That big conservatory mostly,' Amy replied. 'The kitchen and living room would be stacked full of empty bottles of booze and dirty glasses and food was often trodden into the carpet but that conservatory always looked tidy. I thought that perhaps they didn't use it much but, judging from the number of empty bottles, I can't see how they could have fitted everyone into the living room.'

Mac understood why that might be. He also thought that Amy was very smart.

'Amy, please think again. There must be something you saw in that house that might help us,' Mac asked.

He could see that she was tired but she was giving it her best shot. She rubbed her face with her hands and then sat up straight. She'd thought of something!

'I think that I nearly got to meet your mystery man once.'

'Go on,' Mac said.

'Well, it was in the contract that we could only clean between the hours of two to five every Wednesday after-noon. However, I had an early job one Tuesday morning not too far away from the cottage and so I decided to drop in. I'd done it before and the house was always empty. This time someone was there.'

'What did he look like?' Mac asked hoping that they were finally getting somewhere.

'I've no idea,' Amy replied. 'I never saw him. When I opened the front door, I noticed that there was a bag placed just inside. It was one of those flight bags with a laptop bag on top that you see businessmen taking on board planes as cabin luggage. There was no-one downstairs but I could hear someone showering upstairs and so I left as quietly as I could.'

Mac hoped that his disappointment didn't show. Perhaps it had because Amy quickly continued.

'However, I did notice that the bag had one of those luggage labels that they put on at the airport. It said 'ZRH'. I was curious so I had Mark look it up and he found that it stood for Zurich.'

'So, you're saying that he flew in from Switzerland?' Mac asked.

'That's what it looked like. I guessed that he was getting changed before going to a meeting or something. The house isn't all that far from the airport, is it?'

Mac and Leigh exchanged looks. They both knew that this could be the crucial break they'd been looking for.

'Have you any idea what date this was?' Mac asked.

Amy rubbed her face with her hands again. Mac hoped that it was helping her to think.

'It must have been around November last year, I think,' she replied, 'but, if you give me a minute, I can tell you the exact date. The other job I went to was for a lady that I only help out with now and again after she throws one of her dinner parties.'

She disappeared upstairs.

Leigh gave him an excited smile.

'This could be it, Mac,' she said.

Mac responded with a smile. This could indeed be the break that they'd been waiting for.

Chapter Ten

Mac was on the phone most of the way back to the station. He didn't want to waste any time. He asked Martin to check the passenger list of flights coming into Luton Airport from Zurich around November 16th. He also asked him to check if anyone on the list had caught another flight out later that day or early the next morning.

'Do you think that he was staying at the cottage because he was getting another flight somewhere?' Leigh asked.

'While he may have been going to a meeting, as Amy suggested, I think it's more likely that he might have been flying on to somewhere else. In fact, it being so close to the airport might have been part of the reason why he bought the house. Anyway, I'm hoping that he did catch a connecting flight as it should make our job a little easier.'

Once again, the team's room was empty when they got there. Mac took his phone out and put it on the desk. Martin was working on the pub stabbing case in the incident room that they'd set up in Dunstable. He'd told Mac that the new evidence they'd received consisted of some CCTV footage from a shop down the road from the pub. Dan Carter had appealed to anyone in the area who had CCTV equipment to check their tapes around the time of the brawl. A dress shop, around fifty yards away from the pub, obviously hadn't got the message.

That might have been because their camera should have been focussed on the front door of the shop and they didn't expect it to pick up anything relevant to the stabbing. It was only some days later that the owner noticed that the camera was now pointing down the street. She said that a recent storm must have moved it. Martin said that the camera lens hadn't been cleaned for some time and the footage was grainy. However, he was still hopeful of getting something useful. He said that he was happy to help with

Mac's enquiry as it would give him a bit of a break. Apparently, cleaning up CCTV footage is not always an easy or a straightforward job.

Leigh got them a coffee each while they waited. They didn't say anything for a while, they just stared at the whiteboard. They both hoped that they would soon be able to add the first bit of hard evidence to what had so far been mostly informed guesswork.

Mac was about to say something when the phone rang. It was Martin!

'What have you found?' Mac asked as he crossed his fingers.

'Well, I've got the complete passenger list for Flight BEZ 2048 which arrived at 23.55 at Luton Airport on November 15th,' Martin said. 'There were eight passengers that caught flights the next day but I guess that you might only need to look at one of them.'

'Why is that?'

'Does the name of Marcus Kendrick ring a bell?' Martin asked.

It did but Mac wasn't sure why at first. He looked over at Leigh who shrugged her shoulders. Then he remembered hearing the name on one of the news programmes.

'He's a government minister for something or other, isn't he?'

'He was the Minister for Housing and Local Government until he died just over a couple of months ago,' Martin replied.

'Oh yes, I vaguely remember there being an announcement but it was a bit short on details,' Mac said.

'There was a very good reason why his family, and the government, might have wanted to keep it vague. Mr. Kendrick committed suicide and you might understand why when I tell you what he was up to. I like to keep up with anything new that pops up on the police databases and this only came in yesterday evening on the list of upcoming court cases. In a few days a group of men, all of them influential and from the world of business, will be formally charged with being part of a predatory paedo-phile ring and of being responsible for the multiple rapes of young boys over a ten-year period. Kendrick would have been one of them if he hadn't killed himself. It will be all over the news before long.'

Martin let this sink in.

Mac looked over at Leigh who soundlessly mouthed the word, 'Wow!'

'Was Hoar's Cottage mentioned at all?' Mac asked.

'Not as such but I think that it would be a hell of a stretch if Hoar's Cottage wasn't the house that Edward Haskell had described in his statement,' Martin said.

Mac thought so too.

'I can well understand why they kept the case under wraps for so long,' he said. 'I take it that the evidence against Mr. Kendrick was quite strong?'

'It would appear so,' Martin replied. 'Not only that but he also supplied the names of most of the other members of the ring. I guess that was why he felt he had nowhere to run after that.'

'Who's leading the investigation?

'DCI Jenna Bowyer. She works out of Bishopsgate police station.'

Mac knew that the Bishopsgate station belonged to the City of London police and he wondered why they were running the case. Being located in the financial centre of London, they were more usually involved in white collar crimes such as illegal share dealing and insurance fraud.

There was only one way to find out.

He managed to get through to her assistant, a DI John Roberts, who agreed to set up a video call with his boss for five thirty. Mac looked at his watch. They had a couple of hours to wait.

'Oh well, it's better than trying to struggle through the London traffic, I suppose,' Mac said.

'Do you think that we'll finally get to find out why Hoar's Cottage was demolished?' Leigh asked with an excited smile.

'Perhaps but I've got my doubts,' Mac said. On seeing Leigh's puzzled look, he continued. 'It's the timing really. If they're ready to charge a group of people now then the investigation must have been going on for some time. If Hoar's Cottage was part of the investigation then forensics would have turned the place inside out long ago. So, nothing would be gained by anyone in the paedophile ring knocking the house down now. We've been told that it wasn't the owner and I can't see it being one of the victims either. What would they have to gain from it? While it might appear as if the paedophile ring must have something to do with the house's disappearance, I think that we should keep an open mind on that one.'

'I suppose you're right,' Leigh conceded looking mildly disappointed. 'Are you seeing Tim later?'

'No, he said that he's got a few things that he needs to finish off before he goes into hospital tomorrow morning,' Mac replied.

'Well, I guess that makes sense. After all, he won't be doing much for a month or so while he recovers. He's still lucky though.'

Mac looked up in surprise.

'In what way?'

'Well, he's got you and Amrit to look after him, hasn't he? My uncle stayed with us for a couple of days after the operation but he couldn't stand my mum fussing about him all the time. So, he went home. I used to go around and check on him when I had time but he could have done with a proper nurse like Amrit to look after him.'

On thinking about it, Mac could only agree. It wasn't only Tim who was lucky to have Amrit. He would have to do something really nice for her when Tim was able to look after himself.

Mac's thoughts were interrupted by his stomach rumbling.

'Fancy a sandwich?' he asked.

Mac was unusually quiet as they sat in the Magnets eating their lunch.

'Still thinking about Tim?' Leigh eventually asked.

Mac looked at her with some surprise.

'I'm sorry, no. I was thinking about the case actually. I was thinking about how little we actually know. I've not been across many cases where hard facts have been so difficult to come by.'

Leigh gave this some thought.

'I suppose all we really know for sure is that there was a house and that it isn't there now. We know who put the conservatory up and who cleaned the house. We know that the cleaner saw a bag with a luggage label for Zurich on it. That's about it really.'

'Even the luggage label worries me a bit. I often forget and leave them on until the next time I'm travelling abroad,' Mac said.

'Well, let's hope that we learn a little more from this DCI Bowyer,' Leigh replied.

Mac noticed that she crossed her fingers when she said this.

Mac had a feeling of déjà vu when the video conference finally started. DCI Jenna Bowyer was in her early fifties. She had full make-up on and her hair had been recently cut by someone who knew what they were doing. The reason for this was explained by the lavish dark blue evening gown she was wearing.

'No, it's not the new uniform for the City of London Police,' DCI Bowyer said with a smile. 'I'm representing the police at the Lord Mayor of London's dinner at the Mansion House tonight. I'm sorry but that only leaves me around twenty minutes or so.'

'No, please don't apologise,' Mac said. 'We're just glad that you could fit us in.'

He went on to explain what the call was about.

'That doesn't make any sense with regard to our case,' DCI Bowyer said looking somewhat puzzled. 'Hoar's Cottage was one of three sites that we looked at. All of them were used by the ring for their activities. Our teams went all over that house with a fine-toothed comb for weeks and we felt that we'd learned everything that there was to learn. In fact, we had no further interest in it and, when the owner's representatives approached us for permission to sell the house a few months ago, we were happy for them to do so.'

Mac and Leigh looked at each other. There was at least one new fact that they would learn.

'Were these representatives working on behalf of Mrs. Kendrick?' Mac asked taking a gamble.

'That's right but how on earth could you know that?' she asked.

'Just a guess.'

'Well, it was a good guess then. I don't suppose that I should be all that surprised. I'm well aware of your reputation, DCS Maguire.'

'How did you get on to the paedophile ring in the first place?' Mac asked. 'I've worked with the City of London Police quite a few times in the past but it's almost always been around some sort of financial crime.'

'Well, that's exactly how we got involved in this case,' DCI Bowyer said. 'We were investigating a city high-flyer called Dominic Lefebre. He was running what turned out to be a very complicated Ponzi scam and, if I'm honest, it was so complicated that it took us quite a while to realise that's what it was. One of the money streams we invest-igated led to a man who was blackmailing Lefebre. He was an ex-police officer called Don Markey and he was the man who procured the children for Lefebre and his friends to rape. When we pressured him, he gave us the names of the people who paid him, and it was quite shocking as I'd heard of most of them.'

'I take it that Marcus Kendrick was one of those names?' Mac asked.

'Yes, and probably the most well-known one as far as the public were concerned as he was a government minister. The others were all fairly big names but only in the financial world. We questioned Kendrick first and, when we threatened him with a lengthy prison sentence, he quickly folded and gave us everything we wanted. We found more than enough forensic and other evidence to place all of the men in at least one of the three sites and so, luckily for us, they've all decided to plead guilty.'

'Were you aware that one of the boys who was raped by these men had raised a complaint with the Bedfordshire Police just under a year ago?'

'Yes, Edward Haskell,' she replied. 'We came across that when we started building a case against the paedophile ring. It was most helpful. We asked the local detectives to publicly park their case after Mr. Haskell died while we pushed forward with ours in secret. We interviewed everyone who had been at the children's home at around the same time as Edward. In all we found six young men who claimed to have been raped at Hoar's Cottage. All of them identified Markey and five of them are now happy to testify to the fact.'

Well, at least Edward didn't die in vain, Mac thought. It also answered his question about why the local detectives hadn't interviewed anyone else from the children's home and why they had been so evasive about it.

DCI Bowyer looked at her watch.

'I'm sorry but I can't keep the Lord Mayor waiting. If there's anything else we can help you with then ask John here,' she said as she moved the camera to show a man in his thirties sitting next to her. 'I'll say goodbye then.'

Mac heard the scraping of a chair and the rustling of an evening gown. He studied the man on the screen. He was in his mid-thirties, clean-shaven and sharply dressed. He seemed quite nervous for some reason.

'DI Roberts, I presume?' Mac asked. 'We spoke earlier, didn't we?'

'That's right,' he replied with a forced grin. 'If there's anything we can help you with then please contact me. I'll send you all the details if you give me your email address.'

'I don't suppose that there's any chance of getting a copy of your case file?' Mac asked.

'I'm sorry but no,' DI Roberts said. 'We can't release anything until after the trial but if you've got any specific questions then we'll do our best to answer them.'

'I take it that you can give us Mrs. Kendrick's contact details?'

'Oh yes, of course. That won't be a problem.'

Mac gave him his email address and ended the call. He briefly wondered why DI Roberts had been so obviously wound up. He stopped wondering when Mrs. Kendrick's contact details arrived.

They would finally get to meet the elusive owner of Hoar's Cottage.

He ended the meeting and hoped that he hadn't let his nervousness show. He had been asked to keep an eye out for anything new that came up in the investigation around Hoar's Cottage. This was certainly new and completely unexpected.

She hadn't told him what her interest in Hoar's Cottage exactly was and he knew that there was no point in asking.

He'd told her that, as a whole house had gone missing, then there would definitely be some sort of investigation. However, he'd assured her that it would probably only be the local plods investigating and that the chances of them finding anything were slight at best.

He now wished to God that he hadn't said those words. The woman who was paying him handsomely for information wasn't someone who readily forgave mistakes. It was the former DCS Maguire's involvement that worried him the most. As his boss had said he had a reputation and one of the things he was well-known for was for being persistent. He never gave up on a case easily.

He walked out of the police station and down the road, stopping outside a small supermarket. He was going to get a sandwich once he'd made the call. He got his courage up and called her.

He told her about the meeting. He had expected anger but, instead, there was a long ominous silence. Then she spoke.

'See if you can get involved in the case and find out what they know,' she instructed. 'From what you say this Mac Maguire could be dangerous.'

'That might be a bit difficult,' he replied. 'There's no good reason why I should be sticking my nose in someone else's case.'

'Then find one,' she ordered. 'Stop him John, stop him or else.'

The line went dead.

He knew what the 'or else' meant. She had enough on him to send him to jail for a long time and he had no doubt that she would use it if she had to.

An ex-colleague of his had done time. In his case it had only been eighteen months but he said that it had felt like eighteen years. Prison time for ex-coppers was the hardest time of all and there was no way that he wanted to experience what that was like personally.

He would try to do as she asked but he knew that it wouldn't be easy. He started walking slowly back towards the police station.

For some reason he found that he was no longer hungry.

Chapter Eleven

Mac went straight home from the station after speaking to DCI Bowyer but not before he had called and made an appointment to see Mrs. Kendrick the next morning. Leigh was going out with some friends that evening so Mac said that he would take some time to go over the magazine articles on T.B. Power that Sam Ellis had sent them.

He went through the articles after dinner that evening but, while the articles were quite interesting, they didn't really tell him anything new about the case. However, he found something else to fill his time. The Traffic Camera Unit in Luton had finally called him.

They explained that, as the cameras themselves are so expensive, they only have a limited number of them. So, periodically, they move them around from location to location. Luckily, they'd managed to catch some of the tipper trucks on video just the night before the camera was moved to another location.

They had saved him some time by finding out who the trucks belonged to, a rental company located in Middlesex as it turned out. Mac figured that they would be closed for the evening but he called them anyway. He was delighted to find that they ran a twenty-four-hour hotline for their customers. He explained what information he needed to the young woman who took his call and, five minutes later, he had to explain it all again to a supervisor. She told him that he would need to send a photo of his warrant card before they would tell him anything.

Eventually, he discovered that all the trucks that were caught on camera were leased to T.B. Power and were being used on the Dunstable hospital redevelopment.

Everything is leading towards T.B. Power, he thought.

He suddenly felt tired and decided to go to bed early but his sleep was fitful at best.

Mac had woken well before the time that he had set his alarm clock to go off. He went through his usual routine of sitting and then standing up and monitoring how bad his back pain was. He had to admit that it wasn't great but it was still better than he had feared it might be.

He'd been told more than once that, barring a miracle, his pain was going to be a life sentence. Sometimes this depressed him a little but, most days, he was able to ignore it. So long as he kept busy that it. The darkest days were those of maximum pain and minimum things to do to take his mind off it.

Whether it was due to the pain or to what was shortly going to happen to Tim, Mac found that he didn't feel hungry. So, he just settled for a cup of coffee. He drank it as he watched the Coal Tits lining up for their turns at the bird feeder.

He then took his dog Terry out for his morning walk. Although summer had officially started, it was dark and damp outside. Terry didn't seem to mind though. He enthusiastically sniffed each bush and tree along the walk that they always took. On his way back Mac turned into the graveyard and had a chat with his wife Nora. He told her all about Tim and his operation. They had a long chat and, at the end, she told him not to worry. He stood up and turned to walk away. He then heard her voice so clearly that he turned around, half-expecting to see her standing there.

'Have a mass said for Tim, will you? And be careful.'

Of course, there was no Nora there and a sudden pain pierced his heart. He realised then that his 'recovery' from Nora's death was like a thin sheet of ice over a lake of grief. It might crack and shatter in a split-second and he would once again fall through and into its black depths.

He saw his face in the mirror as he hung Terry's lead up on the hook. He looked afraid. No, he looked haunted.

Why would Tim need a mass said? Was something bad going to happen to him? It didn't occur to him to question

Nora's words. He was sure that they meant something but what exactly?

With a start, he realised that it was nearly time. He texted Tim to make sure that he was up.

He was. His bags were packed and he was ready to go.

Mac looked in the mirror again on his way out. He looked like an undertaker's assistant. He hoped to God that he perked up a bit before he reached Tim's place.

Ten minutes later, Mac pulled up outside Tim's shop. Tim emerged pulling a large suitcase behind him and carrying an overnight bag in his other hand. Mac got out and opened the boot for him. He couldn't help noticing that his friend looked more than a little worried.

'So, today's the day,' Tim said nervously as he hauled the large suitcase into the boot.

The suitcase contained enough clothes and toiletries for two weeks. Mac would put it in the bedroom that he and Amrit were preparing for Tim's recovery after the operation. The smaller bag was for his two day stay in hospital.

'God, you look more scared that I do,' Tim said with a smile as he climbed into his seat.

This made Mac laugh out loud and his glum mood was broken.

'Ah well, I suppose that it's always harder for those who have to hang around. As for me I'll be unconscious before very long and I'll either wake up and it will all be over or I won't wake up at all. Either way, it'll all be over,' Tim said with a little laugh.

'If you do peg it, can you send me a message from the grave?' Mac asked trying to look serious.

'Of course,' Tim replied. 'What do you want to know?'

'Where Aston Villa might get a half-decent right back from,' Mac said.

'Now, messages I might be able to do but, as I'm not a saint, I'd guess that miracles would be beyond me,' Tim said. 'However, I did hear about this Spanish guy...'

They happily talked football all the way to the hospital. All talk stopped, however, when the tall white tower of the Lister Hospital came ominously into view. It was early so Mac easily found a parking space on Coreys Mill Lane right opposite the Treatment Centre.

'It is the Treatment Centre you're going to, isn't it?' Mac asked as Tim retrieved the small bag from the boot.

'That's right,' Tim replied. 'We need the fourth floor. They have a waiting room there and they allow one relative or friend in with every patient. You can keep me company until they call my name, if you like?'

'Yes, yes of course I will,' Mac said. 'We're early anyway so we can finish our discussion while we wait.'

They were so early that the waiting room was completely empty. A sign said that it would be staffed in around twenty minutes which left them some time to finish their conversation about their favourite football team.

They carried on until they were interrupted by a grey-faced man in his sixties who had entered the room. He looked around the room in total bemusement before turning and looking back at the doorway. A large woman of about the same age came in and marched straight up to the reception desk. With a thump she placed a large handbag on the counter. She then read the notice.

'Come on, Maurice,' she said in a whining voice, 'we might as well sit down. No-one will be here for at least another ten minutes.'

They sat down as far away from Tim and Mac as was possible. The woman looked annoyed at having to wait and she kept looking at her watch. She then started asking Maurice if he'd brought his slippers. He had. A minute later she asked about his pyjamas, not the old blue ones but the new red ones that she'd just bought him. They too were safely in his bag. By the time a nurse appeared Mac and Tim knew pretty well knew everything that was contained in Maurice's bag.

'Mr. Teagan?' the young nurse asked.

'Here,' Tim said a little too loudly.

'Mr. Menzies?' the nurse asked again.

'He's here,' the woman answered.

'There's just the two of you today,' the nurse said. 'If you'd both like to follow me, I'll take you through.'

'See you later, Tim,' Mac said as he warmly shook his friend's hand. 'Text me when you wake up.'

'If I wake up, you mean,' Tim said looking a little grey-faced but still managing a smile.

'You'll be fine,' Mac assured him. 'It will be over before you know it.'

Tim followed the nurse. He stopped and waved before he went through a set of double doors. A sign above the doors said 'Theatre Preparation'.

It was really happening then. His best friend was going to have six holes put in him and he would be prostate-less in about four hours or so. He said a little prayer and crossed himself. He was surprised by this. He hadn't crossed himself for ages. He turned in case the woman with the handbag had seen him but the room was empty.

Maurice's wife had moved quickly.

He called Father Pat Curran as he walked back to the car. He was more than happy for Mac to drop by at the church presbytery on his way to the police station.

It was only eight o'clock so Mac gladly accepted a cup of tea when offered and even more gladly accepted the offer of some toast to go along with it.

'So, tell me why you needed to see me so early in the day?' Father Pat asked in his broad Cork accent.

Mac had a soft spot for Father Pat. He had been Nora's favourite priest and he had helped him greatly after his wife's death. Mac had been glad to repay the favour when he had been able to clear Father Pat of murder just the year before.[3]

---

[3] Two Dogs – the sixth Mac Maguire mystery

'This may sound a bit daft,' Mac said, 'but I go to the cemetery every few days and I sit down and have a chat with Nora. I did it again early this morning.'

'That doesn't sound at all daft to me,' Father Pat said. 'After all, our stock in trade here is life after death. What did she say to you?'

'It was strange. Normally, she's just a voice in my head but today it was as though she was really there.'

Mac needed a minute as he felt a sudden surge of emotion. Father Pat gave it to him.

Mac wiped away a tear as he said, 'My best friend Tim Teagan is undergoing an operation this morning. It's fairly major too. Nora said that I should have a mass said for him. So, here I am.'

For some reason he didn't mention the rest of what she'd said.

'That's an easy request then,' Father Pat replied. 'I'll be saying mass at ten. I'll mention his name and I'll say a few prayers for him.'

'Thanks, Father. Here, please take this,' Mac said.

He handed Father Pat a cheque. It was for two hundred and fifty pounds.

'Oh, please Mac. You don't have to give me money...'

'Yes, yes I do,' Mac insisted. 'There's quite a few back payments in there too. It's what Nora would have wanted.'

Father Pat gave in and took the cheque.

'Well, I can certainly use it,' Father Pat replied. 'We've had more bad news about the church, I'm afraid. If you remember, I had to move out last year because they found some cracks in the walls. They were only small cracks and the builders said that they should be able to fix it. The only problem is that they've come back, only bigger this time. I've contacted the builders but they've gone out of business. I'm honestly at my wits' end. What should I do, Mac?'

Mac got out his phone and then wrote down a phone number.

'Call this number,' Mac said. 'Ask for a man called Jez Manning. He owns a building firm in Stevenage and I think that he might be able to help. Ask him to do a report on what repairs are needed and tell him to send the bill to me.'

'Thanks, Mac, I will,' a relieved looking Father Pat said.

'Call me when you get the report.'

As he drove towards the station, Mac too felt relieved. He was glad that he'd been able to arrange the mass, as Nora had requested, but it wasn't that. He had the strangest feeling that Nora had sent him there not for any divine intervention for Tim but for some earthly intervention for Father Pat.

He promised himself, and Nora, that he would do what he could.

Chapter Twelve

Leigh gave Mac an exasperated look. They had left a little later so as to avoid the rush hour but it seemed that the rush hour had hung around for them. It had been slow going all the way to the fringes of North London when they were stopped once again on Watford Way by more road works.

'I used to do this run every day,' Mac said. 'Only God knows how I managed it without going insane.'

'It's just as well that we gave ourselves plenty of time,' Leigh said. 'Even so, we'll be lucky if we're not late.'

'If we don't start making some progress soon, I'll give Mrs. Kendrick a call and tell her that we'll be delayed.'

'What you found out about those tipper trucks was interesting.'

'Yes, I thought so too,' Mac replied. 'Everything seems to point towards T.B. Power's company but, unfortunately, it's all circumstantial so far. They probably employ hundreds of people on the Dunstable site and any one of them might be responsible for demolishing Hoar's Cottage. We need some hard evidence if we're going to get anywhere with this case.'

They were both silent while the traffic made a sudden spurt ahead of them. Unfortunately, it came to a stop once again just a few seconds later.

'You were saying earlier that you'd read everything that Sam Ellis from the magazine had sent. Did you find anything interesting?' Leigh asked.

'It was all interesting,' Mac replied. 'The only problem was that none of it really shone any light on our case.'

'Tell me anyway. It's not as if we've got much else to do.'

As the traffic ahead didn't look as if it was going anywhere fast, Mac could only agree.

'Most of it was the classic rags to riches tale. A poor boy from Dublin who became a multi-billionaire by hard work and persistence, you know, that type of thing. However, it was interesting to see the types of building projects that T.B. Power has been involved in recently. They're all massive and the sums of money involved are truly eye-watering. His company is famous, however, for never failing on a contract. It also looks as if the company is expanding as T.B. and his daughter were recently in the Middle East and Singapore to break the ground on some new developments there.'

Mac was quiet for a moment. As the traffic had started moving Leigh concentrated on driving. Two hundred yards further on they once again ground to a halt.

'There must be some temporary traffic lights up there,' Leigh surmised as she looked over at Mac.

He was still deep in thought.

'There was something in those articles though, wasn't there?' Leigh said. 'Something's given you pause for thought.'

Mac turned to Leigh and smiled, 'Well, you're right there. It wasn't so much in the exact wording, which was very careful at times, but, as Sam Ellis told us, it definitely implied that Mr. Power isn't someone who always played by the rules. However, it seems that he never cuts any corners on the quality of his buildings. That appears to be a matter of pride with him but, reading between the lines, I got the feeling that he'd do just about anything else to make sure that his projects get built on time. He certainly seems to be a driven man.'

'I suppose that you'd have to be to get where he is,' Leigh said. 'Is that all?'

'Sorry, no. I just had a thought about Eoin Power, TB's son. One of the articles was about him. He's quite interesting too. He and his father fell out and it seems that they haven't spoken for years. He left home when he was eighteen and, just seven years later, he's co-founded an eco-friendly construction design company with his life-partner who's an architect.'

'What's her name?'

'*His* name is Anders Mellberg. If Eoin's father is like some men I know then that alone might give us a clue as to why he left home. As he's the outsider in the family, I think that he might be well worth talking to. We'll need to speak to T.B. and Nessa Power at some point but I'd like to leave them for a while to see if we can get a little more evidence of their involvement. If there is any, of course.'

'I agree that talking to Eoin Power might be worth a shot,' Leigh said, 'and that we should leave the rest of the Powers until later. Without any hard evidence, I guess that they'd just deny everything anyway.'

'Yes, you're probably right there but let's see what Mrs. Kendrick has to say. As her husband was Minister for Housing and had control over planning permissions and land use, I'd be very surprised if he didn't know Mr. Power. From what little I've learned, Mr. Power would probably have made sure of that.'

It took another ten minutes for them to get on the other side of the temporary traffic lights. After that it was plain sailing and they got there just in time.

Leigh drove them slowly down the narrow road as they looked for the house number. On their right, the road was lined with trees and, beyond them, the green expanse of Hampstead Heath could be glimpsed. On their left, there was a succession of driveways blocked off by high steel gates.

'I looked it up last night,' Mac said. 'A house here would set you back at least six million.'

'Really?' Leigh said with some surprise. 'I wonder what all these people do to get so much money?'

'Well, we know that at least one of them was a government minister,' Mac drily replied.

'Here we are,' Leigh said as she pulled into a driveway.

A high black steel gate stopped them from going any further. Mac briefly wondered if being super-rich was really worth it if you had to serve a self-imposed life sentence behind steel gates. Leigh spoke into an intercom and the gates soundlessly slid aside. Behind them stood a very modern house that seemed to consist of nothing but glass and the odd stainless-steel strut. The front door opened as they pulled up behind a blue Porsche four by four. A woman in her late-twenties with long blonde hair stood in the doorway with her arms folded.

'Being a government minister must pay better than I'd imagined,' Leigh said.

Mac had exactly the same thought.

He looked at the woman in the doorway and, if she was Mrs. Kendrick, then she wasn't at all what he had been expecting. She wore a loose yellow T-shirt with ripped blue jeans and she had a pair of flip-flops on her feet. She had no make-up on but, even so, Mac thought that she was strikingly beautiful.

Although he knew that Tim was probably still in the operating theatre, he quickly checked his phone anyway before he went in. There were no messages. He found that his back was stiff as he climbed out of the car and he hobbled rather than walked towards the woman who was waiting for them.

'Mr. Maguire?' she asked in a North-East accent.

Mac showed her his warrant card and she gestured for him and Leigh to follow her. They walked through an empty and echoing lobby into an even larger empty and echoing room. Two of its walls were sheet glass and the other two were painted pure white. He assumed that this was the living room but it was hard to tell as there was no furniture.

Either Mrs. Kendrick was into extreme minimalism or she's leaving, Mac thought.

She took them through into the kitchen which was also empty except for a small table and four chairs.

'Thanks for seeing us, Mrs. Kendrick,' Mac said.

'Please call me Rachel and, for your information, I'm no longer Mrs. Kendrick. I've gone back to being Miss Rachel Young again. Anyway, you're lucky to catch me,' she said as she gestured towards the chairs. 'This is my last night here.'

'You've sold the house then?' Mac asked as he sat down.

'Yes, I put it on the market a couple of weeks after Marcus...well, after he died. It went in less than two hours if you can believe it. Well, whoever bought it is welcome to it,' she said with a scowl as she looked around her.

'I take it that you haven't exactly enjoyed living here then?' Mac asked.

'It was supposed to be our home but it's been more like a prison for me. This isn't exactly the sort of area where you can just pop down to the shops or the pub or anywhere really. It was Marcus' idea to buy this place. He said that it would be a good investment but I think that he just wanted to have something to show off to his stuck-up friends.'

'I take it that you don't have any friends in the area?'

'No, not proper friends anyway. Everyone down here seems to be playing some sort of game. They say that they're your friend but they'd happily stab you in the back if it suited them,' she said with some bitterness. 'I'm going back home tomorrow. I've got some real friends there and a proper house too, not a glorified glass box.'

'And where's home?' Mac asked.

'South Shields, it's not far from Newcastle,' she replied. 'God, I miss it so much. I miss the sea most of all. When I lived there, I used to go for a walk on the beach every day whatever the weather. I've not walked anywhere in London really.'

'What can you tell us about Hoar's Cottage?' Mac asked.

She shrugged.

'Nothing really. I didn't even know it existed until Marcus died. He bought it with his own money but God knows where he got it from though.'

'His own money?'

'When I married Marcus, he was basically broke. His family are related to royalty and they were once quite rich and powerful, at least that's what Marcus told me. He definitely wasn't rich when I married him though. If he had been then I dare say that he wouldn't have looked at me twice.'

'So, all the money was on your side then?' Mac asked.

'Yes, my dad's officially a 'tech giant' these days,' she replied. 'When I was a little kid, mum used to moan about all the time he used to spend in front of his computer. It paid off though, for him at least. Although it was Marcus who chose this place, it was my dad who bought it for us as a wedding present. He thought that it was great that I was marrying someone like Marcus. I'd never have guessed that my dad would have turned into a social climber but, unfortunately, that's what he is. He never said it straight out but I think he was hoping that me marrying Marcus would help to get him to get a knighthood. Instead of which...'

She left the sentence hanging but Mac knew exactly what she meant.

'What was Marcus like?'

'What was he like?' Rachel said with a frown. 'Oh, he could be charming and persuasive when he wanted to be. That's the side of him I saw before we got married. He was totally lovely and just like the handsome prince you get in fairy tales. I thought that I loved him but I was just young and stupid and all starry-eyed about him and the exciting life we would lead once we were married. God but that seems like a lifetime ago now. Anyway, once he had me, or my dad's money I should say, he became cold and distant. He was quite horrible to me at times but it was never physical. He never hit me or anything like that. Just over a year ago, I told my dad that I wanted a divorce but he talked me out of it. I'll bet that he wished he'd listened to me now.'

'When did you find out what Marcus was getting up to at Hoar's Cottage?' Mac asked.

She stood up and hugged herself. Mac could see tears forming as she turned her back on them and looked out of the window. He gave her a minute.

'The police came here one evening and took Marcus away,' she said as she turned back and leaned against the sink. 'No-one would tell me what was going on. As he was a government minister, I just thought there must be some sort of security thing going on. It was only when the police asked to interview me that I found out that he'd actually been arrested and why.'

'And what did you think about that?'

'That? What did I think about that?' she said with visible disgust. 'I knew that my husband was a liar but I didn't realise how big his lies were. I'm so thankful now that we didn't have children. I wanted to, quite desperately at one time, but Marcus wasn't big on sex. He claimed that it was an old injury but that, of course, was just another lie. But how could he do that to a child? How could anyone? As for Hoar's Cottage, I'm glad it's been knocked down. After what went on there, it's the best thing that could have happened to it.'

'Did you know any of the other men who were charged along with your husband?' Mac asked.

'Only Dominic. He and Marcus were quite close. They'd known each other from when they were small children at boarding school. I guess that's where they picked up their disgusting little habits.'

'That's Dominic Lefebre?'

'That's right,' she replied. 'I've often wondered if Justin was involved too. I guess that he must have been as he disappeared like that.'

'Who's Justin?' Mac asked.

'Justin Reynard used to be Marcus' special adviser. Marcus used to say that Justin was so sharp that he'd cut himself one day. Marcus needed him though and he knew it. While he was the charming front man, it was Justin who put the words in his mouth.'

'What was Justin like?'

'He was young, very ambitious and very good-looking. He was really clever too. He could run rings around Marcus which, I suppose, is why Marcus relied on him so much. He could be very charming too, when he could be bothered, which wasn't all that often. However, if I'm being entirely truthful, he was a snake, Mr. Maguire. Winning was everything to him and I think that he'd have happily run his own mother over if it would have helped him get on in life. You meet a lot of snakes in the political world and Justin fitted right in.'

'When did he disappear?' Mac asked.

'About six or seven weeks ago, I think,' she replied. 'Anyway, it was a few weeks after Marcus died. Apparently, his wife reported him missing and then the police came here and asked me if I knew anything. I couldn't tell them much as I hadn't seen him in well over a month.'

'Do you think that his disappearance was connected to the paedophile ring?' Mac asked.

'I haven't got a clue but I think that's what the police thought. They said that they had no evidence directly connecting him to the ring but they obviously thought that he was involved in some way. It would certainly explain why he left so suddenly.'

Mac was thoughtful for a moment.

'As your husband was the Minister for Housing, he must have known quite a lot of people from the construction industry,' he said. 'Was he close to anyone in particular?'

She gave this some thought.

'We used to throw dinner parties here for some of his so-called friends. Marcus liked going out to eat when he could but he said that he wanted to keep these particular parties discreet and probably for good reason.'

'Do you think that he might have been accepting bribes?'

'I honestly wouldn't put it past him,' she said. 'If he could afford to buy a house then he must have gotten the money from somewhere. I've checked and it definitely didn't come out of our account.'

'Who were these friends of his?' Mac asked.

'Most of the dinner parties that Marcus held here were men-only affairs and so I've no idea who came to those. However, there were a few occasions when some of Marcus' friends insisted on bringing their wives along. Marcus told me that I had to attend these but, if I'm being honest, I didn't mind all that much. It was better than being bored.'

'Can you remember who they were?'

She screwed her face up as she thought.

'Well, the ones who were invited most were Desmond, that's Desmond Salisbury, and Richard Wright. They would sometimes bring their wives with them. Oh, and T.B., of course, but he usually had his daughter with him.'

'That's T.B. Power?' Mac asked.

'Yes, that's right.'

'Was he a particular friend of your husband's?'

'No, I don't think that they were all that friendly. It was all business with T.B. but I really liked him. He was a good talker and he had some great stories,' she said with a smile. 'I suppose that one of the main reasons I liked him was because he wasn't stuck-up like most of the people Marcus brought home. Once they heard my accent, a lot of them seemed to find it hard to speak to me but T.B. wasn't like that at all. In fact, he was very charming.'

'What about his daughter?' Mac asked.

'Nessa? I wasn't so sure about her,' Rachel said with a puzzled expression. 'I only met her five or six times but I could never make her out. She was always nice to me but I had a feeling that it was all a bit of an act. Marcus told me to be careful around her. He said that she had a reputation for being a ruthless operator. What I did notice is that she could instantly put on her 'little girl act' when a man was around. I didn't like that aspect of her character at all.'

'What do you mean?'

'You know the stupid face with the dumb smile that men assume is you hanging on their every word and then

109

moving in so close that they get a good whiff of your perfume and a grandstand view of your cleavage.'

Rachel thought for a moment.

'I suppose that I dislike Nessa now that I think about it but I hadn't realised why until just this minute. I hate women who flirt like that but, from the little I saw, I'd guess that she'd be able to wrap most men around her little finger in no time at all.'

'What does she look like?'

Rachel stopped and gave it some thought.

'Well, she doesn't take after her father that's for sure. T.B. is big powerful-looking block of a man but Nessa must take after her mother. She's tall and slim, quite beautiful really. As pretty as she is, it's her hair that strikes you first. It's red and she wears it really long. I mean, I would too if mine was as beautiful a shade of red as hers. She always dresses really elegantly and very expensively too. However, I had the feeling that she never felt all that comfortable when she was all dressed up. Giselle, that's Richard Wright's wife, told me that Nessa always wore a trouser suit at work and usually just jeans when she went out. Her father still regularly goes for a drink with his friends in the pubs around Kilburn and she always goes along with him.'

Mac raised his eyebrows. Kilburn was historically an Irish area of London but it was still quite working-class and not somewhere that you would expect to find a billionaire.

'How did Giselle Wright know Nessa so well?' Mac asked.

Rachel shrugged, 'I've no idea really but I did hear that her husband and T.B. have been involved in quite a few projects over the years so I guess that she must know the Powers through that.'

Mac made a mental note to give Giselle Wright a visit. If she'd known them for some time then she might know quite a bit about the Powers.

'Did Nessa know any of the others well?'

'Not as far as I know.'

'Was Justin at these dinners too?' Mac asked.

An idea was beginning to form in his head.

'Yes, of course. Marcus relied on him for pretty much everything and, from what I could see, it was Justin who did most of the talking when it came to doing business.'

'Do you think that he knew about Hoar's Cottage and what Marcus got up to there?'

She was thoughtful for a moment.

'Justin tried to make sure that he knew about everything. I think that it's possible that he knew about Marcus and what he got up to.'

'Is there any particular reason why you think that?' Mac asked.

'After one of Marcus' more drunken dinner parties, he managed to get me by myself. He told me that he knew that Marcus wasn't up to fulfilling his marital duties. He said that, as he helped Marcus with everything else, he could help out there too if I liked,' she said as her face wrinkled with disgust.

So, if Justin knew that Marcus wasn't having sex with his wife, he might well know the reason why, Mac thought.

'Why do you think Justin disappeared?'

'If he wasn't directly involved in what went on at Hoar's Cottage then I've honestly no idea,' she said with a shrug.

'Do you think that he'd have easily found another job after working for your husband?' Mac asked.

'Yes,' Rachel unequivocally replied. 'He was a devious, underhanded and totally unscrupulous little man and, from what I've seen of politics, that meant that he'd be highly in demand. Marcus once told me that, the dirtier the political fight gets, the more Justin enjoys it. I'm sure that he'd have had plenty of takers.'

This gave Mac even more pause for thought. He was suddenly very interested in Justin Reynard.

'What other properties have you put up for sale besides here and Hoar's Cottage?' Mac asked.

'Well, Marcus bought a flat not far from the House of Commons, which he used when he was working late, and we also had a place near Aldeburgh which we bought to go for weekends by the sea during the summer. I ended up using it as my little bolt hole. It was nice to get away from all this nonsense for a while and I loved walking by the sea there.'

'Can you tell me why you went to such lengths to keep your ownership of Hoar's Cottage such a secret?'

'It was all arranged by our solicitors...'

'That's Ferrer and Garnet?' Mac asked.

'That's right,' Rachel replied. 'I thought it was a bit of a rigamarole to be honest but they said that it would help to keep me out of the public eye. I was all for that.'

Mac asked a few more questions but didn't discover anything that helped. He didn't mind. He had learned a lot from the ex-Mrs. Kendrick.

As she held the front door open for them, Mac turned and asked, 'What are you going to do now?'

'I'm going back into hairdressing,' Rachel replied with a smile. 'A friend of mine has a little business in Newcastle. I started being trained as a hairdresser before my dad got so rich and I loved it. It will be fun and it will be a new start for me. A new life,' she said as she looked back into the house. 'I want to forget all about this one if I can.'

As he walked towards the car Mac realised that Marcus Kendrick's wife had surprised him in more ways than one. He found that he quite liked her and he silently wished her luck with her new life.

Mac was quiet as they sat in the car so Leigh didn't start the engine up. She was beginning to understand Mac a little better and so she was happy to sit and wait.

'The timeline has been really been puzzling me in this case,' Mac eventually said. 'Nothing seemed to make sense, nothing fitted together. Now, finally, we have something that does. I need to make a phone call.'

As he ended the call, he felt something close to panic. He knew that Mac Maguire had a reputation but, even so, he was surprised at how quickly he had zeroed in on Justin Reynard. Besides Hoar's Cottage, he'd been told that he was to immediately report anything to with Reynard, whatever it was.

He hesitated for some time, his finger hovering above the screen. He pulled the phone away and gave it some more thought. It didn't help. He knew that there was only one thing he could do. He quickly selected her phone number before he changed his mind again.

He hoped that she hadn't turned her phone off. He needed to get this done right now.

'John, what is it?' she asked.

'Mac Maguire, he's now looking into Justin Reynard's disappearance,' he said.

There was a long silence.

'What exactly does he know?' she asked.

'I'm not sure. All I know is that he called and asked me for the contact details of the lead investigator who's looking into Reynard's disappearance.'

'Did he say why?'

'No, he didn't. I asked him several times but he wouldn't tell me anything. I said that I could help him with the case but he, very politely, turned me down.'

There was just silence at the other end.

'Nessa, I shouldn't have even asked,' he angrily continued. 'It's not my case and I shouldn't be poking my nose in. I wouldn't be surprised if he'd smelt a rat. I can't do any more. I really can't.'

He ended the call.

Let her send me to jail, he thought with some bitterness. At least my life would be my own and I wouldn't be at her beck and call anymore.

Nessa was angry too. She could ruin him and perhaps she just might do just that.

Calm down and think, she said to herself. Daddy always told her that decisions made in anger will always be the wrong ones. She poured herself a stiff drink, sat down and let the anger ebb away.

No, she wouldn't ruin her pet policeman after all. It was obvious that he'd done what he could and, probably, more than he should have. No, John was too valuable. She'd keep him safe for another time.

She needed a Plan B. Daddy would have had one, she thought, and probably a Plan C and D too. She didn't want to have to go back to him again for help, he'd done enough for her. She wanted to show him that she could handle this one by herself.

So, how to stop this Mac Maguire from finding out about Justin?

She briefly wondered about murder, after all she'd done it before and they do say that it gets easier every time. While she doubted that this would stop the investigation, it would certainly take Mac Maguire out of the equation. He worried her. She'd read up on him and he was good at his job. Too good.

A memory of her sitting with daddy watching TV came into her mind. It was before he'd met his bitch of a second wife and so she'd had him all to herself. They'd been watching a political comedy that had made daddy laugh a lot. She was too young to get the jokes but she liked watching daddy laugh.

'Daddy, what's masterly inactivity?' she'd asked when the programme was over.

Her father had thought for a while before he answered her.

'There are times when you need to do something positive to get ahead in life but there are also times when things will come to you if you just wait and do nothing. Masterly inactivity is knowing exactly when you should do nothing.'

Although she hadn't understood it at the time, it had always stuck in her mind.

She'd probably already done enough to throw the police off the track so that's what she needed now, she thought. Some masterly inactivity.

This Mac Maguire probably knows next to nothing and, if she kept herself calm, he'll know even less than that. After all, every bit of evidence was either buried under several thousand tons of building waste or laid to rest in the biggest block of concrete in Europe.

This thought made her feel better. She decided that she would do exactly nothing.

However, having a Plan B might still be a good idea.

Chapter Thirteen

They had pulled up just a couple of hundred yards away from the Kendricks' house so that Mac could make his call to DI John Roberts. Mac fell silent afterwards.

'What is it?' Leigh asked. 'Couldn't he tell you anything?'

'Oh, I'm sorry,' Mac apologised. 'No, he was able to give me what I wanted but he also asked a lot of questions about the case. He seemed very interested in what we're doing for some reason and I was just wondering why.'

'Well, I suppose that anyone might be a bit curious about a case involving a disappearing house.'

'No, I think that there might be more to it than that. Anyway, it turns out that the man I need to speak to about Reynard's disappearance is someone I know.'

'You seem to know a lot of people,' Leigh said.

'Well, after nearly thirty years or so of knocking about London, so would you. Anyway, he's agreed to meet us and, as it's just about lunchtime, we're going to meet in a pub called The Stag. It's not far from here.'

Mac looked at his watch. It was now twelve thirty. With any luck Tim would be out of the theatre by now. He said a silent prayer for him.

Even in the London traffic, it took them no more than fifteen minutes before they pulled up outside the pub. It was a large Victorian building that had a corner all to itself. Inside it was shabby chic but there was still enough of the old pub left to give it some atmosphere. DI Jed Salter had managed to get a corner table and he was already halfway down a pint of Guinness.

'So, what's it like working out of West Hampstead station?' Mac asked as he shook hands. 'Have you made friends with many millionaires yet?'

He then introduced Leigh who volunteered to go to the bar for a round of drinks.

'Well, it's certainly different to working in the West End that's for sure,' Jed replied. 'The job's a bit easier and there's less running around, which, at my age, I'm quite grateful for.'

Leigh returned with the drinks. Two coffees and a pint of Guinness. She put the pint in front of Jed.

'Not drinking, Mac? I remember the time when we'd both have a few at lunchtime while we talked through a case.'

'I'm getting old now, Jed, and slowly falling apart,' Mac replied. 'I'd be asleep in no time if I had a few beers in the afternoon now.'

'Yes, it's much the same for me too these days,' Jed replied giving Mac a melancholic look. 'However, as my shift finishes in exactly half an hour, this is one occasion when I don't mind. I've been up over half the night on an aggravated burglary case so sleep sounds good to me right now.'

Leigh looked at Jed and then at Mac. If they were around the same age then Mac had certainly weathered the better of the two. Jed was completely bald and his skin was a shade of grey. She wondered if his hangdog expression was natural or if it was just due to his tiredness.

'So, what's your interest in Justin Reynard?' Jed asked.

Mac took him through the case and the trail that had led them here.

'So, you think that Reynard's disappearing trick and the house being demolished are connected in some way?' Jed asked.

'I think that it's possible,' Mac replied. 'If I'm being honest, not much that we've learned to date makes much sense except for that. Then again, it might just be that Mr. Reynard has taken himself off on an extended holiday and he has nothing to do with the case at all.'

'I think that him being on holiday is the more likely,' Jed replied. 'The night that he disappeared, a suitcase and his passport disappeared as well. There was no sign of a break-in as far as we could see. His wife got a text from him a day later saying that he was okay but that he'd be gone for a few months. We've been keeping an eye on his bank account and credit cards but there's been no activity so far. However, his wife told us that she's fairly certain that Reynard has another account but she had no idea who it was with.'

'Did she have any idea of where he was going?'

'Not until a few days ago when she received a photo from her husband's phone. It was of a waterfall in the Dominican Republic. There was no text but his wife said that they were married in front of this particular waterfall so it looks like it's him alright.'

'It would be the Dominican Republic,' Mac said with a frown.

Jed nodded mournfully.

'Well, if we know that he's there then why don't we get the local police to arrest him?' Leigh asked.

'We don't have an extradition agreement with the Dominican Republic,' Mac replied.

'Besides that, what would we charge him with?' Jed said. 'DCI Bowyer hasn't found any evidence so far linking him with the paedophile ring and it's no crime to just walk out of your house one day and never come back.'

'But there must be some reason why he's done a runner,' Leigh persisted.

'It's my bet that he at least knew and might have even facilitated some of the paedophile ring's activities,' Jed replied. 'We just haven't found the evidence yet.'

Mac thought that, on balance, Jed's guess might be fairly close to the truth. He had to concede that Reynard and the house disappearing at the same time might be just a coincidence. Even so, he wasn't about to give up just yet.

'Where does Mrs. Reynard live?' Mac asked.

'Mrs. Angela Reynard lives just down the road opposite, that's why I suggested that we meet here,' Jed replied. 'I've already checked with her and she's at home. I'll introduce you to her if you like?'

'You've read my mind,' Mac said with a smile.

'And once we've done that, I'm off to bed,' Jed said.

They pulled up outside a Victorian town house. It was a solid brick three-storied house with large bow windows and a red door. It might not be as flashy as the Kendrick's house but, as it was in Hampstead, it would probably cost as much to buy.

Mac got out and looked at the flight of steps leading up to the front door with some trepidation. He'd just have to take it carefully. Before he attempted the ascent, he pulled his phone out and had a quick look.

There was nothing from Tim.

'Before we go in, it might be useful for you to know that Justin Reynard might have been having an affair,' Jed said. 'Mrs. Reynard got a bit upset and let it slip out in one of the interviews.'

Mac did indeed think that it would be useful.

Jed bounded up the steps and waited at the top while Mac carefully inched his way upwards. When he was about halfway up, the front door opened and a woman came out. She was exactly what he'd expected Mrs. Kendrick to be.

She was in her late thirties and she had mid-length hair that had recently been cut. The cut looked more efficient than stylish. She wore a matching dark grey tweed jacket and skirt with black court shoes. A string of large white pearls around her neck stood out in contrast against her black blouse.

She looks as if she's already in mourning, Mac thought.

She smiled palely before she turned and led them inside. They passed through a wide hallway into a grand room stuffed with furnishings and bric-a-brac, all of which looked as old as the house. One corner of the room was dominated by a grand piano and full-length portraits of stiffly posed Victorian gentlemen, all with the most extravagant facial hair, were arrayed across the walls. Mac paused by a sideboard that had some family photos displayed on it. He picked up one of Mr. and Mrs. Reynard drinking champagne.

'Our Third Anniversary' it said in gold lettering along the bottom.

Angela Reynard looked just the same but happier. However, it was Justin Reynard that Mac was more interested in. He was obviously somewhat younger than his wife and, as Rachel Kendrick had said, he was quite good looking. He was sharply dressed with not a hair out of place. His smile seemed more professional than happy to Mac though.

As she sat down Mrs. Reynard delicately smoothed her skirt with her hand so that it wouldn't ride up. She sat forward and looked at her guests expectantly.

'I'm sorry but we've not heard anything new about your husband,' Jed quickly said. 'This is Mac Maguire and Leigh Marston from the Hertfordshire Police. They'd like to ask you a few questions.'

Angela Reynard looked at Mac and then Leigh with a puzzled expression.

Mac told her about the demolition of Hoar's Cottage.

'And you think that my husband was involved with all…all that!' she said with a look of utter disgust.

'No, we've found no evidence so far that might link your husband to the paedophile ring,' Mac said. 'It might just be a coincidence, your husband and the house disappearing at around the same time, but we have to look into it.'

'I suppose you do. However, I can assure you that Justin would have nothing to do with such filth,' she said through gritted teeth. 'I absolutely trust my husband and, if he left the country, it will be for a good reason. Something to do with a new business opportunity, I should think, now that Marcus is gone.'

Mac had to admit that this might well be a possibility.

'If that was the case then why wouldn't he have told you what he was doing?' Mac asked.

'Well,' Angela replied looking a little uncomfortable, 'Justin wasn't the type who believed in social media and keeping in touch every two minutes as so many people do today. When he was working, he was working and he'd tell me what he'd been up to when he came home.'

'And how often did he come home?' Mac asked.

'Not as often as I would have liked him to but I know that Marcus loved socialising and it was a large part of the job too. Marcus needed Justin to be at hand at all times so he often spent nights away from home. Sometimes, he and Marcus would need to travel but more often Justin would stay the night at Marcus' house if they needed to work late.'

He made a mental note to check this with Mrs. Kendrick. He'd been looking at her closely while she spoke and he had the feeling that she didn't really believe a word of what she was telling him. There was a sort of defiant vulnerability about her. She was keeping herself together but only just. He thought that he might as well get the hardest question out of the way first.

'You've told us that your husband might have been having an affair,' he said. 'Tell me about it.'

She gave Jed a hard look and then half stood up before changing her mind and sitting down again. Once again, she smoothed her skirt first. Mac wondered if she'd been taught that in finishing school.

She clasped her hands and stared at the floor. It took her a while to answer.

'Yes,' she said softly still staring at the floor. 'I thought that he might have been having an affair.'

'What made you think that?' Mac asked.

'He was away so much over the last few months. More than normal. He told me where he was staying but, on the couple of occasions that I tried to contact him, the hotels said that they had never heard of him.'

'Did he try to explain this to you?'

'He told me that the hotels had been told to deny he was staying there for security reasons,' she said with a shrug.

'But you didn't believe that,' Mac said.

'Well, it was plausible enough, I suppose, but then everything about Justin is plausible. I never caught him out but I still had the feeling that he was seeing someone. It's over now though, I think, and maybe that's why he left so suddenly. To avoid any fallout.'

'Why do you think that?' Mac asked.

'The photo he sent me,' she explained. 'We were married in front of that waterfall. He was sending me a message. He was telling me that he still loved me.'

She said this with complete conviction. Mac couldn't help feeling that she was just fooling herself.

'You said that your husband wasn't into social media. Are you?'

'Well, yes,' she replied. 'It fills in the time, I suppose, and helps me keep in touch with my family.'

'Did you first hear about Marcus from your husband?' Mac asked.

'Yes, and Justin was angry, as angry as I'd ever seen him. He swore and called Marcus names. He said that he'd ruined them both. He cheered up though when he started getting enquiries from some other government ministers who wanted to give him a job.'

'Then why didn't he accept one of those jobs instead of running off to the Dominican Republic?'

She shrugged, 'I've no idea. Justin never told me much about what he did. I'd guess that it must have been a really good opportunity though, if it meant turning down those job offers.'

'Was your husband short of money?' Mac asked.

'Good God no!' she replied giving Mac an incredulous look. 'We've got a few million in the bank and that's besides all the shares we own. Justin wasn't born rich but he made himself so.'

'How did he do that?'

'He married me, of course,' she replied in all seriousness. 'I knew that he needed my money and background if he

122

was to get anywhere in the party but I also knew that he loved me too. I wanted to help him. I honestly think that he'll make a jolly good Prime Minister one day.'

Mac had no more questions for Angela Reynard. He thought that the poor woman was totally deluded.

Outside, before saying his goodbyes, Mac asked a very tired-looking Jed if he could send him the photo of the waterfall before he went to bed. Jed only had the energy to nod.

Mac then got his phone out and checked it again.

'Still nothing?' Leigh asked as they walked towards the car.

Mac shook his head.

'I shouldn't worry too much,' Leigh said. 'My uncle told me that it took him quite a while to come around after the operation.'

Of course, Mac thought. He gave Leigh a smile.

'So, back to Letchworth?' Leigh asked as she started the engine up.

'I suppose so,' Mac replied. 'I can't think of anything more that we can do today.'

Thankfully, although the traffic was heavy, it kept moving until they ground to a halt at the inevitable jam at the road works on Watford Way.

'So, did we learn anything?' Leigh asked trying to take Mac's mind off his phone.

'Well, we certainly got some insight into Justin Reynard's character and his wife's. I had a look at a photograph of them together and they just didn't look like a couple, if you know what I mean.'

'She is a little older than I'd have thought,' Leigh said.

'It does make me wonder if the love was all on the one side in that relationship and, even though she suspects him of having an affair, it seems that she still wants to think the best of him. He seems to have been an ambitious man yet she's saying that he might have turned down the chance of another job in government. I find that very hard to believe.

If he was the type of person that I think he was then he'd have been drawn towards power. It can be like a drug for some people. I honestly don't think that he'd have given up the chance of climbing the political ladder for any business opportunity.'

'You're talking about him in the past tense,' Leigh said.

'Yes, I am, aren't I?'

Mac was interrupted by his phone. It was a text from Tim!

Op went okay and surprised at not feeling too bad. Text me before you come tonight though Tim.

Leigh didn't need to look over at Mac to know that the news was positive. She could feel the stress field that had surrounded him all day begin to dissolve.

'Tim's okay and the operation went okay too,' Mac said.

'Are you going to see him tonight?' Leigh asked.

'Yes, hopefully.'

'Well, give him my best.'

'I will,' Mac replied.

As he had his phone out, he called Mrs. Kendrick. Leigh could only listen to Mac's side of the conversation. He was thoughtful after the call had finished so she eventually had to nudge him.

'Well?' she asked.

'Sorry, Leigh,' Mac replied. 'Just give me a minute.'

It took ten minutes of scrolling before Mac found what he'd been looking for. Once again, he went quiet. Leigh decided to wait until they got to the station to find out what he'd discovered.

As soon as she pulled up in the station car park, she said, 'Okay, what did you find? You did find something, didn't you?'

'Oh, I'm sorry,' Mac said apologetically. 'I do wander off sometimes but yes, I did find something. Mrs. Kendrick, or I suppose I should say Rachel Young, told me that Justin had never spent the night at her house. He'd asked once or twice but Marcus didn't like him staying over for some reason. He always insisted that Reynard took a taxi home.'

'So, that makes the possibility that he was having an affair even stronger, doesn't it?'

'Yes, it does. I asked her if she knew who Justin might have been seeing and she suggested that I might speak to Annalise Salisbury. Her husband Desmond attended quite a few of Marcus Kendrick's dinner parties.'

'Did she say why?' Leigh asked.

'No, she wouldn't say any more than that. As for this 'business opportunity' in the Dominican Republic, I think that it might be a set-up.'

'What do you mean?' Leigh asked.

Mac passed her his phone. It displayed an entry from Angela Reynard's Facebook page from when she was celebrating her fifth wedding anniversary. She talked about how idyllic the wedding ceremony had been and included some photos.

One of them was of a waterfall.

'That looks just like the photo that Reynard sent to his wife,' Leigh said.

'It is. I've checked and the two photos are identical.'

Leigh gave this some thought.

'I get it!' she said with a smile. 'The photo that was sent from Justin Reynard's phone could have been sent by anyone. It's easy enough to copy images on Facebook, I've done it myself loads of times. What does it mean though?'

'I don't think that it was Justin who sent that photo.'

'His wife seems to be sure that it was him.'

'She's just desperate to have her husband back or so it would seem,' Mac said. 'I think that she'd believe anything at the moment. So, if it wasn't Reynard, then who did send it and why would they have his phone? I can't get the idea out of my mind that Justin Reynard is dead.'

'Do you think that his body might be with the rest of Hoar's Cottage in that waste tip near Luton?' Leigh asked.

Mac shook his head.

'No, I don't. I doubt that the men who demolished the cottage were in on it and there's no reason why they should be. It's a bit of a stretch but, if Justin Reynard was killed in that cottage, then I think that knocking it down was simply the most practical way of getting rid of the forensic evidence. The body would have been disposed of long before the demolition crew arrived. If someone in T.B. Power's company was involved then I guess that the remains of Mr. Reynard might be somewhere where they will never be found.'

Leigh gave Mac a quizzical look.

'And where do you think that might that be…' she stopped in mid-sentence. 'Oh my God, the concrete pour! That was going on at around the same time, wasn't it?'

'That's right. I suspect that the base of Mr. Power's new skyscraper might well contain fourteen thousand cubic metres of concrete and the body of Justin Reynard.'

Chapter Fourteen

The Major Crime Unit's team room was packed when they got there. Dan was giving a briefing on the pub murder case which looked as if it was reaching a critical phase. Mac and Leigh decided to beat a retreat and discuss the case over a coffee and sandwich at the Magnets.

'This case is really annoying me now,' Mac said.

He then took a bite from his cheese and tomato panini and briefly wondered why no-one seemed to do ordinary sandwiches anymore.

'In what way?' Leigh asked.

'In every way. We've now got a theory that explains why Hoar's Cottage and Justin Reynard disappeared but we've got virtually no evidence to back it up. I've had plenty of cases where the body was never found and we won quite a lot of them too. But having no body and no crime scene makes it a little more difficult, doesn't it?'

'Well, I suppose that's what our man, whoever he or she is, was trying to achieve. You have to admit that it's clever though,' Leigh said.

Mac did indeed think it was clever. He wondered if any of the ripples from the investigation had reached 'our man' yet. If so, he or she was keeping very quiet. Mac frowned as he realised that keeping quiet was probably all they would have to do in order to get away with murder.

'So, if we don't have a body or any forensic evidence, how do we catch him then?' Leigh asked.

'We keep digging and we build a case. If we can get enough circumstantial evidence then that, by itself, might be enough to convince a jury. Of course, a few eye witnesses wouldn't hurt.'

'Yes, there's always something to find, isn't there?' Leigh said hopefully.

Mac's phone interrupted the conversation. It was a text from Tim. Leigh noticed his disappointed look.

'Tim's asked me not to visit him tonight,' Mac said. 'He felt okay just after the operation but now he's saying that he feels a bit worse and that he won't be up for a visit after all.'

'My uncle used to play rugby and he said that, when he'd been young, he'd once gotten caught at the bottom of a ruck with two whole teams on top of him,' Leigh said. 'There were stud marks all over his body and he broke a few ribs too. He said that he felt just like that after the operation. Yet, a couple of days later he was up and about and feeling a bit better.'

Mac thought that this made sense. It was a major operation after all and having six holes put in your stomach would definitely take it out of you. He was still disappointed though.

'So, what's next?' Leigh said.

Mac gave this some thought.

'Well, Hoar's Cottage has been the focal point of the investigation so far but, although it's not officially our case, I think that it might not be a bad idea to have a look at Justin Reynard for a while. I have to admit that everything we've come up with so far is based on assumptions and suppositions but I'm going to make another one anyway. However, this one is based on something that I find quite compelling and that's the timeline. Is it just a coincidence that an ambitious politician disappears at the same time as a house, which was owned by his boss, ends up in a waste tip? As far as I can see, this politician had no reason to disappear. In fact, he had everything to gain by staying. His wife thought that he'd make a good Prime Minister and I'd bet that he did too. That being the case, why would he take himself away from the political scene?'

'What about Marcus Kendrick and the paedophile ring though?' Leigh said. 'He could have been involved.'

'I'm beginning to doubt that. It seems that Reynard was into women not little boys so why would he gamble with his future? Becoming involved with something like that would have spelt his political death if anyone had found out. From what I've heard so far, Marcus Kendrick and Justin Reynard were far from being friends and it's my guess that their relationship was purely transactional. Marcus Kendrick was Reynard's ticket into the halls of power and he repaid that by doing a lot of Kendrick's job for him. If that was the case then he may not have known about the paedophile ring after all. If he had then I'd guess that he'd have quietly got himself another job pretty quickly.'

'Well, that all makes sense, I suppose,' Leigh said. 'So, if he wasn't involved, what would he have been doing at Hoar's Cottage?'

'I'm afraid that's where my little theory falls down,' Mac said with a shake of his head. 'I'd guess that being seen at the cottage wouldn't have looked good even after Kendrick's death. Nevertheless, I've still got the feeling that the demolition of Hoar's Cottage and Reynard's disappearing trick are somehow linked.'

'Yes, me too,' Leigh said. 'So how do we follow it up?'

'I think we should try and see this Annalise Salisbury first. If Reynard was having an affair then she might be able to confirm it. I'd also like to know a little more about Nessa Power so it might also be worth paying Giselle Wright a visit. Then I'd like to see if we could have a word with Eoin Power too. As he's not involved in the family business then he might be willing to mark our cards about his father's company.'

'What about Mrs. Reynard?' Leigh asked. 'I must admit that I thought that she was a bit too good to be true. She was like something from the Stepford Wives. Couldn't she have bumped her husband off?'

'Well, it's a possibility, isn't it?' Mac admitted. 'After all, she admitted that she thought that her husband was having an affair and, when it comes to murder, love turned to hate is one of the most compelling motives there is. Who knows? Perhaps she sent that photo from her husband's phone to herself.'

'But wouldn't your friend Jed have considered that when he started investigating the case?'

Mac shrugged, 'I'm not sure but I'll give him a call later and find out. I'm afraid that Jed wasn't one of the most energetic coppers in our team when I worked with him.'

That might explain why Jed Salter was still only a Detective Inspector while Mac had risen to the dizzying heights of Detective Chief Superintendent, Leigh thought. She had been wondering about that.

'Well, it looks like we've got a full day planned for tomorrow already,' Leigh said. 'Fancy something a bit stronger than coffee?'

Mac didn't say no.

Her Plan B was Malky O'Keefe. She decided that she needed to know exactly what this Mac Maguire was getting up to. She had told him to follow Maguire and Malky, being the obedient sort, was only too happy to help.

Only too happy to get me into bed, more like it, she thought.

It would cost her but it would be worth it. She didn't mind the bed bit too much. Malky was older than she was and he reminded her quite a lot of her father. Perhaps that's why she didn't mind so much.

Anyway, she had made daddy happy today and that had made her feel happy too. She'd told him that she'd managed to get that piece of land that he'd needed for his new project in North London. Of course, she hadn't told him exactly how she'd gotten her hands on it and there was a very good reason for that. She needed to get back into his good books and, if she told him what she'd done, he might not have been quite so happy.

Poor Josh! She had romanced him and let him bed her. As she'd planned, the poor fool had fallen in love with her. He'd thought that she was in love with him too which had made it all the easier to convince him that he was on the inside track to making a fortune. He had been a supremely stupid man and, at her suggestion, had signed the land transfer over to her before she had signed the contract. Once she had the land, she had everything that she needed from him. She returned the contract unsigned. The fact that this meant ruin for him didn't matter to her in the least.

Of course, she knew that he'd be unhappy about it. However, she thought that him killing his whole family and then himself was taking it a bit too far.

She had felt nothing when she had heard the news. If he was that stupid then what had that got to do with her?

She smiled. She had made daddy happy and so she was happy too.

Chapter Fifteen

Mac was surprised when his alarm clock went off. He'd felt tired and had gone to bed early the night before. This usually meant that he'd be wide awake hours before he needed to get up but, thankfully, not this morning. For once, he'd had a good night's sleep.

When his brain finally started working, he picked up his phone and checked for any texts from Tim. There was nothing. He sighed and sat up. He then stood up and was once again surprised. For once the pain was minimal. He figured that was why he'd slept so well.

He thought about the case while he showered and shaved. While he made a pot of coffee, he concluded that they could do with a breakthrough and some actual evidence would be nice. He was all too aware that, at the moment, the case was nothing more than a house of cards built out of suppositions. The smallest piece of hard evidence that disagreed with their theory could blow it all down.

Evidence was what they needed. A fingerprint, a shred of blood-stained cloth, an eye witness, anything would be good.

Ever the optimist, Mac decided that today might just be the day that this happened.

He beat Leigh to it that morning and he was already on the phone when she came in. She quickly went back out and returned with two coffees while Mac finished his call.

'That was Eoin Power,' Mac said. 'He said that he'll be able to see us at his office around eleven o'clock. I tried Mrs. Salisbury but I was informed by a somewhat snooty lady that 'Mrs. Salisbury rarely rises before mid-day.' Anyway, she said that she'd tell her that we were coming. I called Jed Salter first. We're going to meet him at West Hampstead station after we're finished with Mr. Power.'

'What about Giselle Wright?' Leigh asked.

'I haven't been able to get through to her as yet but I'll try her again as we drive in.'

'I've got a feeling that today might be the day,' Leigh said excitedly.

Mac just smiled. He didn't tell her that he'd had the same thought. For some absurd reason he felt that it would bring bad luck.

'By the way, how's your mum doing?' Mac asked as they headed towards the motorway.

They had met at one of the police Christmas drinks parties last year. While the word 'bubbly' was way over-used in describing someone's character, Mac thought that this was an accurate description of Mary Marston. She obviously loved a social occasion and she gave it one hundred percent. She'd even tried to drag Mac up onto the dance floor but, luckily, he had his back as an excuse.

Mac sighed at the thought. Even when his back had been alright, he had avoided dancing. He knew the theory behind rhythm and movement but he could never quite catch the beat of the music. He'd start off behind the beat and then overtake it before going behind it again. He looked ridiculous. Nora, on the other hand, could just do it and do it beautifully too. However, it wasn't all bad. He'd gotten quite a lot of pleasure over the years watching his wife from the side of the dance floor.

'Oh, mum's still the same as ever,' Leigh replied with a smile. 'Still doing two jobs, both part-time now, and still going out as often as she can. She had a hard time after dad died so it's nice to see her enjoying herself.'

Mac remembered that Leigh's father had died of a heart attack when she was just twelve and her mother had had to do two jobs to keep the family afloat. It must have been hard on Leigh as her brother, who she's very close to, went off to university not long afterwards.

'And how's your brother doing?' Mac asked.

'Oh, he's the star of the family,' Leigh replied. 'He's in America now. He won an award last year and he's used the money to go and study at a place called Stanford in California.'

'He's a physicist, isn't he?'

'That's right. His speciality is dark matter and it appears to be quite a hot topic at the moment,' Leigh replied.

It was obvious that she was inordinately proud of her sibling.

'He's asked me to go over and see him in the autumn,' Leigh continued with a wide smile. 'I've never been to America.'

'Something to look forward to then,' Mac said.

Mac might have said more but his phone went off. It was a text from Giselle Wright. They could call around any time after three o'clock.

The trip into London turned out to be a little easier than the day before and it didn't take them too long to get to Camden Town.

'Where exactly are these offices?' Leigh asked as they slowly crawled behind the traffic on Camden High Street.

'Just keep going until you see the railway bridge,' Mac replied. 'It's above the Market Hall on your left.'

Mac looked at the crowded pavements. Camden Town was a popular destination, especially with the younger tourists. Among the usual eateries and souvenir shops, there were tattoo parlours and lots and lots of clothes shops. The style of the clothes seemed a little anachronistic to Mac being a cross of punk, goth and biker. However, the bulging bags being carried by the tourists attested that the businesses on Camden High Street were doing okay.

Leigh managed to squeeze into a parking spot right outside the Market Hall.

'We're to look for some black double doors on the left of the building and then go up to the first floor,' Mac said.

They found the doors easily enough. Inside a sign for 'Mellberg and Power' pointed up the stairs. Mac looked around but there was no lift. He sighed and started up the stairs. He took it slowly but, for some reason, he found it a little easier than usual. He wished that he could have more days like this.

The office was smaller than Mac had expected and he was greeted by Eoin Power himself and not a receptionist. He led them to a corner that had two well-worn but quite comfortable-looking sofas. He was not what Mac had expected. He was slim, quite short and his round face was topped with curly red hair. His black-rimmed glasses gave him an owl-like look. He'd seen photos of his father and he had to admit that he looked nothing like him.

'So, how can I help the police?' he asked.

He was smiling and seemingly at ease.

'I'd like to ask you a few questions about your father and his business,' Mac said. 'Would that be okay?'

Eoin's open and transparent look had suddenly become closed and guarded.

'Well, that depends on the questions,' he replied.

Mac decided to ease into the interview.

'What exactly do you do here?'

'Well, my partner, Olaf, is an architect and I studied Material Sciences at university and, as we're both committed eco-activists, we had this idea. Olaf is designing modular buildings with elements that can be re-used and I'm putting together a material database of everything that might go into a building. Between us, we're hoping to design buildings that will be mostly made up of re-useable components so, when their life is over, they can be simply taken apart and used elsewhere.'

'So, no more demolitions then?' Mac asked.

'That's right,' Eoin replied. 'It would be more like dis-assembly than demolition. Of course, not everything can be re-used but we're hoping that we can get it up to well over ninety percent. We're only starting up but we've got some innovative solutions and we think that its time might have finally come.'

Mac noticed how enthusiastic Eoin was when talking about his business.

'So, what did you think about your father's massive concrete pour a few weeks back?'

Eoin's enthusiastic expression immediately turned into a frown.

'Did you know that concrete is the most energy intensive manufacturing process there is? Roughly eight percent of all carbon dioxide emissions in the world come from the production of concrete. Yet, there's dad pouring thousands of cubic metres of the stuff into a hole in the ground and what for? To build another giant penis reaching up to the sky that no-one really needs.'

Mac could see that Eoin was getting quite angry by the time he finished his little rant. He thought that now might be the time to get personal.

'Is that why you and your dad fell out?'

'Yes. Well, that and other things.'

'What other things?' Mac asked.

Eoin stopped and looked up at Mac. He was obviously thinking about what to tell him. Mac held his breath. He knew that Eoin would now either clam up or keep talking. Luckily for Mac, he kept talking.

'I met Olaf at university. It was there that we got excited about the idea of re-useable buildings but we also got excited about something else. Each other. I've known that I was gay since I was eleven or twelve but I always felt that I had to keep it a deep dark secret. While dad's a billionaire businessman and all that, he's also quite old-fashioned in many ways. He believes that people like me and Olaf are unnatural and choose to be gay as some sort of weird lifestyle decision.'

He gave Mac a sad look before continuing.

'He used to go on about it so much that I didn't dare tell him. I was going to come out to him when I'd graduated but, in the end, it was taken out of my hands. I'd come home from university for Christmas but dad didn't seem all that pleased to see me. He then showed me a picture that someone had innocently posted on Facebook. It was Olaf's

136

birthday and we were kissing. I came out there and then and told him that I was gay, that I'd always been gay. He just stood up and walked out of the room. I packed my bags and went to Olaf's. We've not seen each other since.'

'How did your father get the photo?' Mac asked. 'Was he following you on social media?'

'No, dad never was one for stuff like that. It's my guess that the photo came from my loving sister, Nessa.'

It was said in a way that implied exactly the opposite. Mac kept the questions coming as quickly as he could. He didn't want to give Eoin any time to stop and think.

'Why would Nessa do something like that?'

'Because she wanted me out of the way,' Eoin replied with some bitterness. 'Dad had a director's chair in the company warmed up for me for when I finished university. He's quite traditional and he wanted his son to take over the family business after he died. Nessa had other thoughts. So, three months after I left home for the last time, she finally got what she wanted and she was made a director of the company instead of me.'

'It sounds as though Nessa and you don't get on,' Mac asked. 'Why is that?'

'It's mostly on her side, I'm afraid. I think that she's hated me from the day I was born. She's my half-sister and she was eight when mum had me. Her mother had died when she was five and I guess that she'd had dad to herself all that time. I know she resented me but I think she resented my mum even more. I can remember when it was Nessa's fifteenth birthday and my mum, ever the peacemaker, bought her a designer dress. Nessa made out that she loved it because dad was there but the next day mum found a box outside of her bedroom door. Inside it was the dress. It had been cut up into little pieces. That was typical Nessa.'

'I take it that neither you or your mother told your father about this?'

No,' Eoin said with a shake of his head. 'Mum knew that it would only hurt dad and so she said nothing. I'm not sure that he'd have believed her anyway. Nessa was always sweetness and light when he was around. I think he loved her more than any of us.'

'How did your mother die?' Mac asked.

'A heart attack. She'd already had one and she was on medication. The doctors said that they should keep her from having another one but they were wrong.'

Mac could see from his expression that it still hurt.

'How old were you?'

'I was eighteen. It happened just after I'd started at university. I'd been a bit worried about leaving mum but, after she passed away, I was glad to be somewhere else.'

'Why were you worried?' Mac asked.

He was getting very interested now.

'Dad was at work most of the time and I didn't want to leave mum alone with Nessa,' Eoin replied. 'However, mum insisted that I go and she said that she'd be alright.'

'Did you think that Nessa might hurt your mother in some way?'

He nodded.

'I kept telling myself that I was being stupid and that, while Nessa might be a cow, she wouldn't really harm anyone. However, I couldn't even convince myself on that one. I was never sure what Nessa's limits were on anything or even if she had any. Anyway, the doctors said that mum died from natural causes but, if it hadn't had been for that, I'd have been looking closely at Nessa for it.'

'Was she ever violent?'

Mac noticed Leigh giving him a meaningful look when he said this.

'Yes, she could be. She beat me up more than once and I eventually learned to keep well out of her way. Then she went to a private boarding school for a few years. Blissful years they were too. However, our peace ended when Nessa was expelled. She'd had an argument with one of her friends and she beat her up so badly that she had to be hospitalised. I'd bet that dad had to lay out quite a bit of cash to hush that one up.'

'What about since then?'

'I've not heard of anything. Why are you so interested in Nessa?' Eoin asked.

Mac was asking himself the same question.

'Have you ever heard of Marcus Kendrick?'

'God, yes. He killed himself after admitting that he'd raped young boys, didn't he?' Eoin replied with some distaste. 'Are you investigating Kendrick then?'

'Not quite,' Mac replied. 'His advisor, Justin Reynard, has disappeared. We believe that he might be dead.'

'Reynard?' Eoin said his forehead crinkling in thought. 'I've heard of him but I've never met him.'

'Your father and sister knew him. They went to several private dinner parties at Marcus Kendrick's house.'

'I'm not surprised at that. As Kendrick's department managed the planning approvals for several of dad's building projects then I'd guess that he'd have made sure that he knew him.'

Eoin sat up and looked at both Mac and Leigh.

'You don't think that dad or Nessa had anything to do with this Reynard's disappearance, do you?'

'We don't think anything at the moment. We're just trying to find out something about the people who knew him.'

This seemed to satisfy him.

'So, why are you so interested in Nessa Power?' Leigh asked as they climbed into the car.

'I'm not totally sure. It's the love interest angle, I suppose,' Mac replied. 'If Reynard was having an affair then it might have been with Nessa Power. However, from the way Rachel Kendrick said it, it seems that Annalise Salisbury might well be in frame for that too.'

'You're still thinking that Reynard might have been killed by a jealous lover?' Leigh asked.

'Well, it's the most plausible motive we've got so far,' Mac replied with a shrug. 'Let's hope that Mrs. Salisbury is a good talker.'

Chapter Sixteen

They left Camden Town and drove past some very elegant white-rendered Georgian town houses. Mac knew that just behind them ranged Regents Park and the London Zoo. They continued driving through Georgian London past the Royal Artillery barracks until, quite suddenly, they were surrounded by some quite inelegant and very grey nineteen sixties council flats.

Despite having worked in London for well over twenty-five years, this sudden shift from extreme wealth to the workaday still surprised Mac. He remembered someone telling him about a street in London that was being gentrified. At the gentrified end of the street, the renovated houses were worth over six times more than those at the other end of the street. With housing being so expensive, Mac wondered how anyone could afford to live in London.

They came to a grinding halt when they hit the traffic coming onto the Marylebone Road. He knew from experience that it would be slow going from here on. It took four changes of the traffic lights before they were able to insert themselves into the heavy flow of traffic on the main road. They were back in Georgian London again as they very slowly passed the Royal School of Music and, a little later on, the very grand St. Marylebone Parish Church.

'Charles Dickens used to go there,' Mac said as he nodded towards the church.

'Are you doing your tour guide bit now?' Leigh asked with a smile. 'Anyway, how did you find that out?'

'The parish priest told me. There was a case, some fifteen years ago now I should think, that involved that church,' Mac said. 'A man had been stabbed outside a pub near the Edgware Road tube station and he made it all the way to the church before collapsing and dying on its steps. I remember my sergeant joking that he must have had private health insurance as he seemed to have been trying to get to Harley Street.'

'Never mind dusty old churches,' Leigh said. 'Now, that's somewhere I've wanted to visit for ages. What's it like?'

Mac looked across the street and saw throngs of colourful tourists milling around on the pavement.

'Madame Tussauds?' Mac asked. 'I've no idea but, from the looks of it, they must be doing good business.'

'You've never visited it, not even once?' Leigh asked looking surprised.

'No. Nora and I often talked about it but somehow we never got around to it,' Mac replied.

A vivid memory surfaced.

'I remember that we had it all booked up to go once,' Mac continued. 'It wasn't long after Prince William had married Kate Middleton and they'd made some wax figures of them in all their wedding gear. Nora had really wanted to see it but then we found the body of a woman floating in the canal at Little Venice just down the road from here and that was that.'

He remembered his wife's disappointment and he had a deeply sad moment. He knew just how much she'd had to give up when she'd married a policeman. He turned away so that Leigh wouldn't notice. Mac guessed that she already had as she was silent as they continued to crawl down Marylebone Road.

He pulled out his phone and checked to see if he had any messages. He didn't. He wondered what was happening to Tim and that didn't improve his mood any.

'It's left just here,' Mac said breaking the silence.

They turned into Gloucester Place and headed towards Mayfair. Again, more Georgian town houses on either side. These though were only clad in white stone on the ground floor. The three floors above showed the red bricks that the houses had been built with. The doors were large and had ornate wrought-iron fanlights above them. Elegant metal balconies ran along the length of the first floor.

They had to stop while a taxi made a pick-up and Mac noticed a plaque on the wall outside of one of the houses that had been turned into a high-class dentist's office. It told him that Benedict Arnold had lived there until his death in 1801 and described him as an 'American patriot'. He wasn't sure that most modern-day Americans would agree with that statement. It made him smile though. He must have been up and down this street hundreds of times during his working life and he'd never noticed that plaque before. He liked learning something new.

They had to do a bit of a detour along Oxford Street to get to Park Street where Mrs. Salisbury lived. Leigh went slowly as they looked for the house number. Mac noticed that she was also rubber-necking at the houses as they went by, some of which were very grand indeed.

'It's that one there. The one on the corner,' Mac said.

Leigh looked over at a four-storey town house that had a short flight of steps leading up to a wide black door that was framed in ornately carved stone. It was topped with a large stone lintel on which stood the sculpted figure of an antlered deer.

'It doesn't seem right somehow, does it?' Leigh said as they climbed out of the car. 'I mean there's just one family living in there. You could easily house everyone who lives in my block of flats in there.'

Mac could only reply with a shrug.

He made his way up the steps and looked for a doorbell but couldn't see one.

'I think you're supposed to use that,' Leigh said as she pointed to an old-fashioned bell-pull by the side of the door.

He pulled it and a faint tinkling sound could be heard. The door swung open to reveal a young Asian woman dressed in a maid's uniform.

'Yes, can I help you?' she asked in a musical voice.

Mac showed her his warrant card.

'Mrs. Salisbury is expecting us,' he said.

She gave him a smile and asked them to follow her. She left them in a high-ceilinged parlour full of ornate Victorian clutter. However, Mac had to admit that the over-stuffed settee looked comfortable enough.

A few minutes later a sharp-faced woman entered. She was dressed in a black skirt and blouse and her hair was pulled back into a severe bun at the back of her head. A large bunch of keys hung at her waist. She was nothing like he'd imagined Mrs. Salisbury to be. That was because she wasn't.

'I'm Miss Durant, Mr. Salisbury's housekeeper,' she said.

It was the woman that he'd spoken to earlier. She looked just as snooty as she'd sounded on the phone.

'I've let Mrs. Salisbury know you're here but, I warn you, she might be some time.'

She then turned and left, the keys gently clinking as she walked.

'Rebecca,' Leigh said with a smile as soon as the door was closed. 'I knew that I'd seen her somewhere before.'

Mac was puzzled for a moment until he realised that she was referring to the movie 'Rebecca'. He laughed when he pictured Mrs. Danvers in his mind. Leigh was right. There was definitely a certain similarity.

'Do you like those old movies then?' Mac asked.

'Oh, yes,' she replied enthusiastically. 'There's nothing better than cuddling up with a bottle of wine and a classic weepie on Netflix.'

She walked around the room looking at the expensive bric-a-brac that filled it.

'I know all this stuff must have cost a bomb but it's all a bit old-fashioned, isn't it?' she said.

Before Mac could answer, the door was flung open and a blonde woman in a white silk dressing gown wafted into the room. She sat down opposite Mac and lit up a cigarette. She was very attractive and she reminded him of Marilyn Monroe a little. Mac guessed that she was in her mid-thirties. She was only just starting to look it.

She sucked down a lungful of tobacco smoke and expelled it slowly before finally looking at Mac. He showed her his warrant card and introduced himself and Leigh.

'So, what can I do for our wonderful police force today?' she asked in a mocking tone.

'We're looking into the disappearance of Justin Reynard,' Mac replied. 'I take it that you knew him?'

'Oh yes, I knew him alright,' she replied with a sly smile. 'What's happened to him then?'

'That's what we'd like to know,' Mac replied.

He decided to cut to the chase.

'Were you and Justin Reynard having an affair?'

He was a little surprised by her reaction. She laughed.

'An affair?' she said still giggling. 'No, I'd hardly call it that.'

She leaned forward to flick some ash into the ashtray and her left breast fell out of her dressing gown. She sat back and made no attempt to cover herself up. Leigh and Mac exchanged glances.

'So, what would you call it?' Mac said trying to look anywhere else.

'We fucked. We weren't in love or anything like that. We just had sex every time we met, if we could manage it.'

'When did you first have sex with Justin Reynard?' Mac asked.

'Oh, that was after one of Marcus' little dinner parties. My husband was under the weather so he sent me by myself. I think that he just wanted to make sure that no-one was talking about him behind his back. As Marcus wouldn't let Justin stay the night, I offered him a lift home. I pulled up outside his house and he put his hand on my knee. I put it a little further up so he'd get the message. So, we fucked in my car right outside his own house.'

'How often did you and he meet?'

'Not all that often, a couple of times a month, I suppose. I used to look forward to his calls though. He'd think of innovative places for us to go. We did it in a park once, in a taxi cab a couple of times and even in a cinema. I can't remember what the movie was. Anyway, I liked the danger of it all and, apparently, so did he.'

'When did you last meet up with Justin?' Mac asked.

'Oh, that would be at the Kendrick's,' she replied finally tucking her breast back inside her gown. 'It was a week or two before Marcus was arrested for screwing little boys. My husband, Marcus and T.B. were talking about business. Rachel Kendrick and Nessa Power had taken themselves off somewhere. So, I gave Justin the sign. He followed me upstairs to the bathroom and we did it there.'

'You had sex with Justin Reynard in the bathroom? Weren't you afraid that someone would discover you?'

'Oh, there's two more bathrooms downstairs. Anyway, as I said, the fear of discovery made the sex all the better. He had such a lovely cock and he knew how to use it too.'

'Do you think someone might have seen you and Justin in the bathroom?' Mac asked.

'It's possible, I suppose,' she replied with a shrug. 'When I was putting my knickers back on, I noticed that the door was slightly open. We were in such a rush to get at each other, you see.'

'What happened when you went back downstairs?'

'Nothing. The men were still in deep conversation. I doubt that my husband even knew that I was gone.'

'What about the women?' Mac asked.

'Well, I think that Rachel Kendrick suspected something as she had this embarrassed smile on her face when she came back into the room.'

'What about Nessa Power?'

'Nessa?' she replied. She paused for a moment. 'I don't know really. She looked a little sour perhaps but then doesn't she always?'

'Why was that the last time that you and Justin had sex?' Mac asked.

'Well, the whole Marcus thing blew up and Justin said that he was incredibly busy with the hand over to the new chap who was taking over. I tried a couple of weeks later but his phone was dead. It's a shame, I suppose, but luckily I've found this young barman who has the tackle of a stallion,' she said looking straight at Leigh whose face started going red.

'Was Justin Reynard seeing anyone else besides you?' Mac asked.

'Seeing? You mean fucking, don't you?' she replied with a smile. 'I've no idea but, from the little I've learned about Justin, I wouldn't be at all surprised.'

'Is there anything else you can tell us?' Mac asked hopefully.

Again, she shrugged.

'Not really. Justin and I didn't talk much. We just fucked.'

Mac thought that this might be a good time to end the interview.

'Did you find that a little embarrassing?' Mac asked as they walked back to the car.

'Well, yes if I'm being honest,' Leigh replied. 'I found myself feeling a bit sorry for her too. Even though she's got a rich husband and she lives in a fancy house, she didn't seem all that happy to me.'

'Well, she's probably a trophy wife whose only job is to look good on her husband's arm in public. I've met a few women like her before. They make a bargain with life when they marry their rich and, usually, much older husbands but they often quickly regret it.

There was one woman in particular who springs to mind. Looking back, she was quite a lot like Annalise Salisbury. She drank too much and she had a reputation for sleeping around. We were investigating someone she'd had casual sex with and she let something slip which gave me some insight into why she was the way she was. She told us that she was her husband's third wife and that he'd had several children by the first two. As he didn't want them to be disinherited in any way, he insisted that his wife-to-be got herself sterilised before they were married so that there would be no more children. So, she did just that but it was a decision that she bitterly regretted afterwards. Anyway, West Hampstead station next.'

As they drove towards their next appointment Leigh asked, 'Has seeing Mrs. Salisbury made you think any differently about the case?'

'Yes, it has,' Mac replied. 'Two things strike me. The first is that Justin Reynard and Annalise Salisbury weren't particularly trying to hide what they did together. In fact, it seemed to be all part of the thrill. If Justin was involved with someone else then there's a good chance that they found out.'

'You're thinking of Nessa Power again, aren't you?'

'We've got nothing that ties Reynard to Nessa Power yet but yes, I am. It seems likely that Hoar's Cottage might have been demolished by someone with ties to T.B. Power's company and we've heard from her brother that he wasn't sure that there were any limits to what she might do if provoked. What if she had that provocation?'

'You think that she might have been having an affair with Reynard and then she saw him and Mrs. Salisbury at it in the bathroom?' Leigh asked.

'It's possible, isn't it? It's not only that but it appears that Rachel Kendrick guessed what was going on and was somewhat embarrassed by it all. If you were Nessa, think how humiliated you'd feel.'

'Yes, that's definitely a motive for murder but why would Reynard take such a gamble?' Leigh asked looking puzzled. 'Nessa Power is very rich and is only likely to get richer so why take the chance?'

'Yes, it seems a crazy risk to take, doesn't it?' Mac replied. 'However, I get the feeling that Reynard just couldn't resist Annalise Salisbury's charms and perhaps it was the bigger the danger, the better the sex. It's been my experience that people do the strangest things when sex is involved.'

'But what about the timing? Hoar's Cottage was demolished some weeks after that dinner party. If Nessa wanted to get some sort of revenge on Reynard then why wait so long?'

Mac had to admit that this was a good point until he remembered something.

'They went on a long business trip around that time, didn't they? T.B. and Nessa Power, I mean. They went to Singapore and somewhere else. Perhaps that explains it then.'

'She must have been really mad at Justin Reynard to have kept herself that angry for that long,' Leigh said.

'I've known people who would have had no problem at all with that,' Mac said. 'Anyway, there's still too many 'ifs' at the moment, aren't there? But there was something that Mrs. Salisbury said that was very interesting. It was her description of the first time that Reynard and she had sex.'

'Yes, they did it in her car right outside his own house.'

'Well, that started me thinking. Angela Reynard looked like she could be a worrier. It's yet another 'if', I know, but what if she was looking out for her husband's return?'

'Well, she'd have seen the car pull up and...'

A thought struck Leigh and she paused for a moment.

'It would probably have been rocking. The car, I mean.'

'That's right,' Mac said. 'She'd have seen a car pull up, rock for some minutes and then her husband steps out. I think that, even if she was the type who tended to gloss over her husband's transgressions, she might have found that one hard to overlook.'

'So, we're going to look at Mrs. Reynard again?' Leigh asked.

'Well, technically Jed Salter will be, but yes. We know Reynard was having at least one affair, if you want to call it that, and I think that Mrs. Reynard truly loves her husband. I've found that, given the right circumstances, the greatest love can all too quickly turn to hate.'

Chapter Seventeen

West Hampstead Police Station was in a 'nice' part of the city. Indeed, the modern red-brick building looked totally out of place as it was surrounded by century-old 'mansion' flats and Victorian town houses. Jed was in the lobby waiting for them. They followed him to an interview room.

A woman was sitting at the table. She was in her early thirties and she wore a black trouser suit and a crisp white blouse underneath. Her long black hair was held back in a ponytail. She rose when they entered.

'Mac, this is Detective Sergeant Sian Jones. She's been helping me with the Reynard case,' Jed said.

'Pleased to meet you,' Sian said in a sing-song accent straight from the Welsh valleys.

Mac smiled and introduced himself and Leigh.

'So, what have you found?' Jed asked.

Mac told him about Reynard and Mrs. Salisbury.

'So, you think that Reynard's wife might have found out that he was cheating on her? Jed said.

'It's possible. It certainly doesn't seem that Reynard was all that discreet.'

Mac watched the wheels go around in Jed's head. He didn't want to overtly suggest that he looked at Angela Reynard. It would be better if he came to that conclusion himself.

'It certainly puts things in a different light,' Jed finally said. 'What do you think, Sian?'

'I think that we should look at Mrs. Reynard again,' DS Jones said quickly. 'We might also get forensics involved.'

'So, forensics haven't looked at the Reynard's house yet?' Mac asked trying to hide his disbelief.

'Well, it's only been a missing person case to date,' Jed said with a shrug. 'Anyway, Sian and I did a thorough search of the house and we didn't find anything. However,

I think that you might be right. We'll get forensics involved and we'll do a bit more digging on Mrs. Reynard too.'

'I can't believe that!' Leigh said as they walked back into the car park. 'Forensics should have been involved right after Reynard disappeared. What's your friend playing at?'

Mac could only answer with a shrug.

'Have you heard from Tim yet?' Leigh asked.

Another shrug.

'Anyway, just Giselle Wright to see now and, luckily, she lives in St. Albans which is on the way home.'

The Wrights, of course, lived on one of the most expensive streets in the very expensive commuter town of St. Albans. They had to first drive right through the town bypassing the signs for the ancient Roman ruins of Verulamium on the left. The busy High Street was familiar to Mac. On a road just off to the right there stood the St. Albans Crown Court. He'd had to give evidence there on a few occasions.

Sheriff's Drive lay on the other side of the town. As they drove past the huge houses on either side, Mac could well understand why this was one of the most 'sought-after' areas in St. Albans. They found the house and Mac was surprised that it had no electronic gate in front of it. The house had a Georgian feel to it but he reckoned that it couldn't possibly be that old. It had at least eight bedrooms and garage space for three cars. A battered-looking Mini stood on the driveway near the front door.

Mac wasn't sure what he'd expected but Giselle Wright wasn't it. She was probably in her mid-forties but she looked younger and she gave them a genuine smile as he and Leigh walked up to them. She was elegantly dressed in a loose purple top with wide black trousers. Mac guessed that she was the type of woman who would look elegant whatever she wore.

She moved with an effortless grace as she led them inside down a hallway and past rows of family photos. Most of them showed her and two young boys at various ages. Just the one was of her and, Mac presumed, her husband. He was a little older than her and it showed.

She led them into a light and airy living room that looked as if someone actually lived there.

'Can I get you anything?' she asked as Mac and Leigh sat down.

'No, thanks,' Mac replied gesturing for her to sit down too. 'Have you any idea why we've called today?'

Giselle shook her head.

'We're looking into the disappearance of Justin Reynard and so we're talking to everyone who knew him.'

'Justin?' she said. 'I didn't even know that he'd disappeared. I just thought that he was laying low until the stink died down. What's happened to him then?'

'That's what we're trying to find out,' Mac replied. 'What did you think of Justin Reynard?'

She thought about this for a moment.

'Richard, my husband, hated going to Marcus' house and that's why he brought me along. For protection, he always told me. He'd joke about it but I knew that it was at least partially true. He's a good businessman but he knew that he was up against it with the likes of Desmond Salisbury and Justin Reynard.'

'Why those two in particular?' Mac asked.

'Richard always said that Marcus was the one who wound Justin up and set him on people but I wasn't so sure. Justin and Desmond were alike in many ways. They were both double-dealers who'd do anything to get what they wanted. What was for sure was that Desmond had Marcus in his pocket. I even heard him once say that Marcus was 'on a retainer' as if he were a servant or something.'

That might explain where Marcus got his money from, Mac thought.

'If your husband really felt like that then why did he still work with them?'

'Richard knew that it was a bit risky but I suppose it was the only game in town. Being responsible for planning,

152

Marcus could ensure that a building project went ahead smoothly. On the other hand, he could also ensure that a project might get bogged down in red tape and so get delayed, sometimes for years. I guess that he felt that he had to play along. Richard had worked with Desmond on projects quite a few times before but he knew that Desmond would shaft him the first opportunity he got. It was my job to make sure that my husband never drank too much and that he agreed to nothing either verbally or in writing. The fact that the dinners were being held at Marcus' house and not some Michelin-starred restaurant in town was a sure sign that something underhand was being planned.'

'What about T.B. Power?'

Mac noticed an emotion flash momentarily across Giselle's face. What was it? Fear, embarrassment, sadness perhaps?

'T.B. was totally unlike the others. Don't get me wrong, he wasn't above doing an underhand deal if that's what it took to make sure that a contract was completed on time, but he didn't dress it up. While the rest of them used their political weasel words, T.B. would call it what it was.'

'Did Nessa serve the same function as you when she attended these dinners? Mac asked.

She smiled as she said, 'Absolutely not. T.B. never needed a minder and, although he drank, I never saw him drunk. It's my guess that he only attended the dinners because he needed something and it's my bet that he never left without it.'

It was clear that she was an admirer of T.B. and Mac wondered how far her admiration went. He'd ask her about this but there was one question he had to ask first.

'Why are you telling us all this?'

'About the dodgy deals, you mean? I hated all that and whatever I tell you won't hurt Richard anyway.'

'Why is that?' Mac asked looking somewhat puzzled.

Giselle retrieved her phone from a side table. She flicked through several screens before finding the one she wanted.

'That was Richard just a couple of days ago.'

The photo showed a man lying in a hospital bed. He had an oxygen mask on and he was hooked up to an array of electronic machines.

'What happened?' Mac asked.

'Richard's way of de-stressing himself was to go rock climbing. He especially loved doing it with the boys.'

'Your sons, I take it?'

'Yes, they're thirteen and fifteen now and they both love climbing just as much as Richard did. I just thank God that that they were at school when the accident happened.'

'How long ago was that?'

'Nearly two months ago now. They were hopeful at first but...' she stopped and wiped a tear away. 'He's in a coma and they can't see him coming out of it. All that energy spent scrabbling around for money and prestige, Mr. Maguire. Then, when something like this happens, it all seems so ridiculous somehow.'

Mac waited a few seconds before asking his next question.

'How well did you know T.B. Power?'

'Well, we always seemed to be bumping into T.B. at various events over the years so we got to know each other a little, I suppose.'

This was the first time that Mac hadn't believed her.

'What do you make of Nessa Power?'

'Nessa's a strange one. She's beautiful, rich and a good businesswoman too but I've always felt that there was this big hole in her. She follows her father around wherever he lets her go. I think that she's obsessed by him, perhaps unhealthily so.'

Mac's ears perked up at this.

'In what way?'

Giselle seemed stuck for words. Mac gave her time to think.

'I take it that everything I say to you is confidential? You're not recording me or anything?'

Mac assured her that he wasn't. She thought for a while again before she spoke.

'I was lying when I said that I only knew T.B. a little. Things hadn't been going too well between Richard and I for quite a while when I met T.B. by chance in town around a year ago. I'd always thought that he was a very charismatic man and T.B. made it plain that I could take things further with him if I wanted to. I found that I wanted to. We met as often as we could, mostly in a little cottage the other side of Luton. It suited us as we both wanted to keep our affair as secret as we could.'

Mac took his phone out, found a photo and showed it to Giselle.

'Was this the cottage that T.B. took you to?'

'Yes, it is,' she said in some astonishment.

'Please go on,' Mac asked.

'So, we'd go there every second Thursday evening. I used to look forward to meeting him so much. He's a wonderful man and, for someone who's so strong and macho looking, he's remarkably sensitive. It got serious and T.B. asked me to leave Richard and marry him. I was seriously thinking about it when I received an envelope in the post. It contained a single item, a photo. The photo was of me and T.B. embracing outside the cottage. A printed message along the bottom said that the photo would next be posted onto my sons' social media pages.'

'What did you do?'

'I broke it off with T.B. straight away,' Giselle replied.

'I take it that you believed that whoever sent the photo would carry out their threat?'

'I did. I had no evidence but I knew that it was Nessa who had sent that photo. I also had a feeling that she would stop at nothing in trying to break me and her father up. While I might have taken that chance anyway, I couldn't put my sons and the rest of the family through it.'

'Did you ever tell T.B. this?' Mac asked.

She shook her head.

'No, breaking up was hard enough but telling him that I suspected that his beloved daughter was a blackmailer was something I just couldn't find it in myself to do.'

Mac looked at his watch as they climbed into the car. It was nearly four o'clock.

'Let's head home,' Mac said. 'We can get something to eat at the Magnets and talk about what our next steps might be.'

'That sounds like a plan to me.'

Fifteen minutes or so later Mac's phone pinged. He almost dropped it in his haste to get it out of his pocket.

Mac read the message and immediately felt better.

'Was that Tim?' Leigh asked.

'Yes. He said that he's feeling a little better and that I can visit him at six o'clock.'

'I'll drive you, if you like?'

'Thanks. You can come up and see him too, if you want. I'm sure that you'd brighten his day.'

'I don't know about that but it would be nice to see him.'

Even if Mac had been looking, he probably wouldn't have noticed that he was being followed. The scooter had a box on the back with the brand name of a well-known pizza delivery company. There were hundreds of these buzzing around the roads at any one time and it was the next best thing to being invisible. This suited Malky.

He stopped once the police car had turned off the motorway and had headed into Letchworth. He pulled into a service station and pulled out his phone. He told her where Mac and Leigh had been that day.

'Do you want me to do anything?' Malky asked.

'Not just yet,' she replied. 'Keep an eye on them for the next few days and I'll let you know.'

'I'd do anything for you, you know that.'

'I know that and I appreciate what you're doing. I really do.'

'Good. We'll be seeing each other soon, I hope,' he said in a husky voice.

'We will Malky. I promise.'

She was worried. She wondered what Eoin had told them about her. Nothing good, she guessed. Annalise Salisbury didn't worry her at all. She was just a stupid slut who knew nothing but Giselle, now she was different. She briefly wondered if Giselle had told Maguire about the photo that she'd sent her but she quickly dismissed the thought. She wouldn't be that brave. After all, she still had the power to hurt her family.

Oh, look what mummy was doing while poor daddy went rock climbing. Perhaps that's why he fell, thinking about another man shafting his wife.

No, she felt that Giselle would keep her mouth shut.

Still, they were getting too close for comfort and the little surprise that they'd planted to throw the police off the scent didn't seem to have worked as yet.

'Do something, do something!' the little five-year-old inside her head screamed.

Masterly inaction, she told herself.

The problem was that she didn't quite believe in that anymore. She had always solved the little difficulties that life had thrown her way by direct action. That's what the five-year-old wanted and she knew that, before long, the five-year-old would win.

She always did.

Chapter Eighteen

Mac was surprised to see Tim sitting up in a chair when he entered his hospital room. He was even more surprised to see Tim hold his hands up in warning.

'Stay on the other side of the bed, please,' he said.

Mac started wondering if Tim had caught something contagious during the operation.

'I'm sorry,' Tim said with a rueful smile. 'I've got a catheter in and there's a massive bag of piss hanging on the side of the bed here. It doesn't make for nice viewing, believe me. I mean, it's my piss and even I can't stand the sight of it.'

Tim's comical expression of disgust made Mac laugh out loud. Leigh then walked in and Tim instinctively started to rise from his chair. He winced and quickly sat back down again.

'Are you okay?' Leigh said with some concern as she went towards him.

'He wants us to stay on this side of the bed,' Mac quickly said. 'There's a catheter bag on the other side.'

'Oh, I've seen my uncle's loads of times,' she said before going around the bed and giving Tim a peck on the cheek.

This made Tim really smile.

'I'm amazed that you're sitting up so soon after the operation,' Mac said.

He noticed that there was a little bag that contained what looked like blood and water hanging from his stomach. He tried not to look at it.

'Me too but they don't let you laze around in bed for long these days,' Tim replied. 'Anyway, it's not hurting as much as it was this morning.'

'How do you feel?' Mac asked. 'I mean, really?'

'Really? Like I've had a good kicking if you want to know but what surprises me is that, with this many holes in me, I'm not feeling even worse.'

'My uncle said that he started feeling much better after about four or five days,' Leigh said.

'Some hope then,' Tim said with another smile. 'I'm glad you brought her along.'

Although the surroundings were somewhat surreal Mac and Tim chatted away for the rest of the visit as though they were comfortably seated in the Magnets with Leigh chipping in now and then. A nurse had to come in and give them the hint that they had stayed long enough.

'Are you still coming out tomorrow?' Mac asked as he stood up.

'As far as I know but it will probably be early evening before they let me go,' Tim replied. 'They told me that I'd have to be discharged by the consultant first and that I'd then need to see a nurse about getting a supply of catheters. They'll also need to show me how to use them. I'm really looking forward to that.'

Tim's downcast expression belied his words.

'Don't worry, I'll bet that it's going to be nowhere near as bad as you think,' Mac said. 'Now, call me when you're ready and I'll come and pick you up.'

'He wasn't looking too bad,' Leigh said as they made their way out of the hospital.

'You're right there,' Mac said. 'I thought that he'd be still flat on his back with a drip in and monitors…'

Mac was thinking of Richard Wright when his thoughts were interrupted by his phone ringing. It was Jed Salter and he had some surprising news.

'I'm afraid that our day isn't over,' Mac said as he put his phone away. 'The forensic team searching the Reynard's house has found some new evidence and it appears to be quite damning. Are you okay to drive us back into London?'

Leigh was. She had no plans for the evening other than watching something old and romantic on Netflix.

Mac told her what Jed had said as they set off once again down the motorway towards London.

'My God!' Leigh said. 'That changes the whole case, doesn't it?'

'Yes, I suppose it does,' Mac replied, 'but...'

Mac fell silent. While the news should be welcome, he distrusted it for some reason. Perhaps it was Jed that he distrusted. He knew all too well that, if a short cut could be taken, then Jed would always take it. Or was it because it was all just a little too neat?

'But?' Leigh said about five miles later.

'What?' Mac said coming out of his self-induced trance. 'Oh, I'm sorry. I was thinking about something but perhaps I'm getting ahead of myself. Let's see what Jed has to say first.'

Mac chided himself. He hadn't seen this new evidence or heard about exactly how and where it was found. However, as they drove towards West Hampstead police station Mac's doubts still grew.

They met with Jed Salter and Sian Jones in one of the interview rooms. Sian looked angry for some reason.

'This is what forensics found,' Jed said as he laid out a row of photographs on the table. They showed a small suitcase and its contents. One photograph showed an open passport. It was Justin Reynard's.

'And you say that this was found in Reynard's house?' Mac asked.

'Yes,' Jed replied. 'It was in a wardrobe in one of the guest rooms on the third floor. One that Sian here was supposed to have searched.'

Sian didn't even glance at her boss as he said this. Mac could see that she was fizzing.

'I did search that room and I swear to God that it wasn't there when I looked,' she said trying to sound calm and not succeeding.

She looked up at Jed but it was clear from his expression that he didn't believe her.

Mac remembered that, when he was a child, his mother used to have an old kettle that whistled when the water was boiling. Mac used to love watching it as, just before it boiled, the whistle part would move excitedly around all by itself just before it exploded into sound. Sian looked just like that whistle and Mac could feel that she was just about to explode.

He whispered a few words to Leigh.

'Come on, Sian,' Leigh said. 'Let's get a cup of tea, shall we?'

Sian managed to give Leigh a smile through gritted teeth before following her out of the room. Once in the corridor outside she finally erupted and shouted out something in Welsh. Leigh couldn't understand what she said but, from the sounds of the words and the feeling with which they were said, she guessed that they referred to Jed Salter and not in a nice way.

'I'm sorry,' Sian said looking a little calmer. 'It's not like me to swear.'

'Don't worry, in the circumstances I'd be swearing too,' Leigh replied. 'Anyway, I believe you even if your boss doesn't and I've got the feeling that Mac does too. Let's get that cup of tea, shall we?'

Back in the interview room Mac was thinking exactly that as Jed broke into his thoughts.

'It's a shame but she should have done her job,' he said with a look of disdain. 'She'll be suspended, of course.'

Mac was annoyed with his old colleague but he tried not to let it show.

'Have they found any prints or anything else that might give us a clue?' Mac asked.

'They only found two sets of prints inside the suitcase. Reynard's and his wife's,' Jed replied with a meaningful look. 'She's definitely in the frame now.'

Mac wasn't so sure.

'Are you bringing her in?' he asked.

'She's not at home and she's not answering her phone either but I've got someone waiting for her at her house. They'll bring her in as soon as she turns up. Let's just hope that she's not on to us and isn't on a plane on her way to the Dominican Republic or somewhere.'

'Would you mind if I sit in on the interview?' Mac asked. 'If she turns up that is?'

'No, of course not,' Jed replied. 'In fact, I'd appreciate your take on what she might say.'

'Okay then,' Mac said as he stood up. 'I'm going to get a cup of tea. Can you let me know if she arrives?'

Jed said that he would.

While Mac was a little thirsty, he was more interested in talking to Sian Jones.

The canteen was quite full but Leigh had managed to get a table in the far corner well away from everyone else. Sian looked a little calmer now. Mac sat down and looked at her.

'Tell me what happened,' he said softly.

'Well, I was with DI Salter when he first went to see Mrs Reynard. He seemed to take her word for it that her husband was just missing. I said then that we should get forensics in to search the place but he said that it would be a waste of time. He said I could do it, if I liked, while he questioned Mrs. Reynard.'

This rang true to Mac. It would be just like Jed to let someone else do all the hard work.

Sian continued, 'I didn't have time to do a really thorough search but I did look in all the wardrobes and I swear to God that there was no suitcase in any of them. You do believe me, don't you?' she said as she looked up at Mac imploringly.

He glanced over at Leigh. She nodded.

'Actually, I do,' Mac replied. 'I mean wardrobes are always the first place we look, aren't they? For some reason people seem to think they're a great place to hide things. However, please don't tell anyone what I've said just yet, especially Jed. I'm hoping that I'll be sitting in on the interview with Mrs. Reynard before long and we may learn more from her.'

'So, what should I do?' Sian asked.

'Go home and relax. Have a warm bath and drink some wine,' Mac replied. 'And don't worry too much, Leigh and I are on the case.'

She thanked him, gave Mac and Leigh a half-smile and then left.

'What do you think?' Mac asked.

'I think that she's telling the truth. I also think that her boss is a lazy sod who's willing to blame anyone but himself when things go wrong.'

Leigh looked really fired up when she said this.

'Well, that's as accurate a description of Jed Salter as I've heard,' Mac said. 'There's something going on here, isn't there? I'm wondering if all our assumptions and theories might not be too far off the mark after all.'

'What do you mean?'

'Here's what I think might have happened. Someone kills Justin Reynard in Hoar's Cottage and then they break into his house. They fill a suitcase with some clothes and take his passport too. This is to make it look as if Reynard has done a runner and is somewhere abroad. It seems that Jed, who was probably scared of all the paperwork involved if it was otherwise, was prepared to take this at face value. So far, so good. Then we turn up and start poking about. So, the someone who is behind all this still has the suitcase and they think that it would be clever to return it to the Reynard's house. This would then make it look as if Justin Reynard is indeed dead and that his wife was responsible for it.'

'Well, she certainly had every reason to kill him from what we've learned so far,' Leigh said.

'That's true enough,' Mac said dreamily.

He was silent for quite a while and Leigh didn't interrupt his thoughts.

'That's it!' Mac said with some satisfaction. 'The Adventure of the Norwood Builder.'

'What?' Leigh said with a mystified expression.

Mac laughed out loud.

'I'm sorry. Just because I know them so well, I expect everyone else to know them too. It's a Sherlock Holmes story. A young man is very cleverly fitted up for the murder of an older man who had recently changed his will and left everything to the young man. All the evidence is against him and it looks as if he is going to hang when Sherlock gets involved. So, Sherlock forensically searches the house but, disappointingly, finds nothing. Then, the very next day, the police detective, who is almost always incredibly stupid in these stories, triumphantly finds a bloodied fingerprint on the wall. It is, of course, the fingerprint of the young man.'

'So, the young man did it then?' Leigh asked looking no less mystified.

'Well, no. Sherlock congratulates the policeman but then turns to Watson and tells him that the new evidence has, in fact, given him some hope. This is because the young man is in jail and so he couldn't have left his fingerprint.'

'But couldn't it have been left when the murder took place?' Leigh asked.

'Now, this is the point. Sherlock said that he had carefully examined the house, including the wall where the fingerprint had been found, and that it hadn't been there the day before.'

'Oh, I get it,' Leigh said with a smile. 'Someone was manufacturing the evidence.'

'That's right. It turned out to be the old man who everyone thought was dead. He got the young man to seal a document by pressing his thumb in wax. He then used that as a mould to manufacture the fingerprint. So, like many amateurs, he over-egged the pudding.'

'So, if we accept that the suitcase wasn't there when Sian searched the house then what does that mean for the case?'

'I think it means that we might be closer to the truth than we realised,' Mac replied. 'Someone is trying to put Mrs.

Reynard in the frame and we've got a fair idea of who that someone might be, haven't we?'

'Nessa Power,' Leigh replied.

Mac nodded.

'I think that it's time that we gave her, and her father, a visit, don't you? Anyway, another cup of tea?'

Twenty minutes later Mac's phone pinged. Mrs. Reynard had arrived.

Angela Reynard smoothed her skirt before she sat down opposite Jed and Mac. The seat beside her was empty. Jed had asked her if she wanted her solicitor or someone else to be present during the interview but she had just looked at him with a puzzled expression.

'Mrs. Reynard, I'd like to show you these,' Jed said as he laid out a row of photographs.

'That's my husband's suitcase!' she exclaimed. 'Does that mean that you've found my husband? Is he alright?'

She stared intensely at Jed while she waited for his reply.

'No, we haven't found your husband as yet,' Jed replied.

'Then, where did you find his suitcase?' she asked looking puzzled.

'We found it in a wardrobe. A wardrobe in one of the guest rooms in your house.'

'In my house?' she replied looking even more puzzled. 'I don't understand.'

'You told us earlier that you believed that your husband was having an affair. Was that correct?' Jed asked.

'Well, yes. I suppose that was the case but I'm not so sure now. I was probably just a bit overwrought at the time.'

'Mrs. Reynard, did you kill your husband?' Jed said giving her a stony look.

Mac looked up to the ceiling. He guessed that it hadn't ever crossed her mind that she might be considered as being a suspect with regard to her husband's disappearance. Jed had let the cat out of the bag for sure.

'What?' she said in a near shriek. 'No! No, I could never harm Justin. I loved him. Why would I want to kill him? He's had affairs before but he always came back to me. That's the important thing, isn't it? He always came back.'

Mac decided to butt in.

'Mrs. Reynard, can I ask you how secure your house is? For instance, do you have burglar alarms fitted?'

Jed looked at him with some annoyance. Mac ignored him.

'Of course,' she replied looking puzzled again. 'It's London, doesn't everyone?'

'Do you mind me asking what the code is?'

She thought about this for a while.

'Well, I suppose you are a policeman. It's nine-nine-nine-nine.'

'That wouldn't be especially hard for a burglar to figure out now, would it?' Mac said.

'Well, I've always had trouble remembering it, you see. I never was any good at numbers and then there's the maid and the cook who need to get in and out when I'm not there...'

Mac interrupted, 'How many other people know the code?'

'Well, just those two, I think. Oh, there's my sister and her husband, of course, and my cousin Viola who house sits when I'm on holiday.'

'Just those?' Mac asked trying not to sound sarcastic.

'Yes, that's right.' She then turned towards Jed. 'Am I really a suspect?'

'Yes, I'm afraid that you are,' Jed replied sternly.

'Can I change my mind about having a solicitor then?'

'Of course,' Jed wearily replied.

He'd been hoping that she'd keep things simple and confess. He ended the interview and turned off the recorder.

Mac said his goodbyes to Jed who still seemed to be a little miffed at him. It was getting late and he'd had enough for one night. He found Leigh nursing a coffee in the canteen.

'That was quick,' she said.

'Well, in about his second sentence, Jed asked her if she had murdered her husband. She decided fairly quickly that she wanted a solicitor.'

'You look tired. Shall we go home?'

'Yes, please,' Mac replied.

Jed went back to his office. He then shut and locked the door behind him. He waited for a few minutes before making the phone call.

'What have you got?' a man's voice asked.

'You asked me to let you know what was happening in the Reynard case,' Jed said.

'I take it that something's happened then?'

'You could say that. We found Reynard's missing suitcase in a wardrobe in his house. It puts Mrs. Reynard in the frame for her husband's murder.'

'Okay, what else?'

'Mac Maguire was just here too,' Jed said. 'He sat in while I interviewed Mrs. Reynard.'

'And what did he think?'

'He didn't say it directly but, from the questions he was asking, it's fairly obvious that he thinks that the suitcase is a plant,' Jed replied.

There was silence on the other end of the phone.

'I know Mac Maguire from the old days,' Jed continued. 'He's on to something. He obviously doesn't think that Mrs. Reynard is behind her husband's disappearance but it's my guess that he knows who is.'

'Thanks.'

The phone went dead.

Jed had no real idea what was going on and he didn't want to know. All he knew was that he now had a tidy sum to put towards a really nice holiday somewhere. Somewhere sunny and exotic. After all he could easily afford it now.

The Dominican Republic sounded nice, he thought.

She was in a meeting when he called. Even though she was leading the meeting and it involved a billion-dollar project, she asked for a break when she saw the number.

'John, what is it? I'm in a meeting. Can you be quick?' she said.

He was okay with this. He wanted to get the call over and done with as quickly as possible. He knew that she wouldn't like what he was about to tell her.

'Mac Maguire hasn't fallen for your little trick. In fact, he seems to think that the suitcase reappearing shows that he's getting closer to the truth.'

'How do you know that?' she asked somewhat breathlessly.

She felt a shudder of fear as she spoke. This news was the worst possible.

'I know someone at West Hampstead police station who's a bit short of money at the moment. It's cost me three thousand so you'll need to include that in my next payment,' he said. 'Anyway, he thinks that Maguire is on to something. In fact, he thinks that Maguire knows who was really behind Reynard's disappearance.'

She felt panic seep into her veins. Would Maguire be banging on her door next? Or, even worse, her father's? She desperately didn't want him to be any more involved in this than he already was.

'What about the detective who's looking into Justin's disappearance?' she asked.

'Oh, he's more than willing to swallow it all and charge the wife. He'll do whatever takes the least effort, especially if we make it worth his while.'

So, it's just Mac Maguire that's the problem then, she thought.

'Thanks,' she said in a dead tone.

She ended the call. She tried to think for a moment but thinking was difficult. The five-year-old in her head was screaming at the top of her voice now.

'Do something! Do something!'

She decided that she would. She'd show her father that she could handle it by herself. She made the call.

'Malky, I need a favour,' she said.

'What is it?'

She told him.

'Now, that will really cost you. Fifty grand plus a week in that little hotel in Paris with you naked and ready for me to do whatever I want.'

She knew that Malky was mad for her. As he was useful, she occasionally threw him a bone and had sex with him. He was rough and selfish in bed but, in truth, she quite enjoyed that. She had to admit that she enjoyed it all the more because he was not at all unlike her father. She had had recurring fantasies of taking her father to bed ever since she was seventeen but she'd not done anything about it. Yet.

'It's a deal,' she said.

'Okay, consider it done,' he said. 'It'll happen tonight.'

She looked in the mirror and composed herself before she went back into the meeting. She looked fine. The space inside her head was silent, the five-year-old was happy now. She knew that it was a huge gamble, perhaps the biggest in her life, but she had given the order anyway. She had a strong feeling that an inexorable tide of some sort was pushing her along. It was fate that was now throwing the dice and she couldn't fight against it. She had given Malky the order and she knew that he would carry it out. She had never ordered a murder before but she supposed that there was a first time for everything.

Nessa smiled at herself in the mirror. She looked fine. She carried the smile back into her meeting.

Chapter Nineteen

Mac was in a bad way. His battery was nearly flat and his back pain was ratchetting up. He needed his bed.

'Do you think that there's any chance that Mrs. Reynard might have killed her husband?' Leigh asked as they walked towards the car park.

'No, I don't. The code for the burglar alarm was nine-nine-nine-nine and the maid and the cook and her relatives and probably Uncle Tom Cobley and all knew it too. Any burglar with the slightest bit of common sense would have been able to get in and out without anyone knowing.'

'So, what you were saying about someone taking Justin Reynard's case and then returning it to put his wife in the frame seems even more likely now, doesn't it?' she asked.

'Yes, it does,' Mac replied.

Mac had to lean against the car for a minute before he tried to open the door. He hesitated for a moment before he sat down. He knew that it would hurt. It did. A spasm of white-hot pain hit him and all he could do was sit there until it ebbed away.

'Are you okay, Mac?' Leigh asked giving him a concerned look.

Mac turned towards her and tried to smile.

'If I'm being honest, no. I've just been told that I've done too much today. Don't worry, I'll be okay once I'm flat on my back and I've had a good night's sleep.'

As they drove back down the now more or less empty motorway, he hoped that he was right. All he could do was take his tablets and hope that he'd feel better tomorrow.

'So, are we going to try and interview T.B. and Nessa Power tomorrow then?' Leigh asked. 'I must admit that I'm really curious about the two of them.'

'Yes, me too,' Mac replied. 'I think that we had better be careful though and keep it low key. I don't want to stir up a hornet's nest if I can help it.'

'Do you think that they might be dangerous?' Leigh asked.

'I'd guess that both T.B. and Nessa could be dangerous given half a chance. You generally don't get to be a multi-billionaire by being nice to people.'

Mac's phone pinged. He had a text.

'Is that Tim?' Leigh asked.

'No, it's Father Pat, my priest. He sent it a while ago. He wants me to pop by early tomorrow if I can make it. He's having problems with the church as it needs some building work done on it.'

'And you can help with that?' Leigh said looking puzzled.

'No, but I can help with raising the money. I've told him to ask Jez Manning to have a look so I expect that he'll have some sort of building report to show me. I've replied and said that I'll pop by the church first thing tomorrow.'

They made it to the station in good time. Even though every step hurt, Mac insisted on having a look in the Major Crime Unit's room just in case. Luckily, Dan was still in his office. He looked as if he was catching up on some paperwork. He didn't look at all unhappy at being interrupted and he came out to meet them as soon as they walked in.

'Mac! How's the case going?' he asked.

Mac told him where they were up to.

'It sounds like a tough one to me,' Dan said. 'Lots of leads but no solid evidence.'

'Yes, I think that sums it up nicely if I'm being honest,' Mac replied. 'However, I get the feeling that we're getting closer to the truth of what happened in Hoar's Cottage but we'll see. How's your case going?'

'What the pub stabbing? Done and dusted. I'm just finishing off the report now.'

'How did you solve it then?' Mac asked. 'Did the video that Martin was looking at help at all?'

'Unfortunately, no. The main problem was that everyone involved was keeping quiet. I guess that no-one wanted to talk and be thought of as a grass but, in the end, we got lucky. One of the men involved in the fracas found out that the murderer had been sleeping with his wife and, once he knew that, being a grass didn't seem to bother him so much. Once he talked, the rest did too.'

'I wish that we could get a break like that,' Mac said wearily.

'You look tired,' Dan said.

'I am. It's been a long day, too long as far as my back is concerned. I'd better get going. I need my bed.'

He had told her that it would be done tonight and he had meant it. He knew that there would be risks attached but a whole week of sex with her was worth more than anything to him. He had an erection just thinking about it.

He had followed them back to the police station and then watched as they went inside. He had done his homework and he knew the number plate of the car he was looking out for. He also knew that it was an old green Almera. He looked down the entrance to the police car park. It was quite dark so he decided that he'd look for the numberplate first.

All he had to do was wait.

The street was empty and quiet. The doctor's surgery next door was all shut up and no-one was about. It was exactly as he'd have wanted.

Well, not exactly. He'd have preferred using a bomb. He was quite good at bombs and Maguire wouldn't be the first policeman that he'd killed using one. He'd killed three in Northern Ireland but that was in the good old days of the Troubles when there was a war on and you knew who your enemies were. He really missed those times. He'd been young and totally up for it. The first time a bomb of his had worked, he'd been so turned on that he nearly came in his pants. The policeman didn't die that time, he'd just lost both his legs, but it had been a wonderful feeling anyway.

The problem was that you just couldn't get the stuff these days which he thought was a shame.

A car came out of the car park. Its headlights were full on and so he couldn't see who was inside. As he'd decided, he looked at the number plate. It wasn't Maguire's car. He took his hand from the small machine pistol that lay in the delivery box at the back of his scooter hidden under an empty pizza carton.

He looked up and down the street. There was no-one around. He had parked in a bay just opposite the entrance to the police car park, engine running. He doubted that anyone would give him a second glance even if they did see him.

Another set of lights came out of the car park. He read the number plate. It was him!

He put his hand in the box and gripped the machine pistol. He waited until the car had nearly reached the street. The car stopped as he pulled out the pistol and emptied the magazine. The pistol was more or less silent and all he could hear was the snick of the bullets as they went through the glass. He reckoned that at least five bullets had gone through the windscreen on the driver's side.

The car kept coming slowly towards him. He didn't panic. It was probably an automatic and it was inching forward because there was no-one alive inside the car to put their foot on the brake.

He smiled as he sped off down the road. Besides the bullets that were in Mac Maguire, he'd left no evidence behind. There had been no witnesses and he'd even used a 'brass catcher' so that not even a single shell casing had been left behind for the police to find. It had been a good hit.

He turned the first corner and then turned right. He'd memorised the route he'd decided to take. He sped along the back roads into Stevenage and then headed towards Ware. He pulled into a country lane and, using his phone as a torch he carefully overlaid the sticker on the box. He was now no longer delivering pizzas but kebabs for a North London restaurant.

He then kept to the smaller country roads until he hit the A10 into London near Waltham Cross. Here he could just disappear into the city traffic.

As he drove on, he didn't give a moment's thought to what he'd just done. His mind was full of Nessa Power and what he was going to do to her.

Chapter Twenty

Mac struggled to his feet and it was more than obvious to Dan and Leigh how much of a struggle it was.

'Are you sure you'll be alright?' Leigh asked. 'Shall I drive you home?'

'No, I'll be okay,' Mac replied trying to look okay and failing miserably. 'I'll need my car tomorrow. I promised to visit Father Pat at the church before I start work.'

'Give me your keys,' Leigh said holding out her hand. 'I'll drop you off and get a taxi home. I hope you've got some drink handy.'

Mac did.

'Good, I'll meet you out front and save you the walk,' Leigh said as Mac handed her his keys.

He was glad that Leigh had volunteered to drive him back. Even though he was in pain, a chat and a few drinks would be a nice way of winding down before going to bed. Dan locked up and walked out with him. They said their goodbyes as Dan headed off towards the car park.

As soon as Mac went through the double doors onto the street, he knew that there was something wrong. His old Almera had ran into a lamp post which was now at a slight angle. His car was blocking off the narrow street. The engine was still running and the lights were on. He dropped his crutch and ran as quickly as he could to the driver's side of the car.

His first thought was that Leigh must have had a heart attack or something but the bullet holes in the windscreen told him otherwise. He opened the door.

Leigh lay on her side across both seats, her right arm behind her. He leaned over and felt for a pulse but, looking at the four bullet holes in the driver's seat, he didn't hold out much hope. It was faint but it was there. He could hardly believe it but Leigh was still alive!

He pulled his hand away as he realised that it was covered in blood.

'Mac! Mac, what's happened?' Dan shouted as he ran from his car towards them.

'It's Leigh. She's been shot,' Mac shouted back. 'She needs an ambulance right away.'

Dan got his phone out and called for assistance. In no time at all the car was surrounded by policemen. Two of them had been quick thinking enough to bring first aid kits with them. They did their best to staunch the flow of blood.

Two minutes later a paramedic arrived and she took over. She was closely followed by an ambulance and then the police backed off and let the medical team do what was needed.

Mac just stood there, watching it all happen. He felt totally detached. He felt as if none of this had anything to do with him, as if he was watching a movie. He was trying to convince himself that it was just one of his fentanyl inspired lucid dreams and that his friend Leigh wasn't really on the point of death.

He looked away from Leigh and found himself staring at the bullet holes. Five bullets had gone through the windscreen on the driver's side and two through the car's hood just a foot or so below the windscreen. Whoever the shooter was, they knew what they were doing.

'Mac! Mac!'

Someone shook him. It was Dan.

'Come inside. There's nothing we can do here,' he said handing Mac his crutch.

Mac followed him inside and back into the Major Crime Unit's room. Dan sat him down and then started calling the team in. Once this was done, he turned back to Mac.

'There's no doubt that you were the target. Who do we need to protect, Mac? Who?'

He looked up at Dan and suddenly reality came back into focus. He shook his head to clear it. Dan was right. If someone was after him then they might just be after his family too.

'Tommy and Bridget, of course,' he said.

'I've already called Tommy. I've told him to stay with Bridget for now and I'll be sending some uniforms around for their protection. Who else?'

'Tim, he's still in hospital, and my sisters in Birmingham.'

Mac gave him the hospital ward number and his sisters' contact details.

'Oh, and you'd better include Amrit too.'

'Okay, I'll get on it,' Dan said.

Jo Dugdale was the first in the door, closely followed by her husband Gerry.

'Can one of you get Mac a drink?' Dan asked. 'I need to make some phone calls.'

'Sure,' Jo replied giving the eyes to Gerry.

He disappeared to get the coffees.

'What on earth has happened?' Jo asked as she sat down next to Mac. 'Dan only told us that there was an emergency and it looks as if there's been an accident outside. Drunk driver was it?'

'No, it's Leigh who is in the car. Someone shot her.'

'Leigh? Leigh's been shot?' Jo said her eyes wide in surprise. 'But I only spoke to her this morning. Is it bad?'

Mac ran the movie through his head again. While he'd been taking her pulse, he'd seen a deep red blotch on her white blouse and a bullet hole in her trousers near her right knee. She'd also been bleeding from her arm.

'It's bad. I think she's been shot three times,' Mac said. 'I don't know how she's alive though. There were bullet holes in the back of the driver's seat, right where her chest would have been. She should be dead.'

Mac immediately wished he hadn't said this. It didn't take long before the tears started rolling. Jo and Leigh had been partners for quite a while now. They were good friends too.

Gerry stopped when he came into the room and saw his wife's tears. He then looked at Mac. His face was white and he could see the shock in his eyes. He gave Mac a coffee and then gave one to his wife along with a questioning look.

'It's Leigh. She's been shot,' Jo said as she wiped her eyes.

Gerry sat down heavily.

'How?' he asked with evident disbelief.

'Someone shot her while she was driving my car,' Mac said. 'They were aiming for me and they got her instead. It's me who should have been in that car. I wish it was me. She's too young.'

Jo couldn't think of anything to say so she gave Mac a hug instead. They heard the sound of sirens fading quickly into the distance.

Sirens were good, Mac thought. It means that she's still alive.

Andy Reid came in and said, 'I had to go all around the block. Some idiot's ran into a lamp post outside. Is that what we're here for?'

Gerry quickly took him off to one side and quietly told him what had happened. He then positioned himself on the other side of the door and intercepted the other members of the team before they entered the room. They filed in and quietly sat down. No-one said a word. When everyone was in, Gerry sat by Jo and gave her a hug. The tears coursed down her face again as he did so.

They weren't the only tears being shed for Leigh in that room.

The door flew open and Dan strode in. He didn't look sad or tearful. He looked red-hot angry.

'I don't want to be hard but please save your tears for later. One of our colleagues, one of our friends has just been nearly murdered and we have to find the bastard who did it. Forensics are already here so let's start doing our part.'

Dan stopped for a moment and his face softened a little.

'Before I go on, I should ask if there's anyone here who would like to give this investigation a miss. Leigh's not just our colleague, she's been a friend to us all. So, I'll understand if you want to drop out.'

'I'd like to go to the hospital,' Jo said. 'I want to be near her.'

'Of course,' Dan replied. 'I've managed to contact Leigh's mum and she could probably use the company anyway. I'll arrange for some firearm officers to stand guard. Just keep us informed as to how she's doing. Go on, you and Gerry get going.'

Jo didn't need to be told twice. She flew out of the room, closely followed by her husband.

'Mac, do you think that Leigh's shooting is connected to the case you're working on?'

'I'd bet on it,' Mac replied.

'Okay, you'd better tell us what you know,' Dan said.

Mac packed away his shock, guilt and sadness for later and got his professional head back on.

There was a case to solve.

Chapter Twenty-One

He could hear some sounds. Unusual sounds. He opened one eye and looked up at the ceiling. It wasn't his ceiling. He felt seriously disorientated. He briefly wondered if he had put too many pain patches on or something. Then he turned to one side and saw Dan's desk.

He remembered.

A wave of sadness overtook him. He told himself to buck up. He had work to do and he could feel sorry for himself after they'd found the person who had shot Leigh. The sadness was quickly replaced by worry. The last he'd heard before going to sleep was that she was being prepared for an operation and that she was in a critical condition.

He was lying on an old camp bed that Dan had found somewhere. It was surprisingly comfortable. However, he soon found that it was quite difficult to get out of. He had to carefully manoeuvre himself into a sitting position in the exact centre of the bed before briskly standing up. His pain had dialled down a little but it almost felt irrelevant to him at the moment.

Dan had been kind enough to keep him on the case.

It had been entirely selfish, or so Dan had said, as Mac was the expert on the case so far. While this made sense, he guessed that Dan also knew that he'd go mad if he had to sit in his house under guard doing nothing. The only proviso was that he had to keep to the station where he'd be safe.

He'd managed to have a word with his daughter Bridget before he went to sleep and she said that she'd be moving out of their flat and into Mac's house for the duration. That way they could look after Tim when he came out of hospital. He'd thought that this was a splendid idea as it would also make it a little easier to protect them if they were all in the same house. She said that she would send him down all his medication and enough clothes and toiletries for a week later in the day. She told him to stay safe, not that he had any option.

Tommy had decided not to join the investigation. He'd told Mac that he wanted to make sure that Bridget was safe.

Especially now, he'd said.

Especially now? Mac had wondered at those words.

Adil opened the door and poked his head around.

'What's the latest?' Mac asked with a thumping heart.

'Jo has just had a quick word with one of the surgical team and they told her that Leigh's still critical but stable,' Adil replied. 'They've pumped her full of blood and they're patching up the hole in her chest first. It doesn't sound as if it's all that straightforward. The bullet missed her heart but it nicked one of the arteries. Jo said that if they'd got her to hospital even a few minutes later she might have died.'

'What about her other injuries?'

'The bullet wound in her arm caused some bleeding but it doesn't seem to be too much of a problem.'

'What about the one in her leg?' Mac asked.

'Again, they've patched it up. They said that she'll need another operation on her knee or even two perhaps,' Adil said.

Mac knew he wasn't telling him something.

'And...'

Adil shrugged and his eyes watered up as he said, 'They said that there's an outside chance that she might lose the leg.'

'Christ!' was all Mac could say.

'Dan will be holding the briefing in about half an hour or so. Interested in a coffee?' he asked.

Mac managed a smile.

'Yes, please. Just give me a minute.'

It was only six thirty but, except for Jo and Gerry, every-one was already there and a few more besides. No-one was talking and the room was quiet. Mac nodded to them as he headed out towards the shower room.

After he had showered, he picked up his razor and looked at himself in the mirror. He once again wished that he'd been in the car, that he'd been the one who was shot. If only his back hadn't been so bad, if only Leigh hadn't been so kind and had ordered Mac a taxi instead, if only...

If. If.

That weasel word his old boss Rob Graveley had called it. He once again remembered something he'd said. It was never more relevant than it was now.

'You can worry yourself sick about 'What if I'd done this or what if I'd done that' but it won't change a thing and it helps no-one,' Rob had said to Mac. 'Bad things happen and that's it. Whatever you do don't ever let that bastard of a word 'if' enter your head. Just deal with what *is* and you'll be doing your job right.'

It made him feel marginally better. He breathed deeply and made his way back.

'Dan's brought in a tray of doughnuts,' Adil said as he handed him a coffee. 'God knows where he got them from this early in the morning.'

He could see that what remained of the team, plus DI Toni Woodgate and a few others who he recognised from the local detective team, were helping themselves and so he joined in. To his surprise, he found that he was hungry and he managed to grab a couple before they were all gone. He glanced over at Dan's office. He was on the phone and he didn't look at all happy.

Mac watched him as he put the phone down. A look of sadness crossed his face. He looked up and locked eyes with Mac. His normal grumpy expression immediately snapped back into place. He nodded and Mac nodded back. Dan wearily stood up and then joined the rest of the team.

'As you know, I managed to have a word with Leigh's mother last night. She's still with Jo at the hospital,' Dan said. 'I've just now had a word with her brother. He's in

America and it's late evening there. He's been involved in some sort of experiment and couldn't be contacted. He was only told by his mother just now and he called me straight away. Unfortunately, there wasn't much that I could tell him.'

Mac now understood why Dan had looked so sad.

'The shooting of a police officer is always going to be big news. So, they've organised a news conference over at the Stevenage station for nine o'clock. Andy and Adil, I'd like you both to come with me if that's okay. We'll have a proper briefing when I get back and, hopefully, we'll have some forensics reports to chew on.'

'Do you think that forensics will come up with anything?' DS Kate Grimsson asked.

'We're guessing that it might have been someone on a motorcycle of some sort and that they followed Mac and Leigh back from London. They must have had to wait out on the street so we're hoping that they might have left some traces behind. Otherwise, all we've got are the bullets. Luckily, we won't need to wait for the surgeons...'

Dan stopped and breathed deeply. He quickly carried on.

'The shooter fired at least eight bullets as they found six embedded in the car and two of them were in Leigh. The one that injured her arm seemed to have gone straight through. Four bullets went through the driver's seat, roughly around the upper chest area, so it's a puzzle as to how Leigh's alive at all. It's likely that the gun has been used before so forensics have sent information to the Met's Ballistic Intelligence Service in the hope that we might get a match.'

Mac guessed that the shooter waited with his engine running so forensics would probably get enough inform-ation from the fuel residue to hazard a guess about the type of motorcycle or scooter the killer had used. Other than that, unless the killer had been stupid enough to drop a gum wrapper or cigarette end, they'd probably get little else. The lack of shell casings told Mac that the killer was a professional.

The bullets were what Mac was hanging his hopes on. Every bullet fired bore the marks of the gun it was shot from. Microscopic striations on the bullet's side could be matched to bullets found at earlier crime scenes. It was his experience that guns like the one used in Leigh's shooting might be handed from criminal to criminal or even rented out for the occasion. He'd had four or five cases where the evidence gained from a bullet had been crucial in getting the investigation on the right track.

He said a little prayer that this might happen again.

'We'll need to give some thought as to how we're going to structure this investigation,' Dan continued. 'As you can see, with Jo, Gerry and Tommy out of the picture for now, I've gotten Toni Woodgate and some of her team involved. We're already being offered extra resources by our bosses and the neighbouring forces. While this is great, I want to make sure that we keep full control of the investigation. Otherwise, we'll have everyone dashing around, getting in each other's way and duplicating effort. We'll talk about this when I get back.'

Mac knew what Dan was referring to. Throwing more officers at an investigation didn't necessarily mean that you'd get better results. In fact, it can sometimes stop an investigation dead in its tracks as the core team wastes time trying to organise and bring the new recruits up to date. Mac knew all too well that the first few days of any investigation were always the most important. He was curious as to what Dan would come up with.

'It's going to be vital that all information is shared,' Dan continued, 'especially as our team is likely to grow in the near future. So, everything must go through Martin.'

The team glanced over at Martin Selby, the team's computer and data expert, who was diligently tapping away at his laptop in the corner. He raised a hand without taking his eyes from the screen.

'And I mean everything. Every interview, every report, every note, every idea that crosses your mind. I'm afraid that it will be asking a lot of Martin but I'm hoping that Mac can help him out. If Martin can organise and preserve all the information that the investigation generates then I'm hoping that Mac might be able to start piecing it together and get us some leads.'

Dan stopped and looked at Mac. Mac nodded back.

'Good. As Leigh was driving Mac's car when she was shot, we're assuming that Mac was the real target. His family and close friends are already under police protection. That's why Tommy won't be joining us. He's decided to stay with Mac's daughter, Bridget. Going forward, Mac's knowledge of the case will be vital and I wanted to make sure that he was here to help us out. However, for his own protection, he is not allowed to leave the station under any circumstances and any room he's in must have the curtains or blinds drawn. So, no trips down to the Magnets for a quick pint.'

This got a smile from most of the team.

'Okay then. Andy, Adil and I will be working on what we're going to say to the press, so I'd be grateful if Mac could take everyone through the case once again in as much detail as possible. The key to finding Leigh's shooter might well be in there somewhere.'

She got the summons from her father at seven o'clock that morning. She had been busy during the night and she hadn't gotten any sleep. She could always sleep later. After what had happened, she'd been expecting her father's call. He'd probably be angry but she didn't care. It had to be done.

She found him sitting behind the huge desk in his office. The view from the ninetieth floor was sensational but she took no notice of it. She was looking at him, trying to gauge his mood. He was good at disguising his feelings, she knew that all too well. However, she could tell that he was angry but how angry?

'Lock the door,' he ordered.

She did. She gathered her courage and turned to face him.

'I've always known that you could be cold and calculating but I never thought that you were fucking stupid,' her father said.

Okay then. Her father was really angry. He only swore when he was really angry.

'It had to be done,' she replied trying to appear calm. 'He was getting too close.'

'Too close,' he said softly with a shake of his head. 'Did you seriously think that I wouldn't be keeping track of what Maguire was getting up to? After all, thanks to you, I'm up to my neck in this too. I take it that this was Malky O'Keefe's handiwork?'

She didn't answer which was answer enough.

'Well, Malky is a fucking eejit and you're even more of a fucking eejit for using him.'

Her father was shouting now. She had never seen him so angry.

'You haven't heard, have you?' he said with a surprised expression. 'I take it that Malky reported that the job was a success and that Maguire was dead?'

She gave him the faintest of nods.

'The fucking eejit shot the wrong detective. He shot a young policewoman called Leigh Marston who's now in hospital with three bullet wounds in her. It might be murder yet.'

He let this sink in.

'You should have spoken to me first,' he said as he stood up. 'While you might have a pet policeman, I've got dozens of them. For Christ's sake, what were you thinking? The police thought so much of the case that they only put just the two detectives on it and one of them was retired.'

'He was getting close,' she muttered.

'No, he fucking wasn't!' he shouted even more loudly.

She had never seen him this angry before.

'He had his suspicions but he had no evidence,' he continued. 'There was no evidence to be had, I made sure of that. Christ, Nessa, it's a complete mess. Half of the police in the country will be on the case now. What have you done?'

'I'm sorry, daddy,' she said in her little girl's voice.

He looked at her for what seemed a long time.

'Don't do anything else, Nessa,' he said in a near whisper. 'I'll give you up if you do. Even if it means me going to prison as well, I'll give you up, Nessa. I swear it!'

She nodded but said nothing. She got out of his office as quickly as she could.

Her father was right. It was a mess. She had been wrong to use Malky, it had just made things worse. She would do as he asked, after all she'd already done what she had to. Malky was always going to be the weak link and so she had planned to do something about that. She'd stuck to her plan.

Last night, when Malky had returned to his shed, she'd surprised him. He didn't mind as she was naked and in his bed. They had sex. She went on top and, when he came, she put a bullet in his head using the nice little Glock pistol that he'd given her. She hadn't been expecting it but she had the most amazing orgasm when she pulled the trigger.

At least he was happy when he went, she thought.

She dressed it up with a couple of knee-cappings, IRA style, and after that his shed burned nicely. Malky was no longer a problem.

So, it wasn't totally bad news, she told herself. While she quite liked having sex with Malky, a week would have been far too long anyway.

She had better things to do.

Chapter Twenty-Two

Mac had always been a stickler for case reviews when investigations had gotten bogged down so his new role in the team didn't feel at all strange. There would be lots to do and it was his fervent hope that it would take his mind off Leigh for a while. The 'team' right at that moment consisted of just him, DS Kate Grimsson, DI Toni Woodgate and five members of the local detective team. Mac had seen them all in passing but didn't know their names as yet. He started going through the case from scratch for the new members and he'd only got as far as his interview with Mrs. Kendrick when Martin caught his eye.

'It's the ballistics report,' Martin said. 'I think that you'll find it interesting.'

As Martin had a habit of understating things, Mac could hardly wait to open the file. To say it was interesting was putting it mildly. Even though he'd left the team kicking their heels, he still read the report through.

'So?' Kate asked impatiently.

'They think that the gun used was a Skorpion vz 61 machine pistol and it's been involved in quite a lot of criminal activity,' Mac said. 'Most of which seems to have been in Northern Ireland. It appears that Leigh isn't the first member of a police force that the gun's been used on. At least four members of the Police Service of Northern Ireland, or I should say the Royal Ulster Constabulary as it was at the time, have been killed by someone using that gun. As well as that, it was used to execute at least seven civilians, most of which are believed to have been found guilty by kangaroo courts. It was also used in three other murders on this side of the Irish Sea; one in Liverpool eight years ago, one in Glasgow a year later and another in North London just two years ago. All of the people killed were known members of criminal gangs.'

'Do we have any names to go with the gun?' Toni asked.

'Yes, just the one, a man called Conor Mac Brádaigh,' Mac replied. He thought for a moment before he carried on. 'I guess that's Irish for Brady. Anyway, he was an active member of the IRA and he was credited with using the gun in the murders of three policemen. However, nothing was ever proved. Mac Brádaigh was killed in an ambush in Derry in 1993 while trying to plant a bomb but the gun was never found. It was obviously passed onto someone else affiliated to the IRA as one more policeman was killed just outside Derry before the gun crossed over the Irish Sea.'

The connection to Ireland didn't surprise Mac. In fact, it just made his little theory about Nessa Power a little more believable.

'So, it's possible that the man who shot Leigh is ex-IRA?' Kate asked.

'It's certainly possible. However, it's also possible that the gun might have been rented out for the occasion so let's not get too hung up on the IRA connection,' Mac said.

Even as he said this, he was thinking about the IRA connection and how he could find out more about this Conor Mac Brádaigh.

'Having said that, I know a policeman who works in Derry and it might be well worth having a word with him,' Mac said.

Mac texted Detective Sergeant Fin O'Kane of the PSNI in Derry. He and Mac had worked together on what had been, quite literally, an explosive case[4] just the year before. Fin was still quite young but it was possible that some of the older hands in the Northern Irish police might know something about Mac Brádaigh. He could only hope.

'It's quite small for a machine pistol,' Kate said as she handed her tablet around.

A YouTube video showed a man firing a Skorpion machine pistol. It was indeed small but it was nonetheless

---

[4] The Chancer – The eighth Mac Maguire mystery

deadly for that. The ten-shot magazine was emptied in only a second or so. This made Mac wonder if the killer emptied his magazine too. If so then they might find the other two bullets when they did a fingertip search of the area.

Mac carried on explaining the case until Martin interrupted him again.

'Dan will be on in a minute,' he reminded them.

Kate turned on the big screen and got the BBC News channel up. Leigh's shooting was the top story. All that had been released to the media so far was the fact that a police-woman had been shot outside Letchworth Police Station while on an active case. The newsreader had to improvise and tread water while video clips of the crime scene and people coming and going from the police station were seemingly played on a loop. She looked relieved when she could finally hand over to the press conference.

Dan sat very still while he waited for his cue. He nodded to someone off camera and started speaking.

'Yesterday evening, a police detective was shot outside Letchworth Police Station. Her name is Leigh Marston and her family have been informed. The latest we've had from the hospital is that she's still in the operating theatre and that her condition is critical. Leigh is a valued member of the Three Counties Major Crime Unit which is housed at the Letchworth Police Station. We believe that her shooting is related to an active case that is still being investigated.'

Dan paused and looked straight into the camera.

'To whoever did this. We will never give up looking for you. We will find you and you will be punished to the full extent of the law. I'm afraid that's all that I can tell you at the moment so I will not be accepting any questions. I know that the shooting of a member of the police is always news but we would be grateful if the press could keep their distance and let us get on with our job. That's all.'

Dan got up. A barrage of flashlights and shouted questions followed him as he walked off the stage. He ignored them all.

'That was short and sweet,' Kate said as she turned off the TV.

'There's not much more he could say,' Mac said. 'I wish him luck with his plea to the press to keep their distance. I've said the same thing many times myself but it never seemed to change anything.'

'This is a strange day and it's getting stranger by the minute,' Kate said as she shook her head. 'I still can't believe…'

Mac's phone went off and he was more than happy for the distraction. He was even more happy when he saw that it was Fin calling.

'How are you, Mac?' Fin asked.

'Bloody terrible, if you must know,' Mac replied.

'I can well believe that. I just seen Dan Carter on the TV. I've been through this a couple of times myself now and it's always brutal.'

'Whoever shot her thought that it was me. I should have been behind the wheel but my back was playing me up. She was only being kind and giving me a lift home but her kindness nearly killed her. Anyway, I hope that you've got something for me,' Mac said.

'I have,' Fin said. 'I asked my boss and he knew all about Conor Brady, as he was known to us back then. It turns out that my boss was one of the members of the police unit that ambushed Brady when he tried to place a bomb under a police constable's car.'

'Tell me.'

'Okay, Brady was originally from Belfast but, for some reason, he mostly operated around Derry. In fact, he became one of the leaders of the so-called Derry Brigade. He was on the run for four years before he was finally caught. In that time, we reckoned that he killed at least thirty people. He was in the frame for the murder of six serving police officers and eight British soldiers. We think that he was also responsible for the murder of at least seven on his own side who were branded as traitors in kangaroo courts.'

'And the rest?' Mac asked.

'They were chalked up when Brady threw a bomb into a packed pub in the Waterside area of the city which is mostly Protestant.'

'Not exactly a nice person then,' Mac said.

'Definitely not. Anyway, my boss remembered that Brady had an apprentice. He was only a teenager at the time but he became a skilled bomb-maker in his own right. We heard that the Skorpion gun had been passed on to him.'

'His name?' Mac asked.

'I'm sorry but we never discovered that. He was only ever referred to by his nickname,' Fin replied.

'And that was?'

'Malky.'

'Is that short for Malcolm or something?' Mac asked.

'We don't think so,' Fin replied. 'Apparently, this Malky came over to Derry from Glasgow when he was only fifteen. His family must have been in the Republican movement there because he knew exactly who to go to. There's a story about him but I don't know how true it is.'

'Go on.'

'Okay, this Malky had asked to be put on active service but Brady and the rest of the brigade just laughed at him because he was so young. Brady told him that he could make the tea. Malky persisted until, finally, Brady gave in. He gave Malky the Skorpion and a photograph. He then told him to knock on a certain door and if the man in the photograph came to the door, he was to kill him. Malky didn't know it but he was followed. However, Brady needn't have worried as Malky turned out to be the perfect killer. His target opened the door on seeing that it was just a fresh-faced young boy outside. Malky smiled at him just before he put ten bullets in his body. Even after that he didn't panic. He just calmly put the gun back under his jacket and walked off as though nothing had happened.'

'I take it then that this Malky might have been given the gun by Brady?' Mac asked.

'My boss thinks that's a real possibility,' Fin replied. 'It seems that Malky wasn't into the cause all that much. He just loved the opportunity it gave him to damage other people. When peace broke out, we guess that Malky took himself back home to Scotland where he worked for one of the gangs. Someone told us that he later headed to North London somewhere.'

'Do you know why he was called Malky if that wasn't his name?'

'That I can tell you,' Fin replied. 'He was from Glasgow where, so I've been told, to 'dae a Malky' is street slang for committing a murder. I think he took his nickname as a compliment.'

'So, we have the name Malky and you think that he might be in North London somewhere?' Mac asked.

'That's about it,' Fin replied.

It was something. Mac thanked Fin and ended the call. He was deep in thought and he hadn't noticed how silent the room had become.

'Well?' Kate eventually said.

'Oh, I'm sorry,' Mac replied feeling a little embarrassed. 'Did you hear what was said?'

'Well, I got that you're interested in someone called Malky who might be in London and, if he has the Skorpion, then it's likely that he's our man,' Kate replied.

'That's about the size of it,' Mac replied. 'I was just thinking about a grass who I used to use from time to time when I was in the force. His name is Micky Milligan and he's a walking encyclopaedia of anything to do with crime in the North London area. If anyone can tell us about this Malky then it might just be him.'

Mac pulled out his phone and checked. He still had Micky's number.

'I'm going to go into Dan's office and call him from there. I'm sorry but Micky wouldn't appreciate anyone else listening in,' Mac explained.

While he waited for Micky to answer, he remembered the last time that they'd spoken. Mac had been after a safe-cracker and Micky had given him just the man for the job.

'Well, it's been a while, Mac,' Micky said. 'What can I do for you?'

'I'm looking for someone called Malky,' Mac said. 'I'm sorry but that's all I've got. I've been told that he's ex-IRA and likely to be operating in your manor.'

There was a silence. As the silence stretched out, Mac became quite excited. Micky knew something. He was just taking his time in figuring out what he could tell Mac and how much it would cost.

'I might just be able to help,' Micky said, 'but it will cost you. I'd need ten thousand in cash for what you want to know. The lads are involved so you'd have to make it worth my while.'

The 'lads', in this case, Mac knew to be the IRA. He was somewhat surprised at this.

'That's no problem,' he replied.

The police kept a fund to pay grasses such as Micky but Mac didn't wait to ask for permission. He'd pay it himself if he had to.

'Has this got something to do with the shooting of that young policewoman?' Micky asked.

'Yes.'

Mac saw no point in lying. Micky knew.

'I thought so. Believe me, if it wasn't then it would cost you a lot more than that,' Micky said. 'Drop the money down to me in cash. I'll be handing out communion at the six o'clock mass at the Sacred Heart Church.'

'I'll get someone to discreetly drop it off,' Mac said. 'I hope that I won't have to wait until then though?'

Another silence.

'No, you're okay. You happen to be one of the few coppers I trust. The man you're looking for is called Malky O'Keefe. Malky's just his nickname. His real first name is Liam. He lived in a shed in the garden of forty-two Wordsworth Avenue not far from Kilburn High Street using an assumed name.'

Mac knew the road. It was full of old Victorian town houses, most of which had seen better days.

'He lived in a shed?'

'Well, some of the landlords have built sheds in the back gardens of their properties,' Micky explained. 'It's all against the law, of course. They rent them out to illegal immigrants mostly and make a killing.'

Mac had come across this himself when he'd been investigating a murder in a predominantly Asian area of the city. Almost every garden had a shed at the back and some of them had several families living there. They lived in squalor in a shanty town-like building with no proper toilets and the strong likelihood that it might go up in flames at any moment.

'You say 'lived'. Is Malky dead or has he just left town?' Mac asked.

'Oh yes, he's dead. In fact, I'd say that he's most sincerely dead,' Micky said. 'The shed went up early this morning with Malky inside it. I guess that the fire brigade will still be letting the ashes cool down as we speak.'

Mac thought that this was very convenient.

'Who did it?'

'Well, it appears that the lads have been after Malky for a while,' Micky replied. 'Something to do with a gun and fifteen thousand pounds in cash he'd borrowed from the Derry Brigade and forgot to return. You know what they're like, if you cross them then they never give up. Anyway, I guess that's why Malky moved around so much. Even so, it seems that the lads caught up with him at last.'

'Are you sure about this?' Mac asked.

'I have it on the best authority. You can trust me on this one, Mac. I also heard a while back that Malky had a grudge against you,' Micky said. 'Maybe that's why he took a shot at you.'

'A grudge?'

'It seems that you put away a good friend of his a few years back. A man called Pat Grogan.'

Mac had to think for a moment.

'Yes, he beat a man to death with a baseball bat if I remember right.'

'Yes, that's the one,' Micky said. 'Well, Malky and Pat were good friends and, when Pat died in prison, Malky was heard to say that he'd get even with you even if it killed him.'

'As far as I remember, O'Keefe's name never came up in the trial,' Mac said.

'Well, Malky and Pat only did the odd job together but they were quite close. I think that they were from the same part of Glasgow.'

This was something that he could check.

Mac thanked Micky and ended the call. He would normally trust Micky on most things but this wasn't most things. He smelled a rat. A very large one.

He looked up just as Dan, Andy and Adil were just coming into the room.

Mac opened the door and everyone stopped and looked expectantly at him.

'We have a possible lead,' Mac announced.

Or more likely a dead end, he thought with some frustration.

Micky made the call as soon as he'd finished talking to Maguire.

'I didn't even have to ring him,' Micky said. 'He called me first and that will make the whole thing much more believable.'

'He bought it then?' she asked.

'Yes, I think he did,' Micky replied. 'Anyway, it doesn't really matter all that much now, does it? It's the only story he has, or will be likely to have, now that poor Malky has met his maker.'

There was no reply to this.

'I'll also make a prediction that they'll find the gun, in one piece and unharmed,' Micky said.

'It's possible to be too clever, you know.'

'Ah now, you're paying me well for my services and I'll bet that's because you know that I never snitch on a client. When I've done my job then our little arrangement will be totally forgotten and it will stay that way.'

'Fair enough. So, you just need to make one more call now,' she said.

'I know but I'll wait for T.B. to call me, as he surely will. As you've instructed, I'll spin him the same pack of lies that I've told Maguire.'

'Do you think that he'll believe you?' she asked.

'Of course, I've never lied to him before.'

This seemed to satisfy her.

Micky smiled. On top of the ten thousand he was charging Maguire, he was also getting paid fifty thousand for his little lies to the police and Nessa's father. He had just earned sixty thousand pounds in a matter of minutes.

He smiled. Even for him that was a new record.

All he had to do now was convince T.B. Power that his daughter had nothing whatever to do with Malky's demise. He could but do his best.

Chapter Twenty-Three

It was the first day of a potential murder investigation yet, as a team, they'd done next to nothing. They'd first watched Mac on the phone and now they were watching Dan on the phone. He was on it for some time. It was nearly twelve o'clock when they finally gathered around the whiteboard for the briefing.

'I'm afraid that there's nothing more on Leigh as yet. However, it's just been confirmed that a body of a man was found this morning in a burnt-out shed at the back of forty-two Wordsworth Avenue. An initial look showed that the man had been kneecapped and death was probably due to a single shot to the head. We should have some more detailed results from forensics shortly.'

Dan stopped for a moment and gathered his thoughts.

'The Fire Service have found some obvious signs of a propellant being used so it looks as if the fire was deliberately set, presumably by whoever carried out the murder. It seems that the walls of the wooden shed had been clad with thick cardboard boxes for insulation so, once a fire had started, it would have gone up in flames very quickly.'

Dan glanced over at Mac and got an intensely sceptical look in return. Dan continued talking.

'It seems that Liam O'Keefe has a brother who is doing time for rape. We have his DNA on record so hopefully forensics can confirm the identity of the body fairly quickly.'

'So, what do we do?' Kate asked. She strongly emphasised the word 'we'. 'All we've done is sit around so far watching people make phone calls.'

'I can understand your frustration,' Dan replied. 'At the start of most investigations we're usually running around without a single lead...'

'Yet, here we are, not even a day in, and we've been given the shooter, all nicely tied up with a red ribbon and placed on a golden platter,' Mac said interrupting his boss.

'Spit it out, Mac,' Dan said.

Everyone turned to look at Mac.

'Okay, it's my belief that O'Keefe was just a cat's paw for whoever ordered my murder. This thing about O'Keefe holding a grudge, I've checked it out and it's all very plausible but I still don't buy it,' Mac replied. 'This Grogan was a professional criminal and doing time for people like him is just part of the job description. It was just his bad luck that he came across someone while he was in prison who was even meaner than he was. Not only that but Grogan died eight months ago and that seems a long time to bear a grudge without doing something about it.'

'So, you think that your informant was lying when he said that O'Keefe had a grudge against you?' Dan asked.

'Micky Milligan, like most informants, can be bought and, if either T.B. or Nessa Power are behind it, then they could buy him a million times over. Not only that but we don't have any real proof that O'Keefe even knew Grogan. We've only got Micky's word for that and that's the same for the involvement of the IRA which seems a bit far-fetched to me too. Let's just imagine another scenario. I have no real proof for any of this, apart from the fact that our friend Leigh is in hospital. So, I've been trying to figure out exactly what the tipping point was that led to someone wanting me dead.'

He had everyone's rapt attention now.

'I'd guess that someone like T.B. Power would have more than a few policemen on the payroll and I guess that his daughter would know all about that too. I'm not sure exactly when and where but it's my guess that someone let Nessa Power know that we weren't buying their little set-up.'

'Is this about forensics finding that suitcase in Reynard's house?' Kate asked.

'That's right,' Mac replied.

'But why do you think that it was Nessa Power and not her father?' Kate asked again.

'Well, I've learned as much as I could about the pair of them and Nessa would appear to be the more impulsive of the two. I don't think that her father would have reacted at all. He's supposed to be quite nerveless when it comes to his business dealings. Someone also once told me that he's the cleverest man that they'd ever met. If that's the case he'd know that, while everything we know points to the Powers being involved, we don't have anywhere near enough evidence to even start considering a prosecution.'

'Yes, I see where you're going. It was a really smart move demolishing the house like that,' Dan said, 'but the attempted murder of a police officer isn't smart at all. If it was Nessa Power then it looks as if she panicked.'

'That very well might be true,' Mac said. It gave him an idea. 'If she was feeling stressed out enough to order a murder, do you think we could dial up the stress a little more?'

Dan was silent for a moment.

'Yes, I think we could do that alright. I'll ask the Met to keep a twenty-four-hour watch on her and I'll tell them not to be too discreet about it. Mac, what else can we do?'

Mac had been giving it some thought.

'I was going to talk to someone called Liam Flahavan who is managing the redevelopment of a hospital site near Dunstable. It looks as if the trucks and the other equipment that were used to demolish and take away Hoar's Cottage came from that site. Seeing Mr. Flahavan wasn't a priority for me at the time, as he's supposed to be very close to T.B. Power, and I guessed that there was very little chance that he'd tell us anything. However, it might be worth while talking to some of the people who work there, you never know. At the very least it might ratchet up the pressure on the Powers a little.'

'Okay, Andy and Kate can you see to that?' Dan said. 'Take a couple of detectives from Toni's team with you.'

'What else?' Dan asked turning back to Mac.

'If Reynard and Nessa Power were having an affair, even if they were being careful, someone might have seen them together. Reynard might even have told someone, so I was going to start interviewing people he worked with in his government department.'

'A good thought,' Dan replied. 'Adil and I will follow that up and we'll pull in some detectives from the Met to help out. By the way, what's happening with Mrs. Reynard?'

'The last I heard DI Jed Salter, who is looking into Reynard's disappearance, quite likes her for her husband's murder.'

'And what do you think?'

'I can't see it personally,' Mac replied. 'Her husband had had affairs before and she'd put up with it, so why kill him now? Unfortunately for her, I think she loves her husband but it might be just as well to talk to her again.'

'Okay, Toni can you liaise with this Jed Salter and find out what's happening with the Reynard case?' Dan asked. 'See if you can have a word with Mrs. Reynard and ask her if Reynard had any friends outside work. Follow up on that too if you have time.'

Toni nodded.

'Okay, I'm going to ask if Jo and Gerry can, very gently, talk to Leigh's mum and friends,' Dan said. 'While we're fairly certain that Mac was the target and not Leigh, we'll need to cover every angle. You never know, our assumptions might be wrong and someone she knows might have had a grudge against her.'

Mac thought that it was a good idea to cover every base.

'As I've said, pull in whatever help you need and make sure that everything goes through Martin,' Dan said. 'Best of luck.'

Within a few minutes Mac and Martin were alone. Mac had a question.

'Martin, how are you going to handle all the information that's likely to be coming in?'

'Well, I'm putting together a sort of very basic information system. It's one you can help me with, if you like?'

Mac's face showed his scepticism. He and computer technology were on nodding terms only. However, it wasn't as complicated as he might have thought.

'All the hard work is under the hood,' Martin explained. 'All you'll need to do is tag each item as it comes in...'

'Tag?'

'A tag is just a keyword or words that encapsulate what the information is about. Once you tag an item with a keyword, it will automatically go into a folder bearing that keyword. However, you'll normally need more than one keyword.'

'So, a witness statement for instance, can go in more than one folder?' Mac asked.

'Of course. The major tag would be 'Witness Statement' but you could also tag it with the witness's name, who carried out the interview, any people or locations mentioned in the statement and so on. The important thing is to think about what word or words you'd use if you wanted to search for the item again.'

Mac gave this some thought.

'I think I get it.'

'Don't worry, I'll take you through it step by step when the first items start coming in,' Martin said.

The first item to come in was a note from Andy Reid about his interview with Liam Flahavan, an interview that appears to have been very short. While Flahavan agreed that the trucks could well have come from the site, he'd insisted that the company itself had no knowledge of it. He said that, on such a big development, employees sometimes used company equipment on private projects without the company's permission. However, he wasn't aware of anyone who had done this recently. He said that he'd look into it though.

I'll bet that he will, Mac thought with some scepticism.

That was it. Martin tagged it with 'Interview', 'Andy Reid', 'Liam Flahavan' and 'Dunstable' by inserting the words into little boxes and then clicking on 'Submit'.

'And that's it?' Mac asked.

'That's it,' Martin replied.

'And can I add more keywords if I want to?'

'Sure, you can find it in the folders if you want,' Martin explained as he showed him how. 'Also, everything is automatically time-stamped, so you can search for it that way or just enter any of the tags.'

Mac entered 'interview' and it came up. He added 'T.B. Power' and 'T.B. Power employee' as additional tags.

'That was easy,' a very relieved Mac said.

'Well, let's see how well it works once we start getting more items coming in,' Martin said.

More items would be good, Mac thought. He wanted to be kept as busy as possible while he waited for news about Leigh.

He couldn't remember the last time that he'd sworn at his daughter. He regretted it now. She'd think that he was losing it and she might well be right. He realised that he was getting more and more on edge as the sense of events spiralling out of his control increased. It was a feeling that he wasn't used to and one he truly hated.

He remembered an old priest years ago warning him that the road to hell is taken one small step at a time. Looking back, he realised that he'd taken far too many steps in that particular direction.

He'd just spoken to Micky Milligan for news of Malky O'Keefe. He didn't know if Malky being found dead was good news or not. He wanted to believe Micky when he said that he'd crossed the Derry Brigade and now he'd finally got his come-uppance. Yes, he wanted to believe it but...

'Another little step,' a voice inside his head said.

And now the police were poking around the Dunstable site. As he'd expected, Liam had told them nothing. However, the fact that they were going around the site asking questions still unnerved him for some reason.

Liam assured him that they'd find nothing. Stan and his boys had gone back home to Poland leaving no forwarding address. Liam had ensured that they hadn't gone back to the site at Dunstable after demolishing Hoar's Cottage so no word would spread that way. He'd filled their pockets with money and had personally gotten them all drunk and on a plane to Warsaw as soon as the job had been done.

Yet he still had a feeling...but of what? It felt a little like the headache he sometimes got when a big storm was brewing.

He knew that something was coming and, whatever it was, it wasn't going to be good.

Chapter Twenty-Four

Mac was just getting up to speed with his work when he was interrupted by his phone pinging. He had a text. He was surprised to see that it was from Martin. It simply said –

Jo says that Leigh is out of the theatre and out of danger. She still has a long way to go but she's no longer critical.

Mac looked up to see a smiling Martin give him the thumbs up. He had obviously just sent it out the text to everyone in the team. He only realised when he started to relax that anxiety had knotted all of his muscles up. He returned Martin's smile and happily settled down to some serious work.

Things soon started getting hectic but it didn't take Mac long to get back up to speed. He scanned each item as it came in, tagged it and then saved it. He started adding his own tag, 'MM', on anything that he found particularly interesting. He decided that he'd read all of these items properly as soon as he had more time.

Then something really interesting came up.

'Mac, something's come in for you,' Martin said. 'I'll send it straight over.'

It was a short note from Kate Grimsson with a photo attached.

'This was taken in Liam Flahavan's office' was all the note said.

He opened the photo. It showed the edge of a black office chair on the left and a grey filing cabinet on the right. In between there was a cork board with lots of post-it notes, scribbled messages and a few postcards pinned to it.

For a few seconds Mac wondered at the significance of the photo until his eyes focussed on the postcards.

Of course! Mac thought. Kate you're a clever, clever girl.

He expanded the photo so that he could see the post-cards better. The first one was from Ireland, presumably from someone in Mr. Flahavan's family, while the second had 'Greetings from Scotland' emblazoned across the front. The third postcard was just a photo. It excited Mac nonetheless. He guessed that this was what had made Kate take the photo.

The grey squat building style told Mac that the photo was obviously taken somewhere in Eastern Europe. There were tables and chairs outside the building and an awning was drawn down to give customers some shade. Along the edge of the awning there was a name. He zoomed in closer.

Bar i Restauracja Mamy.

Mac copied the name into Google Translate and asked it to detect the language. It meant 'Mama's Bar and Restaurant' in Polish.

Polish!

'Martin, can you come over for a moment,' Mac said. 'I could do with your help.'

They both looked at the photograph.

'I wish that Kate could have gotten a photo of the back as well but this is all we have to go on. Can you find out where this restaurant is just from the photo?' Mac asked.

'Why is it so important?' Martin asked.

Mac told him.

'Okay, I'll have a look then,' Martin said with a smile.

It took him twenty-five minutes.

'The restaurant is in a town called Zyrardow, it's about fifty kilometres south-west of Warsaw.'

'That was quick,' Mac said in something like awe.

'Well, it would have taken less time except for the fact that there are lots of restaurants in Poland with that name. I started off in the Warsaw area and got lucky as that one was only about the thirtieth one that I looked at. It's got a little website and it's got that exact same photo on it.'

'Did you find out anything else about it?'

'Yes, it's owned by a couple, Stanislaw and Alicja Kaminski.'

'Can you look up the name Stanislaw Kaminski on the government databanks and see if he has any sort of an employment history in this country?' Mac asked.

'Sure thing,' Martin replied.

Mac watched Martin as his fingers danced over the laptop's keys. He felt that this might be a game changer.

Or nothing, he reminded himself.

Even so, he started thinking about who he might know in Poland. A picture of a squat bald man wrapped up in an outsized overcoat came into his head.

Of course! Lukasz Tomaszewski. They had worked together on a murder case around nine or ten years ago.

It took Martin just over half an hour.

'Stanislaw Kaminski worked in the construction sector as a Unit Foreman, whatever that is. His employer is officially listed as Polscy Budowniczowie UK.'

'So, it's not T.B. Power then?' Mac asked with some disappointment.

'There's a bit more,' Martin said with a smile. 'Polscy Budowniczowie UK look like they're a sort of Polish recruitment agency for the construction trade. I talked to them and Mr. Kaminski's last assignment was at a site in Dunstable working for T.B. Power Construction. Apparently, he'd worked for T.B. Power on various sites for well over ten years. According to them, he left his employment the week before Hoar's Cottage was demolished. Do you need any more?'

'Get me anything else you can but that's enough for now. Can you find me a number for this man?'

Mac wrote down the name and gave it to Martin.

'He was a Chief Inspector last time I spoke to him and he was working out of the Police Headquarters in Warsaw.'

'Are you thinking that this Stanislaw was somehow involved in making your house disappear?' Martin asked.

'Yes, that's exactly what I'm thinking. I'm hoping that we've just gotten lucky.'

Mac retreated into Dan's office and made the call from there. As he returned to his desk, he noticed Martin giving him an expectant look.

'It's well below his pay grade but, after I told him what had happened, he said that he'd see to it himself,' Mac said. 'He told me that he fancied a drive anyway and that Zyrardow is only about fifty kilometres away from where he works. I've asked him to go easy on Mr. Kaminski as we don't suspect him of any crime. We just want to know who ordered the demolition of Hoar's Cottage.'

'How did you get to know the Chief Inspector anyway?'

'Well, London's a city of immigrants really, isn't it?' Mac explained. 'Over the years I've had to work closely with many of my counterparts in other countries and I got on really well with some of them. Lucasz was one of these.

There was a case some eight or nine years ago now. Two men had been shot while waiting in a queue to get their passports renewed at the Polish Consulate just off Fleet Street and one of them had subsequently died. As it had the potential to become an international incident, I asked for a liaison officer from the Polish Police and they sent me Lucasz. Luckily, we had no language problems, apart from my accent, I suppose.'

'He couldn't understand your accent?' Martin asked. 'I'd have thought that it would be the other way around.'

This made Mac laugh.

'No, when he spoke English, he spoke with a London accent, from the East End of London to be precise. With me being from Birmingham, Lucasz sometimes found it hard to catch my words. He came to this country when he was eleven and stayed until he was twenty-eight. His family lived in Canning Town for the whole of that time and his last job was as a police detective working out of Bromley station.'

'So, he was definitely an East End boy then,' Martin said.

'Most definitely. However, when his family decided to return to Poland, he went with them. He's been living in

Poland for well over twenty years now but his Cockney accent hasn't changed a bit.'

'So, what happened in the case then?' Martin asked.

'Oh, the shootings at the Polish Consulate, you mean? Well, we started off wondering if it was going to be a terrorist attack or something but the motive turned out to be much more mundane. The two men who were shot were brothers. One was an electrician and the other was a plumber.' Seeing Martin's smile Mac added, 'Yes, Polish plumbers really do exist. Anyway, they'd been doing some work on the house of a well-off Polish man who ran a food importing business. He worked all hours while his wife stayed at home. She must have been bored because, within a couple of days, she was having sex with the two of them every time they came to visit.'

'The two of them?' Martin said incredulously.

'Yes, and she videoed some of their sessions which turned out to be bad news for at least one of the brothers.'

'I take it that you're talking about the brother who died but why wasn't this bad news for the other one too?'

'Well, I'll explain,' Mac said. 'The husband came across this video and went to the brothers' flat where he was told by a neighbour that they had gone to the Consulate to see about getting their passports renewed. So, he drove straight there and, without saying a word, he pulled out a gun and shot them both. He got life in prison while the wife got the business and she then set up home with the surviving brother. I have to admit that it was mainly down to Lucasz that we cracked the case. The brothers' neighbour, who was also Polish, wasn't going to tell us anything until Lucasz put his 'bad cop' act on. He's very good at that.'

After that they both got on with their work, only pausing for coffee and the odd sandwich. Mac had his phone on his desk willing for it to ring. When it did finally ring, it wasn't Lucasz but his daughter, Bridget.

'Hi dad. I'm just calling to say that Tim's arrived and we've made him comfortable in the guest room.'

Mac looked at his watch. It had just gone five o'clock. He'd almost forgotten about Tim. Where had the day gone?

'Can I speak to him?'

'Sorry dad, he's asleep. I think the trip over in the ambulance took whatever little energy he had left.'

'But he's okay?' Mac asked.

'Yes, he's fine so don't worry,' Bridget said.

'And you? How are you doing?'

There was a slight hesitation that was unlike Bridget.

'Oh, I'm fine. Tommy too. Even in the circumstances, it's been nice for us to be able to spend some real time together.'

There was an edge to her voice too. Mac started to get a little worried.

'Are you sure?' Mac asked.

'Dad, I've never lied to you, now have I? Not about anything important anyway. I'm fine, Tommy's fine and Tim will be fine now that we've got him home. Don't worry about us. You've got to use all your brain power to find whoever it was that shot Leigh. That's the really important thing.'

Mac thanked her for sending over his things but he had to leave it at that. His daughter was right, she never had lied to him but a residual worry stayed with him after he'd put the phone down. Something was wrong. He had the sad feeling that his daughter was keeping something back from him.

Chapter Twenty-Five

It was eight o'clock that evening by the time that Lucasz called. However, it turned out to be news well worth waiting for. It was good timing too. Everyone had been working flat out and Dan had arranged a briefing for nine o'clock. Martin had already started working on something that had cropped up in his conversation with Lucasz. Mac hoped that he'd have something concrete for the briefing.

While he waited, he thought again about his short conversation with his daughter. It still worried him for some reason. Yet she said that she was fine and he didn't think that she'd lie to him. So, why was it bothering him so? He tried to dismiss it but an annoying niggle still remained at the back of his mind.

The team started drifting in. They all looked exhausted, especially Jo. Dan and Adil came in last. Mac had a quick word with Dan and told him what they'd discovered.

'Okay, let's get on with it,' Dan said once everyone had gotten themselves a coffee and settled down. 'Jo will you go first?'

Dan could see that she'd been put through the emotional wringer. He felt it might be easier if she went first and got it out of the way.

'We had a word with Leigh's mum at the hospital but, if anyone had some sort of grudge against Leigh, she had no idea who that might be. The same with Leigh's uncle.'

'What have you got planned for tomorrow?' Dan asked.

'We were planning on going to the hospital first to see how she's doing and, after that, we were going to speak to some of her friends here in Letchworth. Depending on how long that takes we'll try and fit in a visit to Leigh's old station and we'll interview as many of her ex-colleagues there as we can. It's always possible that someone from an old case of hers might have been nursing a grudge.'

Jo shrugged as she said this. She clearly thought that, while it was a possibility, it was a very slim one.

'Thanks, Jo,' Dan said. 'I know that today has been very difficult and I really appreciate your and Gerry's efforts.'

Jo nodded and very faintly smiled. She reached to her side and took hold of her husband's hand.

'Okay, Andy and Kate,' Dan said.

'We interviewed Liam Flahavan who's managing the T.B. Power development at Dunstable,' Andy said. 'He, as expected, knew nothing about any trucks or equipment that might have been used in the demolition of Hoar's Cottage. He, quite cleverly I think, admitted that someone could have used the trucks for a personal project without his knowledge. He said that it often happens and, depending on who it was, people sometimes turn a blind eye. We interviewed everyone we could at the site but we got no further. My guess is that the word had gone around not to co-operate with us. However, thanks to Kate, we did get something that I believe Mac's following up on.'

'We'll come to that in a moment, if that's alright,' Dan said. 'Okay, Adil and I interviewed Reynard's colleagues at the Ministry for Housing and we've learned a few things. It seems that, like most special advisers, he was someone who was generally not liked. As a special adviser, Reynard had no responsibilities other than keeping his boss happy and it seems that he did most of the dirty work when it came to firings and moving personnel around. However, it didn't seem that his colleagues' dislike for him went quite as far as out and out hatred. We also haven't found any evidence of any affairs as yet but we'll keep digging. Okay then, Toni.'

'We managed to have a few words with Mrs. Reynard and, as Mac said, I don't think she's seriously in the frame for anything. DI Salter hasn't found anything else to back up a charge against her, so I think that we can forget about her for now. We asked about his friends and she gave us some names. We'll try and get around all those tomorrow.'

'Thanks Toni,' Dan said. 'I really appreciate your help. Okay, Mac. Tell us what you've found.'

'Earlier today, Martin passed a photo to me. It had been taken in Liam Flahavan's office by Kate here.' Every eye turned to look at Kate. 'She managed to take a photo, without Mr. Flahavan's knowledge, of a notice board in his office. On this board were pinned some postcards and one of these has proved to be more than useful. The card had a picture of a restaurant on it and nothing more. Luckily, the restaurant's awning had a name on it.'

Martin pulled up the picture on the big screen.

'It's in Polish and it translates as 'Mama's Bar and Restaurant',' Mac said. 'It seems that there are plenty of restaurants with that name in Poland but Martin managed to pin the location of the photo down to a town called Zyrardow which is located about fifty kilometres away from Warsaw. He also discovered that the restaurant is owned by a couple, Stanislaw and Alicja Kaminski and that, until fairly recently, Stanislaw Kaminski had been a foreman working for T.B. Power at the Dunstable site.'

Mac paused and let this sink in.

'I contacted someone I know in the Warsaw police who was willing to go and have a word with Mr. Kaminski. Luckily for us, he's also someone who is very good at getting information out of people and this interview proved to be no exception. After some questioning, Mr. Kaminski eventually admitted that he led the team that demolished Hoar's Cottage and that it was all done on the orders of Liam Flahavan. Mr. Flahavan told him that it was being done for a friend and, as he was being well paid, he didn't ask any questions.'

'That's really interesting,' Andy said, 'but isn't that just this Mr. Kaminski's word against Flahavan's? He doesn't strike me as someone who will cave in easily.'

'That's what Martin's working on now,' Mac replied. 'Kaminski said that right after the demolition had been completed, he and his team were taken straight to the airport where they were paid an extra bonus and given drinks by Flahavan himself before they went through to the departure lounge.'

Dan glanced over at Martin.

'He's looking at CCTV footage, isn't he?'

'That's right. The airport has just sent him everything they have for the day that Kaminski and his team flew home. We've got a photo of Kaminski from the restaurant website and Martin managed to get a photo of Flahavan from a press release announcing the redevelopment scheme in Dunstable. He's hoping that he can get some footage of the two together but it may take a while.'

'Okay then. It's been a long day,' Dan said. 'Go home and get some sleep and we'll meet up here at seven o'clock tomorrow morning.'

The team gratefully went off in the direction of their beds. All except for Dan that is.

'Are you going to wait?' Mac asked.

Dan nodded.

'I don't think that I'd be able to sleep just yet anyway. So, if we get what we want from the CCTV footage then what?'

'You could pull Flahavan in and interview him formally this time,' Mac replied. 'I'd be hoping that we'll get him on tape denying any knowledge of being involved in the demolition of Hoar's Cottage and, hopefully, denying knowing Kaminski too. If the CCTV footage is clear enough then we can at least get him for lying to us. That might give us some leverage. At the very least both T.B. and Nessa Power will know that we're getting closer.'

'That sounds like a plan,' Dan said as he glanced over at Martin.

It took an hour and two coffees before Martin sat back in his chair. The big screen on the wall burst into life.

It showed one of the burger bars at the airport. Mac had seen it a number of times before as he'd queued to drop his bags off before going through to the departure lounge. Four tables had been pushed together and a large group of men were eating and laughing. Kaminski was at the end table, directly facing the camera. A man with two carrier bags came and sat down next to him. It was Flahavan!

He then started talking to Kaminski as he handed around half-sized bottles of clear spirit. The men immediately opened the bottles and started drinking. The two men laughed about something and Flahavan clapped Kaminski on the back. He then handed Kaminski something in a bag. Kaminski took it out and gleefully waved it about until Flahavan made him put it back in the bag.

'That's eight wads of one-hundred-euro notes,' Martin said. 'That's forty thousand in all. It shows up quite clearly when you zoom in and you can see the money bands.'

'Thanks, Martin,' Mac said with a wide smile. 'That couldn't have been any better.'

'Is there any chance that this Kaminski might contact Flahavan and tell him that we've tracked him down?' Dan asked.

'It's certainly something we have to consider but Lucasz, the detective who interviewed him, warned him against doing just that and dropped a big hint that his phones might be tapped.'

'And are they?' Dan asked looking surprised.

'No, but Kaminski won't know that,' Mac replied. 'Anyway, he's retired now and he's a restauranteur. It's Lucasz' guess that he won't want any trouble with the police.'

'Let's hope that your friend Lucasz is right,' Dan said. 'I'll arrange to have some uniforms call on Mr. Flahavan tomorrow morning and I'll get Andy and Kate to interview him again. Good work, the both of you. I might actually get some sleep now.'

She wished that she could be more like her father. The more pressure he was under, the calmer he usually became. Except for when he'd shouted at her though. Perhaps he was feeling the pressure too. She definitely was.

She had to admit that it was really getting to her. She had always prided herself on keeping her nerve, however pressurised the situation might be, but this was different. It wasn't just a contract or money that was now at stake. It was her life.

Everywhere she went they followed her. They didn't even try to disguise the fact. She was getting more and more paranoid and she'd started wondering if the police had bugged her flat as well. The thought wouldn't leave her head so she got someone in to check anyway. She had walked about her flat in total silence for a day and a half until she got the all-clear.

In the silence, it had occurred to her that she might be going mad.

Then daddy told her that they'd been to see Liam and she once again had the feeling that the walls were closing in on her. Prison walls at that.

She'd started carrying around the little Glock that Malky had given her, the same gun that she'd killed him with. She found the weight of the gun in her handbag reassuring. Yet, daddy had told her not to worry. He said that Maguire might suspect the truth but he couldn't do anything without evidence. That evidence no longer existed. He had made sure of that.

Do nothing, he'd told her. Nothing at all.

Yet, the enormity of what she'd done was only beginning to dawn on her. She'd actually ordered the killing of a policeman. What had she been thinking of?

The police will never stop, the five-year-old screamed inside her skull. You nearly killed one of their own and they'll get you. They'll get you!

She ignored the screaming and resolved to follow her father's advice. She would do exactly nothing. In truth, she couldn't think of anything that might help anyway.

That thought didn't make her feel any better.

Chapter Twenty-Six

Mac's phone alarm went off at six-thirty. He lay there for a moment while the realisation slowly dawned on him that he had slept surprisingly well. He was getting used to the little camp bed and it was more comfortable than he would have thought. Then pictures of bullet holes in a windscreen and his hand covered in blood barged forcefully into his thoughts.

He pushed these dark images away. He knew that he would have to process the reality of what had happened to his friend before long but not now. Not while there was work to be done. He carefully manoeuvred himself so that he was sitting in the centre of the bed and then stood up.

It would seem that even his back approved of the little bed. After a shower, shave and change of clothes, he came back to find Dan sitting in his office.

'How do you sleep in that thing?' Dan said by way of hello. His eyes were pointing towards the bed.

'It's really good actually,' Mac replied. 'I used to have one in my office that I used from time to time over the years and that was comfortable too. Have you gotten hold of Flahavan yet?'

'He's on his way in. We'll have our briefing first. An hour or so spent by himself in an interview room might soften him up a little.'

'Any more news about Leigh?' Mac asked hopefully.

Dan shook his head.

'Jo should be at the hospital soon and she said that she'd call me with the latest update on how Leigh's doing before she carries on with her interviews. Unfortunately, I didn't sleep quite as well as you did. I had this thought and then I just couldn't get it out of my mind. While we'll probably have enough evidence to prosecute Flahavan for lying to us, and possibly even the illegal demolition of Hoar's Cottage, what if he just pleads guilty?'

Mac grimaced. That thought had occurred to him too.

'If he takes the fall for his boss then it's my guess that we'll fail in getting either of the Powers. If I'm being honest, I'm surprised that we've gotten this far with so little concrete evidence to go on. After all we've got no body, no crime scene and the man who we think shot Leigh is dead too.'

'By the way, it was a bit late coming but forensics have formally confirmed that the body found in the shed was that of Liam O'Keefe. They've also found the gun,' Dan said.

'The Skorpion?' Mac asked.

Dan nodded.

'They found it buried underneath the floorboards in a tin box. It's in fairly good condition, good enough so that they were able to take some test shots. They've confirmed that it's the gun that was used in Leigh's shooting.'

'How very convenient,' Mac said. 'Unfortunately, while I'm fairly sure that the little story that Micky Milligan told me is a pack of lies, a good barrister would run with it alright.'

'If we leaned on this Micky, do you think that he'd tell us the truth?' Dan asked hopefully.

'Not in a million years. Micky has his own standards and he never, ever snitches on a client. He'd snitch on anyone else as a matter of course but, once he's been paid, he keeps his mouth shut. T.B. Power would know that too.'

'So, if Flahavan doesn't implicate his boss, then the case is as good as dead,' Dan said mournfully.

'That's what it probably boils down to,' Mac replied no less mournfully.

'Come on, let's get a coffee,' Dan suggested.

The rest of the team were waiting for them. Mac guessed from their nervous looks that the make-or-break nature of the upcoming interview with Liam Flahavan had occurred to them too.

Dan went through the motions. He told them about Liam Flahavan and about the discovery of the gun. He then confirmed their tasks for the day.

Toni and her team were going to interview some of Justin Reynard's friends. Dan and Adil were going to follow up on some of the leads they'd gotten from their interviews at the Ministry of Housing the day before. Dan warned everyone that they were nothing to get excited about. Most importantly, Andy and Kate were to interview Liam Flahavan and then follow up on anything arising from the interview.

'Is it okay if we stay and watch the interview with Flahavan first?' Adil asked.

The rest of the team looked at Dan hopefully. Mac knew that his guess had been right and that they all knew of the importance of what Liam Flahavan had to say.

'I'm glad you asked that,' Dan said. 'I'd have had to suggest it myself otherwise.'

That got a faint smile from the team.

'Andy and Kate, can I have a minute?' Dan asked. 'You too, Mac.'

They followed Dan into his office.

'I don't want to put any further pressure on you,' Dan said, 'but have you mapped out what you want to get from the interview?'

'I think so,' Andy replied. 'The first thing we need to do is to, once again, get Flahavan to deny any involvement in the demolition of Hoar's Cottage. We can then ask him about Kaminski. Our hope is that he'll deny knowing him too. Once we've gotten that on tape then we can at least charge him with lying to the police. We can then hit him with the CCTV footage from the airport. It's pretty damning so at that point I guess that he'll have a decision to make. Either confess and implicate his boss or say that it was all his own idea. He could always try and stonewall but we'll threaten him with getting Kaminski and the rest of his demolition team over to testify in court. It's my guess that once that happens then we might also get a more positive response from his employees at the Dunstable site too. With all that, I'll tell him that we will have a good case for a charge of 'Theft in a Dwelling'…'

'Theft of a dwelling, more like it,' Kate said.

This got the first genuine laugh that Mac had heard in days.

'Anyway,' Andy continued still smiling, 'I'll tell him that, considering the value of the house, we'll be going for a Category 1 charge which would carry the maximum sentence of seven years in jail.'

Dan looked over at Mac who replied with a nod.

'That sounds good,' Dan said. 'The best of luck.'

While they waited Mac made a quick phone call.

'Hi, dad,' Bridget said.

'Are you all okay?' Mac asked.

'Yes, we're fine. I'm afraid that Tim was a bit upset this morning though. He was expecting to see you and we had to tell him what had happened.'

'But he's okay otherwise?' Mac asked anxiously.

'Yes, I've had a look at his dressings and he's healing well. How is Leigh doing?'

'Thankfully, she's off the critical list but we're waiting to hear from Jo for the latest update. Can you put Tim on?'

Bridget could.

It was good to hear his friend's voice. After he told his friend how Leigh was doing, he then asked how he was doing. Tim assured Mac that he was okay and that he was getting the best care possible. Mac told him that he would see him when he could but that it might be at least a few days from now.

The big screen TV came on and showed an empty interview room. Mac had to quickly end the call. He promised Tim that they'd catch up later.

He was also hoping that he'd be able to speak to Bridget in person before long. He was certain that she wasn't telling him something but he'd have to save that for later.

Mac saw a red-faced man with grey hair being ushered into the room by a uniformed officer. He was as broad as he was tall and he had hands that were more like shovels. He was dressed in blue jeans and a plain black T-shirt. He placed a black windcheater on the back of the chair and sat down. He didn't look fazed in the slightest.

That might be because he's been through this before, Mac thought. Martin had discovered that Mr. Flahavan had done time. After several police cautions for violent conduct, he was finally charged with an assault in a pub when he was nineteen and he'd been sentenced to six months. He'd somehow become involved with T.B. Power not long after he'd gotten out of jail and there had been nothing since then.

The door opened and Andy and Kate came in and sat down.

'At last. What's this all about?' Flahavan asked in an accent that sounded very similar to Father Pat's.

Father Pat! Mac reminded himself to return his call. It had totally slipped his mind.

Andy ignored his question and read him his rights.

'Am I under arrest or something?' Liam Flahavan asked.

'I believe that the police officers who brought you in asked you to come with them voluntarily,' Andy replied.

'Well, yes, I suppose they did. So, I can go if I want to?'

'Yes, you can,' Andy replied.

He looked at Andy for a while before saying, 'I think that I'll wait until I hear what you've got to say first, if that's okay.'

'Do you want any legal representation?' Andy asked.

This seemed to surprise Mr. Flahavan.

'Will I need it?'

Again, Andy didn't reply.

'Very well,' Andy said as he took his notebook out. 'When we visited you at the Dunstable site you said that you had no knowledge whatsoever of the demolition of Hoar's

Cottage or whether any equipment from your site was used. Do you still stand by that?'

Flahavan looked suspiciously from Andy to Kate and back again. Their faces didn't reveal anything. He thought for a while.

'Yes, I'll stand by that.'

'For the tape, I'd like you to say that you had no knowledge whatsoever of the demolition,' Andy said.

Again, that look from Andy to Kate and back again.

He knows something's up, Mac thought. However, he obviously had no clue as to what it was. It looked as if Lucasz' threats to Kaminski had worked.

'I have no knowledge of the demolition of Hoar's Cottage,' Flahavan intoned.

Andy and Kate didn't react at all to Flahavan's reply.

Good, Mac said to himself, he won't see it coming then.

'Do you know a man called Stanislaw Kaminski?' Andy asked. 'I think you might know him better as Stan.'

'Well, I've heard the name...I think,' Flahavan tentatively replied playing for time.

'Let me refresh your memory then. He worked for you at T.B. Power Construction for over ten years. He was a site foreman, one who reported directly to you. Now do you remember him?'

'Of course, Stan. But he left us ages ago. He went back home, wherever that is.'

'Home, I believe, is Zyrardow,' Andy said. 'It's a little town fifty kilometres south-east of Warsaw where he and his wife Alicja run a restaurant.'

'Really?' Flahavan said with a look of genuine surprise.

Mac thought that he was also beginning to look slightly nauseous now.

'Yes, really,' Andy replied. 'He's also signed a statement that said that he and his team were responsible for demolishing Hoar's Cottage and that it was done solely on your orders.'

Andy gave Flahavan some time to let it sink in.

225

'But it's just his word against mine…'

Flahavan stopped when he saw Andy tapping the screen of a tablet. He passed the tablet over to Flahavan. There he saw himself at the airport, laughing and talking to Kaminski as well as handing over a large wedge of cash.

'Mr. Flahavan, you weren't under formal arrest when you came in here but you are now. We will be charging you with lying to the police on two occasions and other charges will follow. Have you anything to say?'

'Jaysus Christ,' he said in a sort of a low moan. 'I think that I'd like to speak to a solicitor now.'

'That's your right,' Andy replied. 'We can call for a duty solicitor or we can pass a message onto your own solicitor if you would prefer that.'

Flahavan gave them the name of a solicitor's office in Central London. Andy ended the interview. Once outside Kate called the number and arranged for a solicitor to attend.

Andy and Kate entered the team's room. Everyone assured them that they'd done a good job. Coffees were handed around and then the room fell silent again. Everyone knew that it all hinged on Flahavan now. Mac wasn't hoping too hard though. He guessed that Flahavan's loyalty would win over any threat of a prison sentence. He'd been inside once before so it would hold no surprises for him. Flahavan was getting on but, at the most, he would get seven years. With good behaviour, he'd probably only do four or five.

He could only pray that he was wrong.

Dan answered his phone while everyone looked at him.

Once he'd finished his call Dan said, 'That was Jo. She said that Leigh's still out of danger and the doctors say that she's improving.'

Thank God for some good news, Mac thought.

Fifteen minutes after that, Flahavan told the constable guarding him that he wanted to continue the interview. This surprised everyone as his solicitor wasn't due to arrive for some time. They watched on the big screen as Andy and Kate once again entered the interview room. Andy started the recorder again and stated who was in the room.

'We've called your solicitor but they won't be here for at least an hour,' Andy said. 'We shouldn't really be talking until they arrive.'

'I won't waste your time,' Flahavan said. 'I'm pleading guilty to all charges.'

Andy and Kate exchanged worried glances.

'So, you're telling us that you arranged for the demolition of Hoar's Cottage?'

'I did and it was all my own idea,' Flahavan said with a small smile.

'Why did you do it then?' Andy asked through gritted teeth.

'Well, there was this lad working on the site. He was only a young lad, a good worker too. I saw that he was upset one day and asked him what the problem was. He was so upset that he actually told me. He'd been in care when he was young and he said that he'd been raped when he was only twelve and that it had all happened at Hoar's Cottage. He was upset because the police had interviewed a friend of his who'd been at the same care home just the day before and it had brought it all back. I told him that he should go to the police too but he said he couldn't. He was too ashamed.'

Flahavan gave Andy and Kate a sad look.

'It stuck in my mind. It had happened to me when I'd been only ten or so and all that shit started to come back for me too. I started drinking again. I have no memory of it but Stan Kaminski told me that I'd ordered him and his boys to tear the cottage down and leave no trace. He did exactly as I'd ordered. I was shocked when he'd told me what he'd done but, as it wasn't his fault, I told him that he'd done a good job and paid him and his boys off. If I'm honest, I'm not ashamed of what happened and, if I'm being more honest, I never thought that I'd get caught anyway. It just goes to show how wrong you can be.'

'And who is this lad who told you that he'd been raped?' Andy asked.

He knew what the reply would be well before Flahavan opened his mouth.

'I'm afraid that I can't tell you that. He said that everything he'd told me had to be confidential. He said that he couldn't live with the shame if everyone knew.'

It was quite the sob story, Mac thought. There was nothing substantial that they could pick holes in and, given the right jury and a good barrister, Flahavan might even be believed. They would be lucky if he got two years or even less if they could get the ex-Mrs. Kendrick, Rachel Young, to testify that she wasn't all that upset to see the cottage disappear anyway.

A loud sound made Mac look to his right. Dan had kicked the waste paper basket clear across the room. He went into his office slamming the door behind him.

The team just gazed at the basket as it lay on its side. The case was dead and everyone knew it. There would be no justice for Leigh.

T.B. Power and his daughter had won.

Something had happened. Daddy had called her to his office and she knew from the sound of his voice that it wasn't for anything good.

'Liam's been arrested by the police. I've just spoken to his solicitors. I don't know how they did it but the police have managed to track down the team that demolished the cottage. They've got a signed statement from the foreman, Stan Kaminski, that says that it was Liam who organised it all.'

It was far worse than she had thought. If Liam told the police the truth then they would both be in deep trouble.

'It's just this Kaminski's word against Liam's though, isn't it?' she said.

She then saw the look on her father's face and a chill went down her spine.

'Isn't it?' she asked again.

'Liam can't deny that he knows Kaminski. They've got some CCTV footage of Liam at the airport. He was handing the team drinks and an extra bonus. It's pretty damning.'

'Liam is so stupid!' she exploded. 'Why the fuck didn't he get someone else to do the job?'

'Because he's a fair man,' her father said. 'He knew that what I'd asked him to do was illegal and, while he was willing to take any risk to help me out, he didn't want any of his men involved.'

'His 'fairness' is going to see us all in jail,' she said nearly shouting.

'No, it won't. Liam is going to plead guilty and say that demolishing the cottage was all his idea. He even came up with a pretty plausible motive for doing it too.'

'Oh,' she said trying to take it all in. 'So, we're okay then.'

'No, we're not okay,' her father said raising his voice for the first time. 'We're a million fucking miles from being okay. I've known Liam since before you were born. For Christ's sake, he was my best man when I married your mother and

he's been a true friend to me for all that time. Now, because of your stupidity, he might end up behind bars for the next five or six years.'

'But you can always make it up to him,' she said in a conciliatory tone.

'Oh, I can give him back his reputation and the lost years of his life, can I? In the meantime, because of him, we'll still be living a life of luxury but it will all be ashes in my mouth as long as he's in prison. Not only that but, even with Liam taking the fall for us, the police won't give up. Even if they do, Maguire definitely won't. I've met men like him before. He'll keep digging and we'll never have a bit of peace for as long as we live.'

She was silent for a moment.

'Daddy, we don't have to stay here. We could always go away somewhere, just the two of us,' she said in a wheedling tone. 'It's what I've always wanted. You've got lots of money stashed away, enough for a couple of lifetimes, so why don't we just walk away? We could go somewhere nice, somewhere where the police couldn't touch us. Just the two of us, daddy. Wouldn't that be nice?'

He looked at her as though she'd suddenly started speaking in a foreign language.

'Just leave it all behind?' he said with an incredulous look on his face. 'It's taken me a lifetime to build this business up. It's my life and you just want me to walk away from it all?'

'Yes, daddy,' she said moving closer to him.

She felt that it was now or never.

'It would just be the two of us,' she said putting an arm around his waist. 'You could have everything.'

She kissed him in a most undaughterly way while her free hand went down and caressed his crotch.

'Ow!' she screamed.

A strong hand held her arm in a vice-like grip and forced it up and away.

'I've created a monster,' he said.

While the words might have been hurtful enough, the look of total disgust on her father's face felt like a knife to her heart when all she had ever wanted was his love. Her default position in life had always been to retaliate when attacked. She did just that.

'You're so clever though, aren't you?' she shrieked. 'But you're not. You still think that Justin Reynard was the first person I murdered but he wasn't, daddy darling. There was one before that...'

Chapter Twenty-Seven

It was quiet in the Major Crime Unit's room. The waste paper basket still lay on its side and the silence was only broken by the tap-tap-tap on Martin's computer keyboard. Mac sat back in his chair and stared at the ceiling. There were things he could be doing but his heart was no longer in it. His immense sadness was only matched by his frustration at not being able to nail whoever was behind Leigh's shooting.

Jo had updated them again. Leigh was doing well but she was still under sedation. 'Comfortable' the doctors had told her.

Well, that's a lot better than critical, Mac thought.

Jo had added that it would be a long road to recovery for Leigh. Once they had fully repaired her artery, they would need to let her recover for a while before they could consider any further operations. She would need at least two on her knee, they said. That's if they could save the leg. Even if they could, it would be many months at the very least before Leigh would be anywhere near normal.

Thinking about this made him deeply angry.

I won't give up on this one, he told himself. If the day comes when Dan has to drop the case, he promised himself that he'd carry on. He'd make it his life's work if he had to.

His phone rang. It was an unfamiliar number.

'Mr. Maguire, I've sent you an invite for a video call,' a man with a deep Dublin accent said. 'I need you to take it. I can promise you that it will be something that you'll want to hear.'

The call ended. It was T.B. Power! Mac waved at Martin to come over while he opened his email. Martin quickly mirrored Mac's computer so that he could see everything on his own laptop.

'Don't forget to press the record button,' Martin said as Mac clicked on the invite. 'I'll record it too just to be on the safe side.'

Mac hit the button as an image of a man sitting behind a huge desk filled his screen. The man was in his late fifties with black curly hair and broad shoulders underneath his business suit. His square face exuded strength and authority.

'Mr. Maguire, we meet at last,' T.B. said. 'Donegal or Fermanagh?'

'Donegal,' Mac answered.

'Ah, so. Are you recording this?'

'Yes,' Mac replied seeing no point in lying.

'Good, I want this all on the record. I need to explain something...'

Mac saw him flinch for a second. It was a response that was familiar to Mac. It looked as if T.B. was in pain.

'Are you alright?' Mac asked.

T.B. didn't answer his question.

'Can I ask that you let me tell you a story, without interruptions and without anyone knocking down my door? It's important to me.'

Mac had no idea where this was going but he agreed anyway.

'You know, I came to this country with five bob and the clothes on my back. I thought that life was all about making money, the more the better. How wrong I was. Nessa was a beautiful child,' T.B. said with a smile. 'She took after her mother in that way. Those two were so close. I met Teresa Gallagher when I was just starting off my business. She was gorgeous, the most beautiful woman I've ever met but she came from a traveller family and she was wild with it. I liked that wildness in her though, I think it's what drew me to her in a way. I'd guess that our relationship could be described as tempestuous but we really loved each other, I think.

We were complete when Nessa came along, a real family. Then, when Nessa was just five, Teresa suddenly died. She'd told me that she'd been getting headaches but I'm afraid that I didn't listen. I kept not listening and then she dropped down dead one day from a brain haemorrhage when there was only her and Nessa in the house. I'd dropped by the pub for a few drinks on the way home so poor Nessa had been with her dead body for hours by the time I came home.

If I'm honest, I don't really remember the days and weeks after that. I threw myself into my work as a way of helping me with my grief but poor Nessa had no-one. I hired nannies for her but she needed her dad and, may God help me, I went missing.'

He stopped and grimaced. Whether this was due to the painful memory or something else Mac couldn't make out.

'In the years that followed I suspected that something wasn't right with Nessa but I kept persuading myself that she'd grow out of it. I was a fool. She got into more and more scrapes but I told myself that she was just a bit wild, just like her mother. May God forgive me but, when I should have gotten her some help, I only ended up enabling her wickedness.'

That last word was said with some force.

'She killed Justin Reynard. She stole the key from my desk and lured him to the cottage. I got the key from Marcus Kendrick and I used it to visit the cottage while I'd been having an affair with a married woman. I won't say who. My daughter had sex with Reynard there and then stabbed him five times. I, of course, cleaned up after her as I've always done. Another one of my many mistakes.'

Mac was amazed at what he was hearing. T.B. was admitting everything! Mac and Martin looked at each other with disbelief.

'Nessa was also responsible for the policewoman being injured. I hope with all my heart that she'll be okay. Nessa discovered that you suspected her from a policeman called

234

DI John Roberts who was on her payroll. My daughter then hired a loser called Malky O'Keefe to do the job. I can't blame him too much. He was mad in love with my daughter and she used him. We all do crazy things for love, don't we? Anyway, she made sure that Malky died too. She had hoped that would be the end of it but you wouldn't give up, would you? When Nessa found out that you knew about Liam, she totally lost it. I must admit that I did too. Liam was one of my oldest friends and the thought of him doing prison time at his age was killing me. She said that she wanted us to go away together...'

He paused and looked away as tears came to his eyes.

'She then did something that I never thought she could possibly be capable of. I called her a monster and she fought back. In her anger, she told me that Reynard hadn't been her first murder. When Nessa was eight, I married again. Gráinne was a truly lovely woman. She wasn't as beautiful as Teresa or as wild but, in lots of ways, I found that to be a good thing. She was gentle and loving and that was enough for me. After she gave birth to Eoin, we discovered that she had a heart condition. Over time it deteriorated but the doctors said that they could treat it although she'd have to be on medication for the rest of her life. I got her the best care I could but then she died on me too.'

He stopped and closed his eyes before continuing.

'Just a while ago Nessa admitted that she'd substituted some of Gráinne's tablets. Not all but enough so that a heart attack became more likely. She said that she wanted me all to herself and she got her wish. Gráinne was dead and Eoin was at university. Nessa knew just how to push my buttons. She knew that I'd go ballistic when she showed me the photo of Eoin and his boyfriend. It seemed so important at the time but now, pushing him away like that, just seems weak and senseless. I love my son but my stupid prejudices made me forget that. Tell him for me, will you? Tell him that I still love him. Tell him that I always have.'

Mac didn't like the way the conversation was going. T.B.'s voice was getting weaker and he looked exhausted.

'A famous Irishman once said that 'Each man kills the thing he loves' and that's so true. When Nessa told me that she'd killed Gráinne and then went on to tell me how she'd broken up my affair by blackmailing the woman I love, for possibly the first time in my life, I lost all control. I lost my sanity. I've heard about people seeing a 'red mist' when they're really angry and that's so true. I strangled my lovely, warped daughter to death with these very hands,' T.B. said as he held up his hands. He looked at them as though he'd never seen them before. 'The very same hands that held her as a baby. She did turn out to be a monster but I made her like that. I couldn't give her what she needed when her mother died and it warped her. She had a gun in her purse and she shot me as I was strangling her. Can you believe that? Anyway, it's only right that I should die too, a sort of justice perhaps. I couldn't live knowing what I'd done so perhaps it's all for the best. Let the dead bury the dead, Mr. Maguire.'

Mac looked over at Martin who was already on the phone calling for assistance.

'I'm sorry that we had to meet this way,' T.B. said. 'You sound like an interesting man. Do you have children?'

T.B.'s eyelids were fluttering and Mac could see that he was fading fast.

'I do, I have a daughter. She's a doctor.'

'You're a lucky man, Mr. Maguire. A...'

Mac never got to hear the next word. T.B. had slumped down in his chair and his lifeless, unblinking eyes stared straight out at Mac.

'I've sent the police and paramedics to his office,' Martin said.

'Thanks,' Mac said. 'Can you also call the City of London Police Professional Standards and tell them that they've got a bent copper on their hands. If this DI John Roberts has had anything to do with Leigh getting shot, I want to see him behind bars as soon as possible. Tell them that we've got a deathbed confession as evidence.'

'I'll do that right now.'

Mac nodded. He sat in silence and kept watch over the dead body of T.B. Power until the police arrived. He then ended the video call. He stood up and stretched his arms.

'I'm going home,' he said. 'I have to go and see my daughter. Tell Dan that I'll pop into the station tomorrow.'

'Will do,' Martin replied. 'Say hello to Tommy for me, will you?'

Mac said that he would.

Mac was just about to call Eileen, his favourite taxi driver, when he had a thought. He went down to the police cells and asked to see Liam Flahavan.

He looked surprised when Mac walked in. Mac had to introduce himself and explain what part he'd played in the investigation.

'I'm afraid that your boss is dead,' Mac said.

He explained what had just happened. He said that Liam could see the video call if he wanted. Liam believed him. He had to wipe the tears away before he could speak.

'I had a feeling that nothing good was going to come from all of this. He was a good friend to me, Mr. Maguire. The best. I was a wild young man when I first came across T.B. but he showed me that there was another way to go, a better way. We did some great things together, great things.'

'I'm advising you to make a statement, except this time, tell the truth. You'll be free to go home as soon as you do. However, the real reason I came down here was to pass something on. Just before T.B. died he told me that, despite everything that had happened, he loved his son Eoin and he wanted him to know it. Would you be able to tell him that?'

'I would,' Liam replied. 'I'd be proud to. Eoin's a good lad, he always was. It's just a pity that his father couldn't see it until it was too late. Of course, the business will be his now.'

'I think that you might find that Eoin has some very different ideas to his father,' Mac said.

'Oh, Eoin's told me all about re-usability and all that. I'd never have said it to poor T.B. but it just sounded like common sense to me.'

Mac smiled and stood up. He was about to offer his hand when a thought struck him.

'Do you believe in doing penance?'

'Yes, I do, when you've done something wrong.'

'Well, there's a church not far from here that's starting to fall down. The priest is from your neck of the woods and he's worried sick that he might have to close it down. What do you think?' Mac asked.

'I think that we've all sinned, haven't we?' Liam said. 'Especially me. A little penance will do none of us any harm and, after all, people do sometimes use equipment from the site for their own personal projects or so I've been told.'

They both managed a smile at that. Mac gave him Father Pat's name and contact details.

He felt better as he waited for Eileen to take him home but it didn't last. He thought again of Bridget and what she might be hiding from him.

It was time that he found out.

Chapter Twenty-Eight

Bridget stood up in surprise when the police guard showed Mac into his living room.

'Dad, what's happened?' she asked.

Tommy came in from the kitchen. He looked surprised too.

'It's over,' Mac said. 'The people who were behind Leigh's shooting are dead. It's all over. I'll explain later. Is Tim awake?'

Bridget led him into Tim's room.

'Hello, old friend,' Mac said with a warm smile.

'Mac, what are you doing back?' Tim said as he sat up in bed.

'The case is over,' Mac replied. 'I just wanted to make sure that you're okay.'

'Oh, I'm fine,' Tim replied. 'It's nowhere near as painful as it was. How's Leigh?'

Mac told him the latest and tried to make it sound upbeat. Even so he noticed that Tim's eyes became watery.

'It's okay, old friend,' Mac said softly as he took Tim's hand. 'It's okay. It's been quite a case. I just need to have a quick word with Bridget and then I'll come back and tell you all about it.'

He looked up at his daughter. He could see that she felt guilty about something. He knew that look from when she'd been a child. It was time to find out exactly what was going on.

They followed him into the living room where Mac motioned for Bridget and Tommy to sit down.

'There's something going on, isn't there?' he said. 'In all our little chats while I've been holed up in the police station there's been something that you haven't been telling me. What is it?'

Bridget and Tommy exchanged glances while Mac girded his loins for whatever the news might be.

'You're right, dad,' Bridget said as she took Tommy's hand. 'There is something that we haven't told you. We wanted to tell you in person. We felt that it was important that we did it this way.'

'So, what is it?' Mac asked softly.

He wasn't altogether certain that he wanted to know the answer.

Bridget and Tommy exchanged glances again before she said, 'I'm pregnant, dad. Nine weeks now.'

'You're what?' he said in astonishment.

He had been expecting bad news. It was like going out on a dark dank miserable day only to have the sun burst through the clouds.

'I'm pregnant, dad. I'm expecting.'

Mac was more than aware that the new arrival hadn't been planned.

'And do you want it?'

'The news certainly came as a shock but yes, I want this baby more than I've wanted anything in my whole life,' Bridget said as her eyes filled up.

'Me too,' Tommy said with a smile as he gave Bridget's hand a squeeze.

At last, Tommy's words made sense to him.

'Especially now.'

Of course, there was no way he could have left Bridget in her condition when she might be in danger.

'Are you going to enjoy being a grandad?' Bridget asked.

In his delight at Bridget's news, it somehow hadn't struck him that he'd be a grandfather. He only needed a split-second's thought before he answered.

'I'm going to love it,' he replied with a broad smile.

They all gathered in Tim's room and Mac told them the whole story.

'It's like one of those Greek tragedies, isn't it?' Tim said when Mac had finished.

'Yes, I think that you're not far off there. However, it's hard to figure out exactly who's to blame. I can understand how T.B. felt when Nessa's mother died. I hid away for months after your mother died,' Mac said as he glanced over at Bridget. 'T.B. hid in his work but Nessa needed him and it must have been dreadful for her. I know that I was away a lot, too much perhaps, but I knew that you always had your mother. She was my blessing.'

'She was a blessing to all of us, dad,' Bridget said as she took her father's hand.

If only Nessa's mother hadn't died, Mac thought, Leigh might not be in a hospital bed right now. If only.

Later that evening he was in his own bed at last but sleep refused to come. He lay awake as the events of the past few days rolled around his head. He had half-expected to go back into the darkness of depression after the case was over but it just goes to show that life is always full of surprises. Bridget's news had blown a hole in the darkness through which a bright light now shone.

A new life and a new hope.

It would be a hard road for Leigh and also for him. However, when the guilt and the dark sad moments descended on him, as they would, he realised that he had the antidote. He'd just think of the magic word.

'Granddad.'

Four and a bit weeks later

As her energy levels were still very low, the doctors would only allow Leigh one short visit a day. Mac and Tim were close to the top of Leigh's visitor list for which they were thankful. Both of them were dying to see her.

She was surrounded by blinking and bleeping medical machines and her right leg was suspended on wires. She had a bulky plaster cast on her knee and both legs were covered in wadding around which plastic tubes were wound.

'I had those tubes on my legs too after my operation,' Tim said. 'They're to make sure that you don't get a blood clot.'

Leigh gave them a brilliant smile as they drew closer.

'How are you both? Especially you, Tim?' she asked.

'Oh, I'm fine,' Tim replied. 'Never better in fact and you were right. I did feel a lot better after just a few days. The urology nurse had a look at me a few weeks ago and she said that everything's healing nicely.'

'And you Mac?' she asked noticing his glum expression.

'Oh, I'm fine too,' Mac replied.

'You're still not blaming yourself, are you?'

'No, no of course not,' Mac replied.

Leigh gave him a very sceptical look.

'Well, a little perhaps,' Mac admitted.

'Don't, Mac. If you'd been there, you would have taken a bullet for me. I know you would have.'

Mac nodded and tried to let the guilt go.

'So, how are they treating you?' he asked.

'Oh, they're great. I'm getting to know quite a lot of them really well. Plus, I got a visit from my physiotherapist this morning and once this comes off in a week or two,' she said pointing to the cast on her knee, 'I'll be starting my exercises.'

'It'll be hard at first,' Mac said.

'Oh, I know and painful. Noah told me all about it.'

'Noah?' Mac asked.

'He's my personal physio. He's Australian, six feet tall and every inch of him is totally gorgeous,' she said with a naughty smile.

'So, it's not all bad then,' Tim said with a wink. 'Mac told me how you cheated death but it would be nice to hear it from your own lips.'

'Okay, I must have told the story fifty times by now so once more won't hurt. I was just driving out of the car park when my phone went off. I thought it might have been mum calling so I tried to get it out. However, I'd put it in my left-hand jacket pocket and it was trapped there by the buckle of my seat belt. So, I put my foot on the brake and took my seat belt off but, in trying to get the phone out of my pocket before it stopped ringing, I dropped it onto the floor. I was bending over to pick it up out of the passenger seat well when the bullets hit me. That's why they all caught me on my right side. They think that the bullets that hit me in the chest and knee were the two that had first come through the hood. They think that they got deflected and lost some of their energy or it might have been even worse.'

'The best of it was that Martin had a look at her phone and it wasn't her mother after all but someone trying to sell her car insurance,' Mac said.

'I now listen to every spam call I get,' Leigh said with a smile. 'I never buy anything but I always thank them very nicely for calling.'

Tim laughed out loud at this.

'Anyway, both of us were delighted when we heard your good news,' Mac said. 'The second operation on your knee seems to have done the trick.'

'Well, I'm glad that I was sedated most of the time after the shooting, otherwise I don't know how I'd have coped with the thought of losing my leg. I've had it quite a long time now,' she said with a comically straight face.

They all laughed at this.

'You've had some other good news too, haven't you?' Leigh asked. 'I know that Bridget's doing well as she pops in to see me now and again as she only works a couple of floors below me. We talk a lot about the upcoming wedding. Bridget's so excited about it but who would have thought of Tommy being a married man? How is he taking it though? It seems strange thinking of him being a dad.'

'Tommy's absolutely over the moon about it all but he did admit to being a bit scared. I told him that being totally petrified at the thought of being a father was just par for the course.'

'Oh, he'll be a great dad,' Leigh said. 'After all, he's still a big kid himself, isn't he?'

Mac could only agree.

'You know, I've been thinking about that Nessa Power,' Leigh said looking a little more serious. 'How do you think she turned out to be like that?'

Mac shrugged, 'I've no idea. I've been thinking about her too but I've gotten no closer to any sort of an answer. She lost a parent when she was young but then so did you. Her father said that she didn't see much of him after her mother died but your mother was working two jobs so, I dare say, that you didn't get all that much time with her either. Yet, you both turned out to be so totally different, opposites even. People constantly fascinate me and I think that's because there's a deep mystery about why they do the things they do. It's a mystery that I haven't even come close to solving as yet.'

'Well, I still feel sort of sorry for her, if I'm being honest.'

'I'd bet that she never gave a thought to you, even after the shooting, but that's what makes you such different people. I'm glad that you're not bitter about it all though.'

'What's the point?' Leigh said. 'I was told that keeping positive would help my recovery. Anger and bitterness won't help, so why hang on to them?'

'Such wisdom in one so young,' Tim said without the slightest trace of irony.

'Anyway, I'll need all my positivity. Bridget's invited me to the wedding and I mean to go, even if that means going to the church on crutches.'

'Good for you!' Mac said.

'Oh, I was nearly forgetting,' Tim said.

He pulled a package from a bag and handed it to Leigh. Her eyes widened when she saw what it was.

'A new tablet!' she said. 'God, it's massive. It's three times the size of my old one.'

'It was one of the biggest we could find,' Mac said. 'We both thought that you might want to watch some Netflix while you're indisposed. We brought this along as well.'

Mac pulled a large glass bottle from the bag.

'You haven't brought me wine, have you?' Leigh asked with a mixture of disbelief and wonder.

'Not exactly,' Mac replied. 'If this was a movie then it would be a prequel.'

He turned the bottle so that she could see the label.

'Grape juice!' she said laughing.

'Thankfully, you've got a good imagination and you'll need it with that stuff,' Tim said.

They helped, or more like hindered, Leigh as she got the tablet out and set it up. She finally got Netflix up and picked a movie.

'God, it's like having your own cinema,' Leigh said with delight.

Then the door opened and a nurse's head popped through.

'You all sound like you're enjoying yourselves but I'm afraid that your time is up,' she said. 'Leigh will need to take some rest soon.'

Mac thought that the nurse was probably right. Leigh was already beginning to look a little tired.

'As it's only seven o'clock, I take it that your next call will be at the Magnets?' Leigh asked.

'It will,' Tim replied with absolute certainty.

'Have one for me, will you?' she said.

'We will,' Mac said.

Half an hour later Mac sat at table thirteen at the Magnets looking out of the window at the odd passer-by as Tim went to get their drinks. He came back with two pints of lager and a large glass of wine. Tim put one pint before Mac and the other by his seat. He then placed the wine in the space opposite.

'Just so we don't forget her,' Tim said.

Mac smiled at Tim's gesture but he wouldn't need a glass of wine to ensure that he remembered Leigh. The recent events were permanently engraved on his brain.

'I'd like to make a toast,' Tim said in a comically formal voice.

'Go on then,' Mac said with a smile.

'A toast then. To the upcoming wedding; that it may bring blessings to Bridget, Tommy and your grandchild. And also, to Leigh and that we might get to see her there. Even if she is on crutches.'

He had been expecting the toast to be a joke but he could see that Tim was quite serious. It was a good toast and a good thought, one that Mac was more than happy to drink to.

They both stood up, clinked glasses and said 'Sláinte' in unison.

The End

Author's Note – Tim Teagan's experience with prostate cancer was based on my own. If you want to know a little more about this and about prostate cancer in general, I've put up a post on my blog called '*Tim Teagan, Prostate Cancer and what every man should know*' - https://patrickcwalshauthor.com/2021/02/12/tim-teagan-prostate-cancer-and-what-every-man-should-know/

I hope that you've enjoyed this story. If you have then please post a review and let me know what you think. *PCW*

Also in the Mac Maguire detective series
The Body in the Boot

The Dead Squirrel

The Weeping Women

The Blackness

23 Cold Cases

Two Dogs

The Match of the Day Murders

The Chancer

The Tiger's Back

The Eight Bench Walk

https://patrickcwalshauthor.com/

Made in the USA
Columbia, SC
26 January 2022

54832931R00152